'If thou only hadst k
thy day the things th
but now they are hi̶d̶d̶e̶n̶ ̶f̶r̶o̶m̶ ̶t̶h̶i̶n̶e̶ ̶e̶y̶e̶s̶.̶

Scriptures

In This Thy Day

MICHAEL McLAVERTY

poolbeg press

First published 1945 by
Jonathan Cape Ltd.,

This edition published 1981 by
Poolbeg Press Ltd.,
Knocksedan House,
Swords, Co. Dublin, Ireland.

The generous assistance of the Arts Council of Northern Ireland in the
publication of this book is gratefully acknowledged.

Designed by Steven Hope
Cover by Robert Ballagh

Printed by Cahill Printers Limited,
East Wall Road, Dublin 3.

CHAPTER I

WINTER was at an end and the first spring winds blew fresh and cool from the sea, coaxing the hedges to bud and stirring the larks to rise from the withered grass and burst in song. Horses were led along the sea-road to the forge, ploughs gritty with rust were carried in creaking carts, and in the dark barns the doors were flung wide and men were busy riddling the potatoes for seed. On the shore the black and white shelduck were moving in pairs, and farther inland crows were breaking off the young shoots from the trees and flying with them to build their nests. In the fields the ewes, trailing their heavy fleece, their eyes wide with mysterious expectancy, were pressing close to the thin shelter of the bushes or lying amongst the scattered rocks.

A dark-haired girl of twenty-three was standing in the light from her door patching the patches on a pair of her father's trousers and occasionally lifting her head to glance at the fresh blue of the sea or to breathe with quiet gratefulness the salty air that blew around her. Her father was below on the shore, his dog lying near him on a heap of fresh shavings. He was mending his upturned boat, the sail, veined with snail-lines, spread out on the stones to catch the breeze and the hurried blinks of sunlight. The girl saw him lift a white jug of paint and she noticed the two stumps where the handle had broken off. He was holding the jug on the palm of his hand, dipping a brush into it, and dabbing red-lead on the cracks and sunken nail-heads of his boat. She recalled a day last summer when the weather had been dry for weeks, their water-barrel empty, and she had gone to the stream to get soft water for the washing. She had brought the jug to fill the buckets and it slipped from her fingers and the handle had broken against a stone. 'Don't throw it out,' her father had said, 'it'll come in useful some day' — and as usual with him he had told how her poor mother, God be good to her, had bought it over thirty years ago in Downpatrick. She could only remember her mother vaguely, but she could remember how, after her death, her father had looked after them all: herself, her two younger sisters, and her brother, John, and how he used to fill a tub with warm water on Saturday nights, bolt the door, hook the blind to the window, and begin to wash and scrub them all. She recalled how he had rubbed paraffin oil into her hair, combed the smarting scalp, while John put a tiny boat in the tub and Barbara and Tessie lifted the suds in their hands and blew them on to the floor. Then they clustered on stools around the fire, their father telling them stories till their hair was dry and they were drowsy and silent with sleep. 'If only John were sober we'd be happy!' she sighed to herself, blurring the memories from her mind. With her needle she picked out dry clay that was embedded in a button on the trousers and thought again of her brother John, and how one night, a few years ago, he had gone off in a coal boat and had never written a scrape to them. 'Don't worry — he'll be glad to come back some day,' her father always said with a shake of the head. 'My people and your mother's people were never of the roving kind. Some fine day you'll see him come back like the prodigal son.'

Her father straightened his back and looked up at her: 'Mary, see is that tar ready yet,' and he put down the jug of paint and lifted his pipe where it lay on a flat stone.

Mary turned her head and spoke into the cottage: 'Barbara, is the tar ready?'

' 'Tis not!' Barbara shouted back, and heard Mary calling it down to the shore and her father answering: 'I suppose she's admiring herself in the looking-glass. She certainly didn't get her good looks from me,' and he blew through the shank of his pipe and began to fill it with tobacco.

Barbara, crouched before the fire, tossed her head pertly. She was pushing twigs under a bucket of tar that was melting

6

and filling the cottage with a sharp, bitter smell. Now and again as the wind blew through the door a grocer's calendar would rasp against the wall, the twigs hiss and crackle fiercely, turn red, and then writhe like white worms. Because of the steam she couldn't see into the bucket and though she held her ear to it she couldn't tell if it were melted sufficiently to please her father. She went to the door and with the back of her hand brushed away her hair that had fallen over her brow. From the side of the gable she lifted a bundle of withered branches and as she was passing again through the door Mary released for her a thorny twig that was caught in her dress. The hurried sound of horse's hoofs on the sea-road made them turn and they stared at a young man coming towards them, hitting the horse with a bit of a rope. He shouted at them as he galloped past the door: 'My father's dying!'

'He's away for the priest,' Mary said, fixing the needle and thread in the unfinished patch and rolling up the trousers in a bundle: 'Maybe, Barbara, I should go over and help.'

'They mightn't want you!' Barbara said, throwing down her bundle of branches and wiping her hands on her stockings: 'Poor Ned's worried-looking!' and she bit her under lip and listened to the horse's hoofs fading for a moment and she knew he was turning on to the road that led inland to the priest's house. Mary looked to the headland at her right and saw the white gable of Ned's house, smoke coming from the chimney, and she thought of the old man, his father, stretched in his agony of death.

'Did he say anything?' their father shouted up as he sat on the sail fumbling at a ball of cord. He bit at a knot with his teeth: 'Did he say anything?' he asked again.

'Paddy Joe is dying!'

'Time for him — he's eighty-seven if he's a day.... He'll not hear the cuckoo, this year, I'm afraid.'

'Maybe, Father, I should go over and help?' Mary said.

'Maybe you'll do no such thing. Isn't the mother there,

7

hale and hearty, and three fine lumps of daughters. You might be pecking your way in where you're not wanted. . . . What on earth is that girl doing with the tar? If there comes a blatter of rain I'll not get the boat done the day!'

Barbara, with a contemptuous shake of her head, lifted the steaming bucket off the fire and carried it down to the shore. He flapped the steam away with his hat and peered in at the breaking bubbles and craters of tar: 'Man, alive, it's plumping mad-hot this last half-hour! Were you watchin' the tar or admirin' your beauty?' and he stooped to stir the bucket with a dried sea-rod.

'Is that all you want?' Barbara asked, her black hands held out from her cotton dress.

He coughed as the sharp tang of tar caught his throat: 'It'll take another bucketful. I'll call you when I've this brushed in.'

When she came back to the house the kitchen was empty, but on a cracked saucer on the table was a wet bar of soap and a few bubbles. Presently Mary came out of the room with her hair combed and an old red-knitted jumper under her arm. She noticed Barbara's questioning look.

'I'm going down to the stream to watch the geese. The school children lamed one of them the other day!'

'Och, the geese is well able to look after themselves.' Barbara spoke sharply, knowing that Mary would sit near the road to meet Ned on his way back. 'You may clean up that before you go!' and she glanced at the splashed table. Without a word Mary put the saucer in a corner of the dresser, wiped the table, and went down to the stream.

She sat in the shelf of a bank and began to rip out the red jumper and roll up the wool into a ball. Behind her the wind sifted amongst the dried wrack and now and then eddied the sand at her feet and settled it on the cracks in the stones and on the empty limpet shells. Nearby the geese nibbled at the grass that grew on the bank of the stream. Presently barefooted boys on their way from school raced towards the stone bridge, leaned over it and dropped blades of grass on the surface of the stream, shouting excitedly to one another: 'Look at my boat! . . . Oh, look at the speed of mine!' The noise and chatter disturbed the geese and they rose from the crushed grass and hissed and stretched their necks. But safe behind the parapet of the bridge the children continued to shout, crane over it, and spit on the water, watching their spits flowing seawards or being lost in the scallops made by the jutting stones. They didn't notice Mary where she sat in the nook of the bank. She was smiling at their antics, but when they mounted the bridge and hopped across it on one leg she shouted at them: 'Get down out o' that! Do you want to fall and break your necks!' For a moment they stood still, frightened by the unexpected nearness of the voice. She made to rise at them and they jumped from the bridge, lifted a handful of gravel and flung it at the swimming geese.

Mary shook her fist: 'I know you all — every one of you. I'll tell Miss Drennan to-morrow!' And when they heard the schoolmistress's name they held down their heads trying to change their appearance in some grotesque fashion. Mary smiled to herself: 'It's good to hear them laughing. . . . It'd be a lonely place only for them!'' and she continued to rip out the red jumper, and occasionally glanced up the road or looked at the long grass combed out below the surface of the stream.

The priest rode by on his bicycle but he didn't see her. And then she heard the sound of a trotting horse and she speedily ripped out great lengths of the wool and got to her feet. Ned jumped off the horse, holding the rope-reins in his hand.

'I'm terribly sorry, Ned, about your father. . . . With God's help he'll pull through.'

'He's very bad, Mary. He's done. The doctor has given him up. . . .'

She rolled up a bit of the loose wool, looked into his

9

saddened eyes and said hesitantly: 'Would you like me to go over? I could help your mother and the girls.'

He dug the toe of his boot into the gravel on the road, raised his head, and looked away seawards: 'No, Mary, don't come over yet. . . . Wait for awhile. . . . I'll let you know if anything happens.'

The horse moved to the edge of the stream, sniffed at it, and began to drink; its front hoofs sank in the mud and the long hair on them floated on the water. Ned wound and unwound the rope-reins, glancing at the wool on the road and the bits of straw clinging to it as she rolled it up. The horse jerked its head, the water dripping from its wet mouth on to the stones.

'I'll try and see you in the evening,' he said, and she heard a loose shod on his boot striking the road as he jumped on the horse. He waved to her, and she sat for awhile on the bridge, peevish now at the knots in the wool. 'At least he could have let me go over when I asked,' she said to herself — a wearisome mood of doubt and jealousy fidgeting at her mind. She got up and walked along the shore, gathering the sticks that lay entangled amongst the wrack. The waves broke close to her, but she paid no heed to them, her fingers rooting amongst the piles of wrack, her feet crunching on the limpet shells. Back again she came to the stream and drove the geese in front of her, the sand on the road gathering on their wet feet. They walked slowly and awkwardly, their voices scolding and bad-tempered, and then as they neared the house they stretched their wings and ran forward in great haste. The disinfectant smell of tar drew Mary's attention to the shore and she saw her father, his foot raised on a rock, lacing his boot. She stood beside him and admired the boat.

'There'll be rain afore night,' he said, 'but I'll get her finished for her timbers is dry as hay,' and his eyes scanned inland towards the hills that had gathered a snuff of cloud about their tops. 'A plout of rain would loosen the soil for

the potatoes. It'd do good once I have the boat finished.'
Presently there was a scream and Barbara came rushing out
of the house. 'The tar! The tar!' she yelled. 'It over-
flowed...it's on fire...everything!' Already long streamers
of flame stretched up from the square of the chimney
and twisted rolls of smoke crushed out through the door.
'Call the neighbours!' the father shouted as he scrambled
up from the shore. 'Get buckets!'

He crooked an arm over his eyes and ran through the
smoke-filled door. Inside he saw spurts of tar leaping into
the fire and trickles of flame wriggling down the sides of the
bucket and across the floor. A bundle of branches was
burning on the hearth and the clothes on the line over the
fireplace were ablaze and the thatch below them flaming
red. He lifted the bucket of drinking-water from the side
of the dresser and flung it over the flames; then he took the
oil-lamp from the wall and hurried out with it to one of the
girls. He turned and went into his room, put his hand into
one of his Sunday boots that were below the bed and
smashed the window with it. Through the window gap he
tossed out his Sunday clothes, blankets off the bed, his razor
and soap, and finally the contents of a chest of drawers.
Outside, the men gathered quickly; the blacksmith had seen
the flames from the open door of his forge, and other neighbours who were bushing gaps in nearby fields all rushed
towards Luke Devlin's cottage. As Luke blundered about
the room he could hear them calling to children and sending
them for buckets. When he came stumbling out through the
door he saw that they had made a chain of buckets from the
edge of the sea, and others were carrying their coats filled
with sand. The blacksmith rolled the empty water-barrel
to the front of the house and when buckets were handed to
him he flung them over the thatch.

With a rising anguish that squeezed all thought from him,
Luke saw threads of smoke wavering like feelers through the
thatch. They rose faster, merging in a web that soon

covered the whole roof. He clenched his fists, feeling as it were the strain and stress of the flames underneath as they scratched and tore ready to leap in fury through the first gap. Bucketfuls of water hissed amongst the smoke, but near the chimney, flames burst through and the thatch around it shrivelled like burnt paper.

'It's gone now!' a man said.

'Keep at it! Keep at it!' Luke yelled. 'If only John were here it'd never best him!' And he dashed through the door again and emerged with a chair, a stool, a drawer from the table, bowls and plates. Mary and Barbara took the things from him as he came out and put them under the hedge, and, as they hurried, Barbara would lament: 'I put a big armful of twigs under the bucket to hurry it up . . . and then I went into the room to wash my face . . . and when I came out the whole bucket was burling with flame.' She cried bitterly as she shook out the blankets and folded them up: 'Och, everything seems to go wrong with me! And to think of Tessie over in my granda's with nothing to worry her!'

'It was you was asked to live with my granda,' Mary said impatiently, 'and you wouldn't do it. "Do you think I'm going to slave and attend any old man!" was the words you said.'

'I wish I was with him now! I'd be out of all this trouble.'

'Och, you're never at rest. You don't know what you want. Anyway, this is no time to be listening to your cries and lamentations!'

Little boys with pieces of bread in their hands yelled at three mice that ran along the edge of the thatch; the mice stopped, sniffed undecidedly and looked with stupefied astonishment at the smoke and the harsh rattle of the buckets and the splash of water. A man flung a bucket of water at them and they scurried into a hole in the thatch, but the heat chased them out again and they made off over the roof to the other side where little boys chased after them with branches in their hands. But Mary saw nothing. Ned had suddenly appeared amongst them and, with a rag round his mouth and a spade in his hand, he had rushed through the smoke-filled door. He stood on the table and lunged at the thatch with his spade, making holes in it to break the spread of the flames. And now Luke had smashed the window of the girls' room and was pitching everything he could find out to them. Ragged gaps could be seen in the thatch, and now and then the gleam of Ned's spade and smoke trailing from the blade of it. Water began to trickle out across the threshold. A man climbed on to the roof and, sitting astride the roof-tree, he jabbed at the thatch with a pitch-fork, and when he saw the flames trapped in one corner, he showed the men where to fling the water and sand.

A woman screamed and the men stopped. Ned's mother, pale and wild-looking, was standing in the midst of them. 'Where's my son?' she was saying in a voice harsh with anger and exhaustion. 'Where is he? . . . He has disgraced us forever. . . . His poor father . . . not cold yet.' Ned, his face covered with dirt from the falling thatch, came out to her.

'Come home at once, Ned, for the love of God. . . . You're a disgrace. . . . You've no respect for your dead father!' and she wrung her hands and flung back her hair, seeing no one but her son. Ned tried to speak calmly as he pointed to the smoke and the flames: 'We've nearly it beat! I'll see it out to the end!' and he beckoned with his eyes to Mary and Barbara to come over to her.

His mother caught him by the arm: 'Come now!' she screeched, and, turning to Mary and Barbara, she stared at them: 'It's you has his head turned! . . . Not one of you will get him! Not one of you! . . . With your good-for-nothing father and a drunken brother!' Ned put his arm around her shoulder: 'Mother!' he said and drew her to the edge of the crowd. The priest was standing there leaning against his bicycle, and when she raised her head and saw him her

13

voice stifled in her throat, her lips stiffened, trembled, and she sobbed brokenly: 'We're disgraced, Father! . . .'

'Ah, now, Mrs. Mason, he has done no harm! Don't take it so seriously! He's a good lad! . . . A misunderstanding.' She held her head down and her eldest daughter came running up and put her arm around her and led her home. Ned ran back and spoke to Mary: 'Don't heed what she said. She doesn't mean it! She's worn out with sitting-up! . . . I'll go on home with her.'

Suddenly the roof-tree broke above the kitchen and the sound of the falling thatch and the gush of sparks brought the men back to the house and away from the scene that was already forming a tangle of thoughts in their minds.

'It's gone this time!' the blacksmith said, 'But we'll be able to save the two bedrooms,' and he jumped from the barrel and looked into the kitchen at the heap of smoking sods, the burnt-out dresser, and the glowing ends of thatch that edged the walls. They sent boys for graips and flung water over the roof above the rooms and shovelled sand on the burning heap that lay on the kitchen floor. But even amidst the vigour of their toil there infringed upon their minds the sight of Ned's mother and her piercing wail. Had Ned Mason done right? Coming out like that and his father a corpse in the house? Each one had the same thought, turning it over secretly, fumbling for an answer. They yearned to discuss it openly, but knew that Luke was watching them, aware of what they were thinking. They wished they had at last finished with the fire and were on their way back from the wake where they knew that with their minds enlivened by a little drink they could find some answer to their restless questioning. All the time Luke worked without ceasing, getting Mary and Barbara to put all their belongings in one of the outhouses. Then he sent them inland to their grandfather's, where they could stay the night, while he himself would sleep in the barn in case the flames would break out again. Before they left he called them aside. 'I

14

want the two of you to go to the wake,' he said quietly. 'But you needn't stop too long. Come home early and not be upsetting your granda. You can all sleep with Tessie in the one bed.' They hesitated. 'But, Father . . .' Mary was ready to speak when he interrupted her. 'Don't talk, girl! When a man is dead it isn't the time nor the place to hold spite!' He turned away from them and walked anxiously to the barn where he broke off the lids of old boxes and hammered them against the windows he had smashed.

In ones and twos the men moved away, but Luke continued to work, locking the fowl-house, giving hay to the cow, and before the spread of light left the sky he made a bed of straw for himself in a corner of the barn. Only a few children lingered about the cottage searching amongst the smoking sods — one finding a sharpening stone, another a red-burnt trowel and a horse-shoe. Luke chased them home and stood against the sycamore tree at the side of the house and gazed at the ugly gap in his cottage and wondered if he should put on one of those new-fangled roofs of corrugated tin. Behind him the sea-birds cheeped as they clustered on the shore for the night, and out at sea the winking light that marked the entrance of the lough grew in strength under the falling hood of night. People going to the wake called to him when they saw the swaying light of his lamp as he made across the yard to his outhouses. Then Tessie arrived, carrying a can of tea and warm potato bread wrapped in a clean cloth.

'You're not going to the wake?' he asked her when they were seated on bags in the barn, the hurricane lamp hanging from a nail in the wall.

'I'd like to go,' she said, peeling off the husk of a grain of corn she had picked from the floor. 'But my granda wasn't out the whole day. He has a load of cold on his chest and when he's like that he always likes to have someone moving about the house.'

'Och, when the others are there you may as well stay at

home,' and as he put the can to his head he wondered if Mary and Barbara had told her about the insults Ned Mason's mother had flung at him. He'd say nothing about it; she'd hear about it time enough. He ate in silence, the dog watching him. Tessie put the grain of corn between her teeth, stretched out her hand and pulled the dog towards her. She ruffled his coat and picked out bits of shavings that were entangled in his hair. He struggled away from her and she held him tightly. He wrenched himself free and went back to Luke and put his nose on his knee.

'Ah, Tessie,' said Luke, 'There's the best watchdog in Ireland. . . . He watches every bite that goes into your mouth,' and he threw a piece of bread in the air and the dog snapped at it before it reached the ground.

Outside someone whistled on the road, and Tessie lifted the can and impatiently squeezed on the ill-fitting lid, and when her father offered to go a bit of the road with her she smiled shyly and said she had no fear of the dark. She combed her black hair and put a clasp in it, and he stood back admiring how she was growing into a fine young girl.

'You'll do all right. I'm thinkin' you're nearly as vain as Barbara. Go on now before he lets another whistle out of him.' She ran from the door and he heard them laugh as the lid sprung off the can and rattled on the road.

He was content now as he lit his pipe and had a last look round the house, knowing that before long the rain would fall. He loosened the laces in his boots, spread an empty sack for the dog, and tossed up the straw in the corner where he would sleep with the sail of his boat covering him. Around him was the cool quiet of the lamp, lighting dimly the things in the barn: his bundle of lobster pots with their rotted cord and nail-split sticks, the brass buckle of a belt, and the loops of nets hanging from the rafters. He puffed at his pipe thinking of the heap of work that was before him: a new roof to put on the house, fresh hazel rods to be cut for the lobster pots, new twine needed for the nets, potatoes to be set — and there was little help the girls could give him. He took his beads and began to say his prayers for the night, but the sight of Ned Mason's mother pressed in upon his mind, distracting him. A drunken brother and a good-for-nothing father! That was a way for anyone to talk about John! John that could throw a fifty-six pound weight about like a boot-last! And then Mary and Barbara in at the wake; it was foolish to send them, and maybe the neighbours eyeing them with contempt and whispering amongst themselves: 'Aren't them Devlin girls the bold, brazen hussies, coming here where they're not wanted . . . annoying the poor woman!' His thoughts jumped madly; it doesn't matter what they think — he had done the right thing! The sudden fall of rain on the roof brought back his mind to the beads in his hand and to the lamplight shining quietly on the straw. He held the beads tightly in an effort to stem his wayward mind. Presently he had finished and he blessed himself and quenched the lamp.

The rain fell heavier, drenching the dark with cold, and as he felt it blow wet under the door he got up and twisted an empty sack across the threshold. Then he burrowed into the straw, drawing comfort from the noising rain, aware that it would pinch out all specks of flame. And in his mind he saw the rain falling through the gap of the broken roof, slithering down the walls and carrying with it bits of burnt straw and flakes of limewash. He pulled the sail around him and his breath came back from it warm and moist and smelling of tar. ' 'Tis well the boat got one coat, anyway,' he said aloud to himself, and the dog, hearing him, came over, licked his hand in the darkness and lay on top of the sail beside him. Outside the rain rattled forlornly on an empty bucket and slapped in blowy gusts against the door. A goose in the fowlhouse stirred, scraked, and then tucked its neck under its warm wing. Down on the shore the sea-birds with their cold feet crouched closer to the shelter of the rocks, and farther to the right the rain washed the sand from the beach-stones, fell on the bare fields, and trickled down the lighted windows of Ned Mason's cottage, where men and women had gathered to sympathize, to gossip and to pray for the soul of the dead man.

CHAPTER II

GLEAMING sheets of corrugated zinc leaned against the front of Luke's cottage, and Luke himself was standing on a ladder, putting on the new roof. The priest who was coming from Ned Mason's stopped to chat with him, his hands behind his back leaning on his walking-stick.

'I see, Luke, you're not wasting much time in getting the house in order again.'

Luke took the nails from his mouth, looked down at the priest, and brandished his hammer playfully: 'It'll be a sweet roof when I have finished with it and a nice skin of tar on it to keep down the rust. Do you know, Father, but the thatch is a bothersome roof — you're never done mending and patching it. Indeed, I wonder why I put up with it so long. In ways it was a God-send that the oul roof did go afire — not a bit of me would have stirred hand or foot·to put on these new-fangled fellows. They're a handy roof and a cheap roof.'

'And maybe a cold roof,' put in the priest. 'You'll find it much noisier in the winter-time when a few waves break across it.'

Luke scratched the back of his head with the handle of the hammer: 'Och, Father, it'll be the life of me to hear the sound of it falling like gravel on the tin! And as for the cold — I'll put on a low ceiling of well-seasoned boards. God have mercy on my old father, but he used to say: "If you want a warm house build a low roof." '

The priest dug the ferrule of his stick into the soft ground, making a pattern of holes, and went on talking casually about the fishing, the price of dulse, and the sheep that had lambed; and occasionally he would glance at the sea where a ship's funnel was scribbling a charcoal line along the sky.

'Tell me, Luke, do you ever hear from John at all?'

Luke paused and hammered a nail through the tin.

'Not a scrape, Father, not a scrape!' and added with feigned light-heartedness: 'John was never a good hand with the pen. . . . But never fear, he'll come home some day!' and with great vigour he drove another nail into the roof, but this time it went in crookedly and he had to lever it out again with the hammer and drive in another.

At that moment Barbara came round the gable carrying eggs in her apron, and seeing the priest unexpectedly, she blushed and tried to lower her apron to cover a patch in her skirt. The priest noticed her embarrassment and pointed his stick at the roof: 'Your father will need your help some of these days when he is going to put on the tar.' Barbara smiled, turned sideways, and, lifting one of the warm eggs from her apron, she blew off a tiny feather that clung to it, and as the priest watched her innocent movements there came from the edges of his mind the scene with Mrs. Mason on the day of the fire, and he wondered what they thought about it and if, like many another trivial thing about the countryside, it would grow into a long-lived spite between these two families. He tried to get them to talk about the fire, but neither Luke nor Barbara would refer to it.

On his way home along the road he noticed the fresh green on the hedges and the catkins like yellow caterpillars dangling in the wind. A spider was weaving its web, sometimes sliding down the silver threads. A goat with its long-eared kid nibbled at the tiny leaves on the bushes, and from the fields came the continual bleat of the young lambs. 'What blight is coming over this land!' the priest thought to himself, 'that the only things making life are the animals in the fields and the flies in the dung-heaps!' He looked round the fields that were stubbed with whins and saw in some of them the outline of grassy ridges that showed that they once were tilled. Hadn't he told his people time and time again from the altar that in another fifty years their land would be dead; that there were more wrecks of houses than good ones; that there were more old men than young children. Wastrels he called them, but they were quick and proud to take offence, and one of them hadn't entered the chapel door because he thought the priest had eyed him during the sermon. As he recalled these things his face grew stern and he found himself whacking at the grass that curved the edge of the road. He took off his hat and let the cool breeze ruffle his thinning hair, and then suddenly he drew up near the hedge when the words of old Mason's will sang through his mind: *I leave all my possessions to my wife for her day.* He had tried to persuade him to leave the small farm to Ned, but the old man was immovable: 'My wife will do all that's good for him. I can set my mind at rest about that!' The priest clicked his tongue as the memory of the old man's death came before him. Why didn't he leave the small farm to Ned and let him marry before he is too old and too cold to have children! Everything for her day! How often had he seen the same words in the wills of dying men! It was like a formula in this part of the country or like an old song that had been handed down from one generation to the next!

The shouts of three little boys attracted his attention and he saw them walking along a bank that edged the road and saw a little path they had worn on it with their bare feet. How shy they were before him! They held their heads down looking at their bare toes, the eldest fiddling with the safety-pin that fastened the strap of his school-bag.

'How many slaps did you get the day?' he asked them. They giggled and glanced up at him from under their long lashes.

'Head or harp!' and he tossed a penny into the air and

trapped it between his palms. They all guessed at once and he gave them a penny each, ruffled their hair, and playfully smacked their bottoms with his stick. He smiled as he left them, but when he came in sight of the chapel gates and saw the untidy graveyard with the grass fringing the plinths of the graves, his face once more became solemn. He would get the grass cut before the new growth would rise. And then the bishop was due any time to confirm the handful of children. He would speak to his people on Sunday about that and ask them to get wire brushes and soap-suds to scour all the headstones. He would like to have things in good order for his lordship. And that damp, mildewed wallpaper in his sitting-room; he would push the book-case against that until the bishop had departed. He had done his best with that damp spot, but nothing would keep out the rainy, south-west wind.

He opened the door of his house and saw the streaks in the wall where he had scored it with his bicycle. He would see to that, too.

From the kitchen came the sounds of his housekeeper poking at the range and shouting at the cat. She was slightly deaf and consequently noisy, but she was kind to him and obedient, and as he mounted the stairs to his sitting-room he thought of some of the housekeepers he had endured during his twenty-five years on the mission and of the domineering one he had encountered on his first curacy, where he had shared the same house with an old parish priest who had already forfeited his freedom to his house-keeper. He remembered how, if he had been late of an evening, she would have ordered him into the kitchen for his tea, and how he had to stoop below the clothes-horse to get to the table, afraid to raise his eyes lest the housekeeper would think he was scrutinizing the garments on the line. 'She was a Tartar!' he smiled to himself as he reached the head of the stairs and turned into his sitting-room. The window was open and the door slammed shut from his hand,

and a few papers lying on the table were blown on to the floor.

'Kate believes in fresh air,' he said as he closed the window and stood gazing at the green fields spreading flat to the sea, and above them a silver light combing out between the clouds. He lit a cigarette and went to the head of the stairs.

'Kate!' he called, leaning over the banisters. There was no answer, although he could hear the hum of the range and the tick-tock of the clock from the kitchen. 'Kate!' he called a little louder — 'as deaf as a post' he said to himself. He could hear her cutting bread at the table, and he knew she would be getting him some tea. 'Kate! Kate!' and he padded with his feet on the landing.

She poked her head out of the kitchen door: 'Did you call, Father?'

'A little!' he said with a wry smile. 'Before I forget — would you mind giving the brass candlesticks and the crucifix on the altar an extra spot of brasso?' and she looked up at him with soft, steady eyes as he told her in detail how to sharpen a point on a match and gouge out the verdigris from the crevices in the candlesticks.

'To be sure, Father. . . . To be sure! Is there anything else you'd like me to do?' and she passed a bread-knife from her right hand to her left and took out a handkerchief from her apron pocket.

'I think you should tell Jimmy Neil to give the doors a lick of paint and spruce up the garden.'

She held down her head and stroked the blade of the knife with her forefinger: 'I'm afraid, Father — not that I should say it — but from what I hear poor Jimmy's not doing well. He was found — not that I should say it, Father — in a ditch some weeks ago, and the rain pouring on him like you'd think he was an old sack and the empty bottles rattling at his feet. It was Paddy Boden and Tessie Devlin found him and brought him to Dan Scullion's in the cart — only for them he'd be foundered and famished. But, Father, it was no lesson for him; he was hard at it again — as drunk as the drunken sailor. I hear he's sprawling somewhere about Downpatrick and that he has an ass and cart all of his own.'

'Don't mind, Kate. I'll see him myself when he turns up here again,' and he flicked the cigarette ash into a flower-pot that stood on a mahogany stand.

'Och, Father, not that I should say it, but he's a sore torment to me when he's in the kitchen. He ruined a table-cloth on me and broke a cup the last time he was mending the punctures on your bicycle. His hands is all shaky like a dangling branch.'

'Maybe you could bring in a trough for the occasion,' he tried to say gravely as he turned into his room.

He crossed to his book-case, took out a copy of St. Paul's epistles, lit another cigarette, and sat down to prepare a sermon for the following Sunday. He heard the door-bell ring, and he paused with a finger in his book as Kate came to tell him that it was Ned Mason to see him.

CHAPTER III

WHEN Ned came into the room the priest greeted him jovially, forced him to take a cigarette, lighted it for him and talked about the grand spring weather. But Ned was only half-listening, glancing sideways and twisting his cap. He held the cigarette between his forefinger and thumb and smoked it rapidly. At last he blurted out: 'Father, I came to see you. . . . You were one of the witnesses of my father's will. God be good to him, but he told me if anything happened him he would see that I got the wee farm, and the home-place be for my mother and sisters.' The cigarette fell on to the rug and he scooped it up and flung it into the fire. 'And you know, Father, how the will was made . . . I'm left nothing!'

'I know, Ned. I know,' the priest said sympathetically.

Ned opened and closed the stud in the peak of his cap: 'But this is the fix I'm in. I'm going with Mary Devlin for the past two years and we said we'd get married as soon as my father'd give me the wee farm and the house on it.'

'I understand everything. But don't say anything for a while yet. There's plenty of time. Go slowly. After all, Ned, your father is only a little while in his grave and it would upset your mother to be . . .' and he paused and toyed with cigarette ash on the table . . . 'to be finding fault with your father's arrangements.'

'But I told my father about me and Mary a year ago and he agreed with me. "Mary Devlin's a fine lump of a girl and I'd like to see you settled" — them's the words he used.'

'Your father, Ned, was a reasonable man.'

'But he didn't do fair by me in his will,' and Ned held out the empty palms of his hands: 'There's what I get — nothing! And while other fellows were out sporting themselves on a Sunday I was always about the place working the very flesh off my bones,' and he looked at the priest with a hard gaze.

'Now, Ned, take an older man's advice. Go about your work quietly,' and the priest smoothed the air with his hand. 'And you'll find, with the help of God, that an upright man like yourself will get all that he desires. And your mother . . .'

'But she treats me like a boy that's just left school. She doesn't want me to be seen next nor near the Devlins. You remember, Father, what happened at the fire.'

The priest joined and unjoined the tips of his fingers and, with his head to the side, looked at Ned with an expression of great gentleness. 'When there are so many people ready to remember that — you, at least, you should try to forget it. Your poor mother's nerves were strained with worry about your father. She hasn't mentioned that incident to me and I am sure she regrets it.'

'Indeed, Father, she hasn't softened one bit to the Devlins — she has more kind words for the tinkers and beggars that ramble about the countryside.'

The priest with his finger-nail scratched at a little stain on his sleeve: 'She doesn't mean half a word of it, Ned. She thinks — sure all mothers are the same — that she'll be able to marry you to the richest girl in the diocese,' and he gave a light-hearted little laugh and was glad to see Ned smiling and twirling the cap in his hand. 'And as for the Devlins, they are all decent, quiet girls. And there's fine stuff in Luke and in poor John, wherever he is.'

'When you're over in the house, Father, maybe you'll speak to my mother . . .' and he stood up to take his leave.

'Don't worry, Ned, I'll do all in my power to help you. . . And by the way if you see Jimmy Neil tell him to call to see me. I want him to cut the grass.' And he went down the stairs with Ned and put a hand on his shoulder as he opened the door to let him out. 'Take things easy, Ned, like a good man.'

A wind swirled round the corners of the priest's house tugging at the grass that edged the path and rasping the unpruned roses that straggled along the top of a wall. Ned plucked some of the young leaves from a hedge and put them in his mouth, and at the graveyard-gate he turned in and standing at his father's grave, on which the grass was sprouting through the faded clay, he said a few prayers and tried to dispel any feeling of hardness that had come to him since his mother had shown him the will.

At a turn off the road he saw old Scullion digging at the back of his cottage and Tessie Devlin following him with a white basin and planting the seed potatoes in rows. Near them was a heap of manure with a graip stuck in the top, and a few gulls flitted over the clods waiting until the old man had passed up the field.

'Don't plant them too close together, girl. Give them room to swell,' and the old man spat on his hands and plunged the spade into the soil. Ned watched them through the thin hedge and smiled at old Scullion when he rested on the spade and glared with affectionate contempt at the girl coming on her knees behind him.

The soil was black and cool. Smoke was rising from a heap of withered stalks, blowing thickly over the field, sometimes covering the two workers. Tessie would give an odd cough and cover her eyes with her hand until the wind swirled the smoke in another direction.

'Bad luck to it for a bad-tempered wind — it hasn't made up its mind what way to blow!' the old man grumbled when he saw the fire harried and teased by the wind and the smoke blown as flat as a blanket across the drills.

'Take it easy, Granda,' Tessie said, looking at him with eyes that were smarted by the smoke. 'You've done enough for one day and my father could open the rest of the drills with his plough.'

'Do you want me to be the laughing-stock of the whole countryside — a plough and a pair of horses in a bit of a field that you could cover with a few bed-sheets. If you're tired bendin' your back leave the seed be and I'll put them in myself,' and he lifted a big stone to fling into the hedge and saw Ned Mason smiling at him.

'Your soil's in perfect health, Dan', Ned said, and old Scullion stuck his spade in the ground and came stumbling over the clods. He spat on his hand and held it out to Ned: 'Leave it there! I'm proud of you! There's plenty who talk and plenty who don't understand and plenty who don't think — all ignorant galoots of men that get their knowledge out of a newspaper. But no matter what they say you done the right thing in helping to put out Luke's fire. Aw, I had it out with some of them in O'Hare's pub the other night — giving off their opinion as if it was ex cathedra!' and he cleared his throat and spat with haughty contempt through the hedge. 'And what does Father Toner think of it?'

Ned broke off a thorny twig from the hedge: 'You know

26

what Father Toner is!' and then he added quickly, trying to draw the old man's mind in another direction: 'Tessie's a great help to you, Dan.'

'No, he'd be careful in making a pronouncement,' Dan went on, following the track of his own mind. 'He's better to say nothing — not give a theological opinion. But there's plenty would dare to speak for him.'

Ned poked out the dirt between his finger nails with the thorns on the twig and hastily made an excuse to be off, the old man shouting at the top of his voice and sending spittle over his beard: 'You're going the sea-road, I warrant! You'll see Luke hammering on the lazy man's roof. Thon will be an ill-natured contraption. Och, he'll live to regret the warm straw! Work that takes time and thought is good work. Tell him from me it's only a makeshift.' Ned laughed and flicked a piece of clay over at Tessie, but she paid no heed to him, thinking in her own mind that she would treat him coldly for the way his mother had behaved on the day of the fire: 'We're every bit as good as the Masons,' she said to herself, 'even they have sixty acres of land.'

Ned put a blade of grass in his mouth and walked off, his cap at the back of his head, his thick black hair bunched out over the peak. From the road he heard old Dan shouting at Tessie and saw him with the spade over his shoulder marching to the burning heap of weed and with his back to the wind scatter the ashes in fury over his field. The gulls rose up in fright and flew overhead looking sideways at the soil covered now with countless twirls of smoke.

Luke's hammer echoed sharply from the sea as Ned came to a rise in the road, and when he reached the cottage Luke had fastened the end of a rope to a staple in the wall and was flinging the other end over the roof where Mary stood with upraised hands to catch it.

'That's a brave day, Luke. Can I give you a hand?'

Luke turned and when he saw it was Ned he nodded dryly, and without haste went round to the back of the house to tie

27

the other end of the rope. 'Ned Mason's here — so you stay where you are,' he said to Mary as he tautened the rope to hold down the roof against the winds from the sea. 'We've three more ropes to put on and I'll sling them across to you.'

'You've made a fine tidy job of it!' Ned said when Luke came round to the front of the cottage.

'Aye,' Luke said and lifted a rope, spliced it with his pen-knife, and after tying it to a staple above the door he threw the free end over to Mary. Ned ran round, caught it and swung on to it till it scringed tight against the hip of the roof. He pressed her hand when they were lapping the rope round the staple and she whispered to him: 'My father's a bit stubborn the day. But it'll soon wear off. Your mother's words are starting to rile him.'

'See how it's holding at the other end,' Ned shouted with pretended good humour, aware of the sour greeting Luke had shown him. 'Tell him to give it a belt or two with the hammer.'

Mary came back again to Ned: 'He's not putting the other ropes on this evening,' and she bit her lower lip and gave a confused smile.

He noticed the uneasy look in her eyes and added quickly: 'I'll be going to the town in the morning . . . I'll see you at the usual place — about seven o'clock,' and when he came round the gable Luke was nowhere to be seen and for some reason Ned lifted a few pebbles and tossed them on to the roof and heard them rattling over the ridges of the tin and falling to the ground. Crossing over the little bridge he saw Mary's geese preening their feathers, and then he heard the defiant ping of Luke's hammer striking the iron staple. 'I know Luke too well to mind that!' he smiled: 'A couple of bottles of stout would soon cure him!'

His lonin gate was swinging to and fro, the white pillar deeply grooved by the loose bolt. He closed the gate for the wind was blowing strongly, fluttering the ivy on the trees and humming in the three rows of bull-wire that closed the

28

gaps in the hedges. As he drew near the house he noticed where the bark of one tree had bulged over the wire like two swollen lips. Hens ran in and out of the orchard where a stone wall sheltered the crouching apple trees from the sea winds. None of the trees had blossomed yet, and as he peered at them from over the hedge he saw where the hens had tramped down some of the daffodils. As he stood there wondering if he should close the gaps with netting wire Sarah, his eldest sister, moved across the yard with two buckets, while his sheepdogs came barking to meet him. He threw a stone at a hen that was scraping in the orchard and hurried up the yard.

His mother was baking bread on the griddle when he entered the warm kitchen. With one glance she saw that he was wearing his good boots. She vigorously scraped the griddle with a knife, swept the scrapings with a goose's wing on to a plate and flung them on to the cobbled yard.

'Surely you didn't put on your good boots to go to the blacksmith's,' she said as she carried the dough in her two hands and spread it on the griddle.

'I wasn't at the blacksmith's!'

'I thought you were over about the broken plough,' and she stooped over the griddle to blow off smuts that flickered on top of the bread.

'I'll see about the plough to-morrow!'

'And where were you to this time!'

'Out!'

'Out where?'

He didn't answer her. With slow deliberation he took off his boots, looked at the sole of each in turn, and put them on the rungs of a small table. She stood erect beside him, turning her wedding-ring on her finger, and with clenched lips watched the damp imprint of his feet on the hearthstone and the slow way he broke off the clay from his old boots before putting them on his feet. She rattled the brush from its place behind the door, spread a newspaper over the bread on the griddle, and brushed the hearth. She put the brush back and it fell with a clatter on the floor.

'Get me a few pieces of kindling to save the coal,' she said, taking the newspaper from off the bread.

As if he weren't listening to her he gazed at the tracks of the brush on the hearth and the red glow of the fire under the griddle. Again she asked him to bring in wood and he looked at her and said quietly: 'Sure you know the wood's all done!'

'Take the axe and chop up the plank you got ashore last October. I don't know what you want that ornament for — propped on two stones and your initials cut out in it like any schoolboy. It's about time you grew up!'

'It's about time you stopped treating me as a child! Do you think the labouring man hasn't his eyes open and sees what's going on!'

'You'll not have James long if you take many holidays off like you did the day. Poor Sarah and Ann and Delia and himself have been toiling and moiling all day putting in the potatoes. And you! — gallivantin' and philanderin' about the countryside. Go on now before dark and do a bit of work. Cut up that plank!'

'It'd be useful some day,' he said quietly and took a glowing twig from the fire to light his pipe.

His mother turned the bread on the griddle, and as a burning smell spread over the kitchen she clicked her tongue and scraped the burnt part off the bread with her knife. Then she stood stiffly beside him, her arms folded across her apron, her mouth set.

'It only makes a shelter for the hens. But I suppose you'll keep it till it crumbles to pieces in the wet and damp, till the toadstools grow out of it, and it brings a nest of snails crawling up the walls and into the house!'

He puffed slowly at his pipe: 'It's a good plank and it'd be a crime to mangle it with any axe. It's a saw it wants and the saw needs to be set.'

'Anything for an excuse!' and she plunged her knife into the bread, withdrew it and looked to see if the blade were clean. 'If you don't do it I'll do it myself! I suppose you want it for a certain party that could be doing with a new roof — that's why you'll not touch it!'

He wiped his mouth with the back of his hand, took the axe, and strode across the yard to the grindstone. He drenched the stone with a tin of water, and rapidly turned the handle; and from the window his mother eyed him, listening to the hasky grit of the revolving stone and the sparks running from the blade.

The plank lay at the side of the house propped on two stones, and after chasing out the hens that sheltered underneath it he rested it against a huge boulder and began hacking it in the middle, and without speaking, his mother came out and carried the chips and scallops in her lap and brought them into the house. Presently his sisters, Ann and Delia, trudged past him on their way from the potato field, scarfs tied about their heads, and their sack aprons spotted with damp. They went over to a tub of water, Ann holding out her hands while Delia poured water over them from a tin. Then James came with the two horses from the field and when the girls had finished washing their hands he gave the horses a drink at the tub and led them to the stable.

Ned took off his coat and when he had hacked the plank into convenient lengths he began to chop some of them with the hatchet. Sarah worked about the yard seeing to the fowl and the cows, and occasionally she would come over and ask him to come for his tea and not be bringing a head of sweat out on himself. With a silent stubbornness he ignored her and when he came to the butt of the plank where he had cut out N.M. he scraped out the dirt that was embedded in the letters and he carried it into the house and placed it on the fire, his name standing out as clearly as the marks on a milestone.

'You needn't make me anything to eat till I come in again,

There's a wind rising and I want to see that the boat's all right,' and he lit his pipe and went out, his two dogs at his heels.

When he topped the little hill at the back of the house the wind met him with great force, whistling like wire in the grass, and swirling the hair on the necks of the dogs. He made down the cliff-path to the shore, watching the hurrying waves breaking and spreading a hem of white on the sand. He put an oar under the forepaw of the boat, lifted the sand-soaked rope, and hauled up the boat till it lay on the grass above the farthest tide-mark. He didn't want to go back to the house until James had finished his tea, so he walked along the shore and stopped once to look at a dead cormorant with empty eye sockets, and when he kicked it out of the withered wrack a hive of sand-lice fistled from underneath it. He left the shore and struck up over the banks where the dogs chased rabbits in and out of the tall bent grass and his sheep with their lambs moved away from him. He saw a few bones of a rabbit with fur sticking to them and beside them the rusted wire of a forgotten snare. Above his head the peewits disturbed from their nests kept up a melancholy cry and dipped around his shoulder when he stooped to look at a hoof-mark containing three eggs the colour of a thrush's breast. When he reached the top of the banks some of his sheep were lying in hollows out of the wind, their lambs quiet around them now that the light was fading and the first stars arriving in the sky. At the wooden gate of his potato field a few potatoes lay mashed in the wheel-ruts and as he passed through he counted the drills the girls had finished without his help and looked in the unharnessed cart at the boxes of seed potatoes covered with sacking to protect them from the cold night-air. The field lay dark and shelterless, for only a few scraggy thorns hunched and starved by the sea-winds served as a hedge. He walked down between the drills and at the foot of the field he saw a light spring up in the Devlin cottage and he thought of Luke and his ropes and wondered if Mary would be able to meet him in the morning.

He crouched under the bull wire at the foot of the field and came up to the back of the little house which his father had bought about six years ago and which they now used as a store for corn and meal and potatoes, and where they stabled the brood mare and reared a few pigs.

The pigs grunted when they heard his foot on the stones. He went into the stable, lit a small hurricane lamp, and pitched some hay to the mare. He stood near her, running his hand over her huge glossy sides, watching her tugging the hay from the manger and turning her moist eyes to look at him. She was thriving well. In another few weeks he would have to sit up with her — and with his father dead and a labouring man that feels he's overworked, he knew that he'd have to watch the mare himself.

It was dark when he left the little house and when he reached his own lonin he saw a light in the upstair windows and he hoped his mother had gone to bed, but when he entered the kitchen she was seated at the small table with a note-book in her hand and beside her an ink-bottle with a red pen in it.

'Ned,' she said when he was taking his supper at the big table and Sarah pouring out the tea for him: 'Did you settle for the six cases of stout O'Hare sent up at your father's wake?'

'I did.'

'Did he give you a receipt?'

'I didn't ask him for one. It'll be all right — Jimmy O'Hare's not the kind of a man that'd bill you again,' and he split a farl of bread in two and plastered it with butter.

Her pen scratched something into her book and she took off her glasses, blew her breath on them, and wiped them on the hem of her apron. 'You're getting very careless of late! Your father never did business like that!'

'You'd think Jimmy O'Hare was a black stranger — the way you talk! Didn't we go to school together!' And as there was a touch of hardness in his voice Sarah, who was

C

stirring yellow meal at the fire, raised her head and signed to him with her eyes to keep quiet.

'I know! I know!' his mother answered, making a few meaningless squiggles with the point of her pen.

There was silence for a moment. Sarah skimmed off soot that had fallen into the meal, scraped the wooden spoon on the rim of the pot, and lifted it on to the hob.

'You'll ask him for a receipt?' his mother said, her left hand smoothing her brow.

Ned had a piece of bread raised to his mouth and he stopped, put the bread down on the plate, and stared sharply at his mother bent over her book. But Sarah quickly lifted the teapot from the hob, and as she poured out more tea for him she nudged him with her toe.

'All right,' he said, shaking his head. 'I'll ask him for one. But sure it'd make no differs anyway.'

His mother closed her note-book, wiped the nib with a corner of the blotting paper and put the ink-bottle on the ledge of the window. She got to her feet and holding the brass stand of the table-lamp in one hand she pulled the little chain of the extinguisher and quenched the light. There was no light now in the big kitchen except the glow from the fire and a feeble light from an oil-lamp nailed to the wall. From a shelf under the stairs Sarah got her mother a candle and wrapped a piece of paper round the butt of it so that it would fit tightly into the socket.

'Don't be staying up too long,' she said to Sarah. And then she halted for a minute at the foot of the stairs, looking at the candle in her hand, the grease melting around the wick and the flame brightening. 'And you, Ned, you should have been in for the Rosary — and your poor father not long dead!'

She looked thin and worn standing in black before him and the flame of the candle haggering her features.

He combed his fingers through his hair and unconsciously smoothed the back of his neck with his hand.

'I was down foddering the mare and I didn't know it was that late.'

As she climbed the stairs the shadow of the banisters waded and closed across the kitchen like a fan. Then the wind hummed through the house when she opened her room door, and when she shut it Ned came to the fire and Sarah put the dishes in a basin and scalded them with water.

'Take the easy way with her, Ned,' she said with a slight ache in her voice. 'She's getting old and you'll have to humour her. She thinks more of you than of any of us.'

'That might all be. But if she'd think less — I'd be happier.'

' "There's nothing good enough for Ned"— I've heard her say time and time again. She wants the very best for you.'

'But what she thinks is best for me is not what I think. I want left alone — to live my own life in my own way. Since my father's death — aye, and months before it when he was ailing she was for ever watching me and asking me where I was and who I was with — just as if I was a youngster out of school. I'm thirty-three now, and even I am the youngest in the house it's time I was allowed to think for myself.'

'But you never give way to her wishes in anything. There's always a row even when she asks you to harness the trap of a Sunday and take her to see Aunt Rose.'

'There's one thing certain — she'll not fall down in this house for the want of support,' and he stooped to unlace his boots, pondering on what Sarah had just said and trying to remember when he had refused to do anything his mother had asked him. He took out his pipe and was searching for a piece of paper to light it when he saw chips of wood on the hearth— bits of the good plank his mother had ordered him to hack up. He wondered if he should mention it to Sarah but when he saw her take his boots from below the table and polish them for the morning and thought, too, of the wan look on his mother's face he kept silent. Presently she came over to the fire. She took a pair of his socks from a line below the

35

mantelpiece, shook the dust from them and stretched her hand into them in search for holes. The table-lamp crackled as it cooled slowly and the sleepy cat opened an eye and looked at it. Ned smoked his pipe, and outside the wind blowing up from the sea hurled itself in great gulps at the house.

CHAPTER IV

DURING the night it had rained. Puddles lay in the farm-yard and drops dripped from the cart-shed on to sodden straw. All the doors were closed and the white walls seemed cold and shrunken in the mists that blew up from the sea.

Ned was early astir, and when he came into the yard he looked at the sky and at a few stars that were struggling to keep alive against the stretch of dawn. He went to the hill at the back of the house, and the rabbits that were nibbling the wet grass bounded down the cliff rattling pebbles on to the stones below. Some of his sheep were chewing their cud, their fleece moist and curled by the night's rain. He looked at the Isle of Man smothered in mist and the smoke from a few ships lying in broken smudges above the sea — it'd be a good day, please God. He turned to go in when the blob of a rowing-boat off the point attracted his attention and he wondered if it was Luke lifting the lobster pots. God knows what made him spend so much time at the fishing! What was to be had out of it except colds and damp and rheumatism. And John was the same — never out of a boat. There was one thing certain — if he had a few sons out of Mary he'd try to keep them from the sea. It's all right once in a while when the herrin's in and you can shoot a net like many another — but to be always at it and have no settled hours: cutting dulse, setting lobster pots, and fishing with the hand-line for a few cod and whiting. Fishing and farming don't mate well — how often he had heard his father saying that!

Presently the boat pulled away from the point and he saw the man ship his oars, go to the hump in the stern, lift a dark object and drop it into the sea; and he knew it must be Luke for he had to do everything himself now that John was away. He hurried from the hill for Mary would have the fire reddened long ago and might be out ahead of him.

He got out the horse and yoked her to the cart. He took off the tail-board, spread out some straw and hoisted up three pigs that he was taking to the fair. Sarah rapped the kitchen window, and when he came inside she had his break-fast on the table, and on the floor a pair of ducks with their feet tied which she was sending to her Aunt Rose in Down-patrick. One of the ducks nebbed at the cord on its legs, and as it flapped its wings it whirled the ashes from a shovel which Sarah was carrying out to the midden. The cold air rushed through the open door and Ned watched the horse eating an armful of hay and pricking its ears when Sarah tapped the ashes from the shovel.

He was hurrying his breakfast in case Mary would be waiting for him. Then he heard the banisters creak, and his mother came down the stairs with her coat and hat over her arm.

'I think I'll go with you, Ned. I have a few calls to make in the town and I may as well do them now as not.'

'They're not that important that they can't wait,' Ned tried to say casually, and he forked the last piece of bacon on his plate and put it in his mouth. 'What'd the neighbours say if they see a woman of your age sitting on a bare cart and maybe get your death. You should go back to bed and rest. What do you think, Sarah?'

'Heed what Ned says, Mother! You're taking too much out of yourself. You're getting too old now to be jarveying in to town on a draughty cart. Sure Ned will do all you want.'

'Ned can't do these things. I've a few things to look after since your father's death and I have a longing to see your Aunt Rose.'

'Sure I'll tackle the trap some fine Sunday when the days are warmer and take you to see Aunt Rose,' and he wiped his mouth with the back of his hand and took a hat from a peg below the stairs. He opened the door and the horse looked over at him with hay in its mouth and the two dogs crushed past him and ran across the floor on wet paws.

'There's a sour look on that sky,' Sarah said, gazing over the roof of the cart-shed at a dark swirl of crumbling clouds. But her mother paid no heed to her as she stood near the looking-glass, stabbing a hat-pin into her hat. 'Well, if your mind's made up to go, Mother, wait'll you get a bite to eat itself,' Sarah said, putting the pan on the fire.

Ned leaned against the jamb of the door, his back to the kitchen, his hands thrust deep in his pockets. From the sitting-room he heard the grandfather clock strike seven, and at the last stroke he raised his voice: 'I'm late as it is! Sure you can wait till the next fair!'

'I'm going this morning should I tramp it,' his mother answered, a cup of tea raised to her lips.

He was unable to stifle the feeling of anger that was setting him on edge, and he was afraid of what might happen when they met Mary on the road. 'The best of the fair will be over by the time we arrive,' he said sharply, and spat out on the cobbles. 'I'll loose out the horse and stay at home.'

'Sarah!' said his mother, pertly putting down her knife and fork. 'Go outside and waken James! I'll get him to drive me — and live down the disgrace of it!'

'A headstrong woman!' Ned said to himself as he strode across the yard. He kicked the hay away from the horse and the horse startled, upsetting the pigs on top of one another. They squealed and moved stupidly about on the straw, grunting and shaking their flabby ears. Ned put his foot on the felloe and jumped into the cart. His mother, dressed in black, an umbrella over her arm, came out of the house and was half-way across the yard when she turned back for a rug. Ned jerked at the reins; the horse tossed its head and he yelled at it to keep still. Presently his mother came out with the rug. Sarah helped her on to the cart and told her to keep herself warm and to come home early.

Ned set off briskly, the briars in the hedges scratching against the wheels as the cart swung in and out of the holes in the lonin. His mother sat stiffly beside him, her lips compressed, her gloved hands clutching the umbrella, its ferrule thubbing on the boards.

'Don't go so fast, Ned,' she managed to say, at the same time wondering why he wouldn't get a load of gravel from the shore and fill up the pot-holes. She was ashamed of the state of the lonin, and as soon as she'd get back she'd tell James to attend to it. In the hedge a wren with its tail erect hopped from twig to twig giving out a little cheep as if it had lost something, and then, as the cart jolted close to it, it flew off and hid in the ivy that shivered around the trunk of an old tree. The lonin gate was closed, and as Ned swung it open, the raindrops on the bars ran together and fell with a slap on to the wet ruts.

At the wee farm two rats ran across the road and Ned felt his mother's hand on his arm: 'Were the cats in when you were down with the mare last night? The rats would make a quick feast of Delia's chickens.'

'They couldn't get into the kitchen. I've it well sealed,' he answered, his mind on Mary, almost hoping that she would not meet him this morning.

'I was against your father buying that poky wee house. It's hatching with rats and falling to bits with the damp.'

'What's poky about it! You could turn a cart in the kitchen! And forby it's sheltered from the sea!'

'It's no use to us except for the bit of land. We could store all it holds up in the home-place. And look at the state of the front door — hacked with names and scribbled with things you wouldn't dare to say aloud. There's plenty could be doing with the house — some poor pensioner out of the workhouse. It'd be a charity.'

39

'And would you let him have it rent free?'

'They don't appreciate anything for nothing in this country.'

'Then where's the charity?' he said bitterly.

'Taking him out of the degradation of the workhouse. Giving him a house of his own and making him feel free — that'd be the charity,' and she poked her umbrella at the dirt between the floorboards of the cart.

A strained silence came between them as the horse turned its back to the sea and trotted on to the main road that led to Downpatrick. The wind was freshening and blades of sunlight cleaved up between the clouds and glittered on the puddles on the road. About a quarter of a mile off he saw Mary standing under a tree at a bend in the road — their usual meeting-place. He felt his blood throbbing in his head. He stood up in the cart, slowed the horse to a walking pace, and held the reins slack. He'd face it out. 'Are you going to Downpatrick, Mary?' he'd say. 'Hop in and I'll give you a lift!' But as he was fumbling and arranging his words he saw her leave the road and disappear through the hedge, and he knew she had seen his mother seated in the cart. He urged on the horse and when he had turned the bend in the road he suddenly pulled in to the side, scrambled over the pigs, lifted out one of the pins of the tail-board, and pretended to his mother that he had lost it and had heard something drop a short distance behind them. He ran back to look for it and met Mary cleaning the mud from her shoes against the grass on the roadside. He looked at her hair, wet with drops that had fallen from the branches, and a scratch of blood on the back of her hand.

'I saw your mother!' she said, giving a joyless laugh and looking at him with anxious eyes.

He took her hand firmly: 'Come on, Mary, and face it out with me! It has to be done some time!'

'I couldn't, Ned. I couldn't. Not now!' and she glanced furtively down the road, expecting his mother to appear round the bend. He told her about the pin, and she bit her lip and patted the brown paper that covered a hole in the bottom of her basket.

'I might get a lift in another cart and see you in the town,' and her lips quivered as she spoke, and, drawing her towards him, he put his arm around her and kissed her.

'She'll come back!' and she broke away from him, but, noticing the grieved expression on his face, she added: 'I'm not blaming you, Ned. It's not your fault!'

He pressed her hand: 'Mary, we'll make up for this some day!' And when she had hurried him away and told him that she would surely get a lift in another cart and see him in the town, she stood about on the road listening with a gathering feeling of sorrow to the rattle of his cart as it moved off. She licked the line of blood on her hand, undecided what to do or where to go, and at the same time walking slowly homewards. But suddenly she stopped as she thought of what Barbara or her father would ask her: 'God knows you were out early enough to get a lift!' her father would say; and Barbara would say when she got her alone: 'Did Ned not turn up!'

Mary shook her head and turned in the direction of Downpatrick, looking around now and again to see if a cart were coming her way. The sun shone warmly, polishing the varnished buds of a chestnut tree and gleaming on the furrows in the ploughed fields. She spread the brown paper from her basket under a hedge and sat down, idly plucking the petals from a primrose and yielding to a hostile feeling against Ned. He should have let her know that his mother intended to go with him, and not have her sitting about on the roadside like any tinker! She got to her feet, dusted the petals from her coat, and with a twig scraped the dirt from the crevices of her shoes. The road was drying; larks were splintering the air with song, and finches, swaying on the topmost branches of the hedge, kept up a nervous pink-pink.

She had walked about two miles when a cart overtook her

41

and she was glad to see it was Paddy Boden, and when he pulled up and spoke to her, her grandfather, who had been stretched out on the bottom of the cart, raised his head and peered at her with a grotesque expression: 'In the name of God, where did you come from!'

When at last she was comfortably seated Dan lit his pipe, covered its bowl with a tin-cap, and lay back on the straw, his two hands under his head, his feet crossed in an attitude of great contentment. She noticed his thick grey stockings, the neat patches on the knees of his trousers, and the broken peak of his cap stiffened underneath with a piece of cardboard, and she reflected how fortunate he was in having Tessie to look after him and not Barbara — a girl who thought of nothing only her own self. And as they ambled up the hills with the roads drying rapidly under the sun and the whins in the hedges blazing in a yellow that was too bright to look upon, Paddy began to sing and Dan closed his eyes, grateful for the little breeze that fingered his beard and rustled the straw in the cart. Mary, seated beside Paddy, looked sideways at his red-complexioned face and thought of his love for Tessie and how her granda encouraged them. Then there was her own love for Ned — her father tugging her away from him, and Ned's mother with her tight-lipped mouth and her scornful insults. And the more she pondered on it the more it twisted and wound itself in an implacable gloom about her mind. She sighed heavily and lifted the basket off her lap and placed it at her feet. She joined her hands and scanned the road, hoping they wouldn't overtake Ned. With her lips closed she smiled at a blue bonnet with a feather in its mouth flying into a hole in a wall, and then she looked through the leafing hedges at the ploughed land or at the cows, out after the long winter, moving stiffly across the fields.

The sun came out stronger and the larks combed the air with tiny drills of song. Paddy raised his head and sang with loud passion:

42

Dear thoughts are in my mind,
And my soul soars enchanted,
As I hear the sweet lark sing,
In the clear air of the day . . .

and as the sad loveliness of the tune fell in swathes about
her ears, a choking heaviness came over her and she turned
her head away from him, and through the tears that formed
in her eyes she saw, as through a prism, the blurred colours
of the countryside. Then suddenly Paddy stopped, caught
her arm, and pointed to a flock of birds flying high above a
hill and hanging like the tail of a boy's kite. And as the line
of birds looped and twisted, changed and turned, dangling
and describing their curious curves, they debated loudly as
to what kind they might be until old Dan sat up, shaded his
eyes and peered at the sky.

'Them's wild geese,' he said with a longing in his voice.
'Them's wild geese! Bad weather's chased them from Scotland and they're heading now for a lake amongst the hungry
Mournes.' His eyes glazed, and the wrinkles on his face
bunched tight together as he raised his stick to his shoulder
and recounted how he had shot six barnacles one hard
December night. 'I did in troth — not a feather escaped,'
and he lowered his stick and eyed the birds again. 'They're
going now!' he shouted, as he saw one bird disentangle itself
from the line. 'In every flock you'll always get one lad to
know the road. The rest will follow him. But if he ever
hesitates they'll lose faith in him,' and he spat over the side
of the cart and wiped the spittle off his beard with his sleeve.
Then from the town came the slow, ponderous strokes of
the Angelus bell and he took off his cap, held it in front of
his breast, his eyes travelling over the fields to the red-
bricked asylum and to the inmates scattered about the
grounds or walking in groups escorted by a uniformed
attendant. His mind wandered from the prayer he was
saying and struggled with a thought that mixed wild geese
with the inmates of an asylum.

43

'God help them and their people,' he said, pulling on his cap and waving his hand towards the fields sloping up to the building.

' 'Tis terrible for anyone to be shut up there!' Paddy said, clicking his tongue at the horse as it climbed the hill.

' 'Tis worse on them that has anybody in it,' Dan went on. 'The patient is all right — his mind has cut the tether and he's roaming in a land of his own. But it's a purgatory on earth for their kith and kin — visiting them, week in, week out; year in, year out. And always hoping and hoping for the best! Poor girls crossed in love or poor fellows tortured with scruples or a man or a woman burdened and broken with worry — that's what fills them places!' He shook his head, ' 'Tis a sad and misfortunate sight!'

'I heard someone saying you should be locked up in it,' Paddy said with a smile, bringing the rope-reins down on the horse's rump.

'Begod, you're right,' Dan said angrily. ' 'Tis a wonder half the Irish race isn't in it. Look at all the years we have suffered — downtrodden, famined, evicted, exiled, and workhoused! Begod there's great spirit in us somewhere!' and his fist shut tight over the bowl of his pipe. His eyes blazed as he recalled how, over sixty years ago, his mother had him praying night and day that his father's mind wouldn't break, for his father had opposed the landlords, and because he had refused to sign a landlord's paper to avoid Land agitators he was evicted from his house. He remembered, too, as a boy how his father used to shout: 'All this land will I give you if falling down you'll sell your birthright . . . A man that'd deny his country for a job hast lost his soul . . . It's like marrying an oul hag for her money!' And now he repeated these things to Paddy Boden and with a scornful laugh added: 'You don't understand a damned word of what I'm saying. The young people is no good — they're all out for coortin' and cards and drinkin' and dancin'.'

Alongside the asylum wall they rattled down the steep hill

44

into Downpatrick and saw below them the smoke crawling over the rooftops, and saw between the lovely tower of the Protestant cathedral and the spire of the Catholic church, the outspreading fields stripped clean by shadows that trailed the sun.

' 'Tis a sight to lift the heart,' Dan said, and then jerked his thumb towards the wall. 'But if I was in there I'd die of heartbreak looking out at it.'

Mary wasn't listening to him. She had felt a stab of pain when he had talked about girls who were crossed in love, and now as the cart jolted along the street to where men were shouting and brandishing sticks at the cattle she tried to quell the whirring thought in her mind.

CHAPTER V

DAN counted the money in his pocket—four shillings in all. Then he clambered out of the cart, stamped about to ease his feet, and with his pipe well alight, set off as briskly as he could, cracking his stick on the pavement and looking like one who was bent on important business. He went along the main street which was crammed with carts. Against a wall on the sunny side of the street a woman in a white apron sat on a box, her knitting on her lap, and spread out on straw at her feet was a cluster of hens with their legs tied. He inquired the price of the fowl, and the old woman answered him without taking her eyes off her knitting. He prodded one of the hens with his stick: 'Hm, I wouldn't give that price for year-old turkeys let alone hens,' and he walked further up the street, halting beside a few men who were gathered round a young mare. Dan rested his two hands on his stick, and with his head to the side gazed intently at the mare. The owner looked at Dan and then shouted to the lad who held the mare by the head: 'Give her a skelp there, Johnny, and run her up and down ... There she goes, my hearty

45

fellows, every hair in her tail worth a guinea.' He came over to Dan: 'There she is in clinking condition — her coat as glossy as a new shoe. Make me an offer.'

Dan took the pipe from his mouth and spat loudly on to the street. He examined the mare's mouth, inquired her age and how often she had foaled. He spat out again and walked off.

'Forty quid and a harness thrown in with her,' the owner called after him.

'I'll be back again,' Dan said.

'You'll be too late,' the owner said. 'Snap her up at once and good luck to you.' But Dan shook his head and hurried towards the library where he wanted to have a free read of the newspapers.

When he entered the unnaturally quiet room with its polished floors and its notice, NO SMOKING, hanging in four places on the walls he saw that a few men were bunched round his favourite paper, each reading a different page of it, and so he leaned against the wall waiting his turn and cursing the authorities for not providing a few seats where one could sit in comfort. Then he took the pipe from his mouth, unscrewed the shank and flung a swipe of spittles on the floor: 'Blast them and their notices! How could you enjoy a read and you without a pipe in your mouth.'

All the men were as old as himself, each of them with his jaws continually moving and his nervous fingers trembling as he held a page to turn it over. One man had a soft hat and polished shoes and Dan wondered that a man like that wouldn't buy a paper and not be disgracing himself edging his way in like an inmate of a workhouse. Impatiently Dan paced up and down, but when another man tiptoed into the room searching in his pockets for his specks, Dan darted across to the paper and began to read the advertisements with the aid of a rough-edged magnifying glass. He noted the price of a setting of Leghorn eggs, the price of a house with fifteen acres of land, and the amount of money people had left in wills and the occupations each had followed.

46

'Begob there's money in hardware!' he would say aloud to no one in particular as he pointed with his finger at a hardware merchant's will: 'And I suppose that man, more power to him, started as a message boy ... And there's a publican — dead as an empty bottle — leaves twenty thousand quid behind him! Begob there's money in drink! And there's a solicitor leaves a paltry three hundred pound — now that's not much for a solicitor to leave! But I could tell you the kind of man he was and I never met him — he was a decent, generous man with a big family: that's what he was. May the Heavens be his bed! There's no pockets in a shroud!'

A library attendant looked in: 'Silence there, please. Silence!'

Dan buttoned his coat and with his stick over his shoulder like a rifle he strode past the attendant: 'A reading room should be a place where men can smoke and talk.' And he turned his head to the surprised room; 'Look at it — you might as well be in a bloody morgue! Good day to you — I'm not coming back here again!'

He crossed to a timber yard and for a few pence bought odd scraps and ends of wood that would make frames for fishing lines or nest-boxes for his hens. His next call was to a hardware store to buy some nails, and as he followed a young boy down the shop that was packed with brushes and buckets and lamps and washboards he was thinking of the man's will he had just read and how much profit there must be on all the articles that cluttered the shop. Down in the cool store that was lighted by one window the boy showed him bucketfuls of nails and as he weighed some into the scale, dropping them in two at a time, Dan eyed him with contempt: 'You'd think it was sweeties you're weighing. Empty them in, son, you'll not wear out the bottom of the scale!'

'Have you anything to put them in?'

'I've boards to drive them in. Wrap them up for me in a cardboard box and tie a bit of string round it. You'll be a bad business man!' and he began to tell him about the hardware merchant's will he had just seen in the paper: 'And do you know how he made his money? I'll tell you. He was never stingy with his customers. When you're generous with a customer you get more customers; when you're stingy you lose everything. And what's more — you'll have a bare funeral.'

The lad parcelled the nails up in a cardboard box and made a loop in the string for Dan's finger and Dan, realizing that the lad was bent on pleasing him, asked to see a few saws, spokeshaves, penknives, and razors. He would hold a saw perpendicular to the ground, tap it with a ruler, and listen to its ping: 'I wouldn't give the tail of my shirt for that one. Let me see another like a decent fellow!' He inquired the price of each article he handled, bought nothing only the nails, and finally departed with a catalogue in his pocket and the cardboard box dangling from his finger and a bundle of small pieces of wood under his arm. He crossed the road to a drapery store to buy a handkerchief for Tessie.

There was a warm, heavy smell of new clothes in the shop, the floor was sprinkled with water, and in the far end, which was darkened by frocks hanging from the ceiling, there was the glare of gaslight. The shopkeeper, with a pencil behind his ear, an inch-tape round his shoulder, leaned on the counter with the palms of his hands and spoke to Dan about the lovely weather and the quiet fair they were having and Dan, now that he had found somebody that might talk to him, began to launch forth about the old fairs until he was interrupted by two women who entered the shop, fingering bales of tweed that were stacked on one corner of the counter.

'Give us a handkerchief that'd suit a nice wee girl,' Dan said aloud, determined to be served before the women, and when he got what he wanted his shopping was finished for the day and he made off to the railway where he rested for a while on an iron seat and smoked his pipe. The station was deserted and the sun shone through the glass roof on to his bundle of boards making them give off a sweet, warm

48

smell. With great contentment he spat over the platform on to the sleepers and stared at a row of wagons covered with black tarpaulins, trying to read the chalk-markings on their sides which indicated their future destinations. A peaceful feeling of ease and freedom came over him and he imagined himself to be the station-master and how he'd have wire baskets with moss swinging from the girders, a flowerbed instead of that slag heap, and he'd get rid of that weighing machine that was always out of order and he'd do something about that old pipe in the lavatory that seemed to hiss perpetually.

Three sparrows began to squabble over a crust of bread on the platform and he whistled to frighten them but they only stretched themselves thinly and continued to fight. There was a rattle of keys and presently a porter passed wheeling a bicycle with a flat tyre, a label flittering on the handlebars. When he had gone off, the station was very silent and the sparrows came back to the crust and screeched at one another. Dan flung his stick at them, and then getting up he went to a row of carriages on a siding, selected a second-class compartment, put up the windows on each side, stretched himself out on the seat, and with his cap over his face fell asleep.

The noise of an engine awakened him and he opened his eyes in the sunny compartment and saw the shadow of the engine's smoke on the varnished partition. He hurried out of the carriage to get something to eat, but when he looked at the station-clock he realized he had been sleeping for nearly two hours, and when he entered an eating-house he found the place deserted, nothing but salt cellars and pepper castors on the wooden tables and a greasy smell hanging thickly in the air.

A girl came wearily to attend him, and as she lifted up the salt cellar in one hand and wiped under it with a cloth he kept up a chat with her, trying to find out where she came from and how much in tips she'd make in a week. She laughed good-naturedly at him, and when she had gone to the kitchen to re-heat some potatoes and cabbage he noticed a streak on the wall beside him where someone had killed a fly, and knowing that it would disturb his appetite he crossed to a table at the other side of the room. The girl reappeared with an empty plate and smiled as she flicked the crumbs off his new table.

'It's cooler at this side,' he explained, but when he raised his head and saw a portrait of Queen Victoria frowning imperiously down at him he once more lifted his para-phernalia and sat at a table near the window where he could see the people passing by.

'Man alive, if you take another hop you'll be out on the street,' the girl said, leaving down his bacon and cabbage and six roasted potatoes.

'It's like this, daughter, I have to keep a look-out for a fellow in case he'd leave on his cart without me — the young fellas is very forgetful nowadays,' and he lifted his knife and fork. 'Like a decent girl, I wonder would you fetch me a jug of buttermilk and I'll not give you another bit of bother.'

When she had brought him the jug of buttermilk, he blessed himself, opened the top button of his trousers and stabbed one of the potatoes with his fork. Through the window he saw on the sunny side of the street a blind man on a stool; in one hand a tin mug drooped between his legs, a piece of bread was in the other, and sparrows hopped fearlessly around his feet picking at the crumbs.

'Aw,' says Dan to himself, 'it's a pity he couldn't get his sight back for a minute or two and throw his tin mug at them cheeky bastards. They'll be building their nests soon but let them try to hatch in Dan Scullion's thatch!' and he gripped his knife and fork and held them in front of him like two candles. He stabbed another potato and was peeling it when he saw Jimmy Neil sitting on the shaft of a donkey-cart and jumping to the ground as Ned Mason hurried towards him across the road.

'Father Toner's scouring the country for you,' Ned was saying, smiling at the donkey with no winkers and the broken breech strap mended with a bit of cord and a spoke missing from each wheel.

'I'm heading for your country now and tell him I'll give him a call,' Jimmy said, fiddling at a row of pins in the lapel of his coat. He twisted and grimaced, shrugged his shoulders, shut one eye and then the other as if he found difficulty in keeping still. He had one button on his black coat and every time he buttoned it it would spring loose because the hole was too big. 'Do you see that coat? that's one of Father Toner's. And it was him gave me them boots and that hat!'

Ned smiled, because since Jimmy was always dressed in black Dan Scullion had nicknamed him 'The Curate'.

'It does your heart good to work for him,' The Curate went on, taking a pin out of one lapel and fixing it in the other. 'He's always cheery — and a cheery man is a saintly man!' He had no collar and he kept fingering the brass stud in the neck of his shirt. Then he pushed his hat back and the sun shone on his sallow face and the soot on his cleft chin. He held Ned by the arm and whispered in his ear: 'But do you know? I'm afraid of Father Toner's health — he's as light as a kite and you could blow him off your hand. The cigarettes is killin' him. But I often wonder where he got thon cross-eyed blade of a housekeeper. I bet she's an inlander for she's always peckin' at me through the curtains.' They walked towards a pub for a few pints of porter and before going in The Curate tied the rope-reins to the spokes of the wheel and lifted up an old canvas cover in the cart: 'Look, Ned, I'm at the chimney-sweepin',' and he showed him his set of worn brushes, their handles tipped with brass. 'They're not great brushes but they're better than stickin' a whin bush up the chimney.'

When he had taken his first draught of porter he wiped his mouth with the back of his hand, leaned his elbow on the counter and affected a moist and polite accent as if he were talking to a rich and standoffish old lady: 'My dear lady, I'll do your chimley, clean and hygienic like a pan wiped with a newspaper — nothing like soot in your garden as a fertilizer and grub killer,' and he brought his fist down with a thump on the counter, and Ned smiled reassuringly when a few customers looked over to see if there was going to be a fight. The Curate buttoned his coat: 'But do you know what I'm going to tell you? The people near the sea is patienter and decenter than the inland people — they see nothing, their minds is cramped, turned inwards with scallying at themselves. But a man that looks at the sea: take old Dan Scullion — his mind's that broad you could sail a ship in it. And John Devlin — a powerful decent fellow! Many's a good pint he stood me! All the Devlins is decent. There's Tessie brought me down to Dan's some weeks ago when I had the dregs of a few drinks in me and old Dan let me stretch on the settle. But these inland folk — they're a prying, pestering, parcel of suspicious gets!' He took another drink and turned up the whites of his eyes till they looked like peeled eggs.

Ned laughed, pleased at the good word he had for the Devlins, and ordered another pint for him: 'Tell me, Jimmy,' he said, trying to tease him. 'Is it true you turned your coat when you were working for a Presbyterian minister?'

'That's a damned crooked lie. I wouldn't turn my coat nor betray my country for the best job on this earth. 'Tis true that I work whiles for the Reverend Hope — and if I do he treats me damned decent. I cut his grass and cleans the leaves out of his spoutins and he gives me a good jorum of whisky — and whisky's as scarce as holy water in any manse. He's from Scotland and he lilts a few Scotch tunes for me till I can play them on the mouth-organ. And the other day he said to me and walked away after it: "Scotland's dead! Scotland's dead! Soon it'll be nothing only a name on a map." Aw, he's a decent gentleman and I wish he was one of us!'

'You're well in with the clergy on both sides!'

'What'd he mean by Scotland's dead?'

'Divil the know I know. Ask Father Toner when you see him.'

'I might and I mightn't,' The Curate said, taking a mouth-organ from his pocket and tapping its teeth against the palm of his hand. 'But I asked him a while back is there any harm in working for a Presbyterian minister and do you know what he said: The only harm'd be if I didn't work hard enough! — them's his very words. Wait a minute till you hear one of the tunes the minister learnt me. *Deirdre's Farewell to Scotland.*' And The Curate holding the mouth-organ in his two hands moved it across his lips.

'I have to go now and I'll see you when you're round in Dunscourt,' Ned shouted and left him standing in the middle of the floor, The Curate shaking his head in assent.

As he hurried towards his Aunt Rose's where he was to meet his mother he ran over in his mind all the incidents of the day, from the wrangling in the morning to the broken meeting with Mary. He hadn't seen her all day in the town and he felt that she had returned home; and the thought of her disappointment had coiled tight about his mind and only now, after his meeting with The Curate, did it slowly unwind leaving a light feeling of freedom behind it. He walked quickly and wished that he could see her amongst the people who passed him or in the carts that were moving out of the town. He smiled to himself as he walked up the pebbled path to his Aunt Rose's house with its neat lawn and three white terriers playing about on it, for his Aunt had married late in life and having no children she kept dogs.

His mother and Aunt Rose were sitting on a settee in the bay window and beside them on a round mahogany table was a tray with a bottle of sherry and two glasses. His mother had been crying, a handkerchief was crushed in her hand, and she tried to turn her face from the light when he came into the room.

'We better be on the road if we want home before dark,'

he said, swaying from one foot to the other, and refusing the sherry or tea which his Aunt had offered him.

'I'll go and get on my hat and coat,' his mother said, picked up a few crumbs of cake which had fallen on the carpet at her feet, and went out of the room. And when she had gone Aunt Rose closed the door which was left ajar, lifted a cut-glass candlestick on the sideboard and put it down again, and with her little finger scraped at a speck of dirt on the arm of the settee and then stood at the window looking out at the terriers on the lawn. She told Ned to sit down, asked him about the kind of prices going at the fair, and then she sighed heavily, fingering the tassel on the window blind: 'Ned, I'm afraid for your poor mother's health,' she managed to say. 'Since your father's death, God have mercy on him, she's ten years older. Her nerves are gone!'

'I've been telling her to take things easy and rest herself. But she'll not heed me — and look at her coming in to-day on a draughty cart,' and sitting on the settee he stretched out his finger to a Persian kitten that was gazing at him from behind a chair-leg.

Aunt Rose with a wry smile took her finger from the tassel: 'She's terribly broken-hearted, Ned . . . about you.'

He said nothing, and the kitten standing on its hind legs sparred at his protruding finger and then rolled over on its back, trying to catch the finger in its mouth.

She went on in a plaintive tone about his unbecoming behaviour on the day of his father's death and how he had disgraced himself putting out a fire for the Devlins and the country swarming with lazy able-bodied men.

'It's only what any man'd do,' he said quietly. 'My father was dead and there was nothing I could do except pray for his soul.'

Encouraged by the quiet tone of his voice she sat on the arm of the settee, and the kitten ceased playing with Ned and eyed with narrowed pupils the swaying tassel on the blind.

'Ned, like a good boy, have nothing to do with the

Devlins. I'm sure Father Christy wouldn't like it — bringing the Devlins close to him ... in marriage,' and she cleared her throat and raised her eyes to the photo of her wedding group with Father Christy standing at the side.

'I'll not ask him to marry us, anyway. He didn't bother himself to come to my father's funeral,' and he stretched out his boot towards the kitten and it jumped to the side and pawed at the laces. 'I'm afraid it's you and my mother is claiming the relationship with him. If he's a friend of ours he must be a very far out one.'

'Ned, you're very hard. He didn't forget to send five shillings of an offering.'

'Father Toner will do the job for me when I get my mother talked round.'

'Sure you have plenty of time for marrying.'

'Aye,' he said, thinking of the terriers running about on the lawn.

'And as for the Devlins there's not one of them a suitable match for you.'

'Am I not allowed to have a life of my own — even a thought of my own. My mother pulling at me every day and now you.'

'But, Ned,' and she put her hand on his shoulder: 'It's for your own good I'm advising you. You deserve better than the Devlins. The whole breed of them is a good-for-nothing pack. There's not one of them with a penny to bless themselves with!'

He put her arm from his shoulder and got to his feet: 'Why do you always talk of love in terms of money? There's too much of that in this country. I'd rather be under seven feet of clay than lie with a girl I didn't love.'

His mother came into the room, and with an aggrieved smile Aunt Rose saw them off, standing at her gate and waving to his mother perched on top of the cart.

Ned walked by the horse's head up the long hill past the asylum wall. Behind them the lowering sun stretched rafters of light along the ceiling of the sky and the smoke from a train chugging out from the station reflected a dull gold. At the top of the hill he put his foot on the felloe of the wheel and jumped into the cart. The air was clear and cold, and his mother told him to put on his overcoat. Ahead of them the land switchbacked to the sea, all its little hills saddled with a ploughed field and all the white gables of the homes catching the last of the sun.

'Have you a candle for the lamp?' she asked him.

'I have but we'll hit home before dark. There's an hour's daylight in the sky.'

And then as she settled down with the rug around her and her prayer beads in her hand she discovered she had left her umbrella behind her.

'Let it go now,' he said. 'Sure I'll drive you over some fine Sunday. A good jaunt would knock a bit of the freshness out of the pony.'

She rubbed the back of her hand, smiled because of the warmth in his voice, and asked about the price he got for the pigs. For a moment he hesitated for he always kept a secret pound for himself out of every deal, but when he handed her the money she returned him a ten-shilling note: 'That'll keep the devil out of your pocket for awhile. They were puny little things and it was a decent price you got for them.'

A woman with a barefooted child was taking in her washing that was spread out on the tops of whin bushes and Mrs. Mason suddenly thought of cool sheets and how sweet they smelled after a day's airing in the sun. She sighed wearily. Her head ached as the cart knocked its way up and down the hills. The day seemed very long. But she was glad she made the journey for she was sure that Rose gave him a bit of her mind about the Devlins. Presently the horse of its own accord drew in at a pub and Ned jerked it forward.

'Ah, Ned, it doesn't take a horse long to learn a habit — good or bad.'

56

' 'Tis little I could afford to take at any time!'

His mood was changing again. He gave the horse a flick with the rope and it broke into a trot, its mane rising and falling, and the dust in the cart forming and reforming in little heaps.

'It's a lovely evening, thanks be to God,' she said. ' 'Tis well the rain kept away. I'm sure the girls got the field of potatoes finished to-day.'

He said nothing. Two or three stars, hard and bright, appeared in the sky. He kept the horse at a trot, conscious all the time that if Mary were with him, they would have sat close together, his arm about her waist, and they would have lingered on the road, waiting to see the moon rise like a Host above the sea.

CHAPTER VI

WHEN The Curate left Downpatrick in his donkey and cart he headed for the sea and, on his way, halted for a few days amongst the little by-roads, cleaning chimneys in the early morning, and at night sleeping under his cart in a hammock made out of old sacks. He would drive the donkey into a nearby field, and in the mornings before the sun would have dried the dew on the spokes of the wheels he would be awake, light a fire on the sheltered side of a hedge, make himself some tea and boil a couple of eggs. And in this way before the women of the countryside would have had time to kindle their morning's fire he would be at the door begging to clean their chimneys, and while they would debate with him from the bedroom window and assure him that they didn't need him, he would pretend that he was hard of hearing, cup his hand to his ear, nod his head, and stride towards the door with the bundle of brushes balanced on his shoulder.

'I won't be more than a few minutes, Missus,' he would

say when the door was opened. 'Don't be afeared for I'm a good clean worker. You could leave your washing on the table and divil a speck would fly on to it.' And once his foot was in the kitchen he would give out a streel of talk and occasionally incline a deaf ear if the woman were unbending. He would then spread a sack over the cold fireplace and with a tremendous show of energy and a spate of talk he would begin his work. And when he would be nearly finished and the children arriving in the kitchen in their shirts he would say: 'Go out, Missus, and see is the Jolly Roger on top of the mast!'

'She's up!' the woman would shout, seeing the circular brush like a grotesque golliwog covering the top of the chimney.

'Watch her spin!' The Curate would shout, and he would twirl the brush, spin a shower of soot from it, and push it up and down to hear the children laughing as they ran in and out through the open door.

When he was satisfied that no trace of his work remained on the fireplace he would ask the woman if she had any clocks to be cleaned or locks to be mended. Then he would whistle like a blackbird to please the children, play a tune for them on his mouth-organ, and when he would be driving off again on his cart the children would give him a cheer for himself, and the mother, standing at the door with a tear of joy in her eye, would shout after him: 'Don't forget to give us a call next time yer round.'

'I'll do that, Missus!' and he would sweep off his black hat to her and rattle away.

In this way he ambled up to Father Toner's house one morning when the priest was finishing his breakfast. He knocked at the door and the housekeeper, seeing who it was, told him sharply that Father Toner was engaged.

'All right,' said The Curate dryly, and turned on his heel. She called him back: 'Are you wanting him particular?'

'Not at all!' he shouted and continued to walk away from

her. 'Not at all! It's Father Toner that wants me!' He had now reached the donkey and was taking the reins in his hand when the housekeeper hurried down the path to him.

'Mr. Neil, a minute, please,' she cried. 'Don't go away till I tell him you're here.'

He sat on the shaft of the cart and spat loudly on to the road. The donkey's head was round the gate-post eating the edge of the priest's lawn, and as The Curate backed it on to the road the wheel of the cart cut into the loose gravel which the housekeeper had raked yesterday.

'Wait a minute!' she cried again, her voice husky with temper and vexation.

At that moment Father Toner himself appeared, a cigarette in his mouth: 'I'm glad you didn't desert us entirely,' he greeted The Curate, smiling at the donkey and searching the shaft for the owner's name-plate. 'Is it your own turn-out, Jimmy?'

'It isn't mine yet, Father, but it will be soon. An old friend of mine is in the workhouse and he left me all his belongins till he comes out again. But the poor man's done! He's only a rake — not a pick on him! He'll never sit at his own fireside again!'

'I thought, maybe, it was the Reverend Hope presented you with it,' smiled the priest, but noticing the grieved expression on Jimmy's face he was sorry for what he had said and hurriedly tried to drag Jimmy's mind from the remark by outlining the jobs he wanted done.

Jimmy untackled the donkey and drove it into a field, and when he came back the priest was standing at the back of the house, his hat on his head, his bicycle against the cart.

'Tell me, Jimmy,' said the priest, raising his foot on the lowered shaft, and putting on his bicycle clips. 'Why don't you settle down here? Sure you could get a good job on a farm.'

'A farm!' and Jimmy screwed up his face. 'I wrought on a farm once but never again. It's no work for any gentleman.

There's no leisure in it. You're going all the time like a cow's tail. I'd rather be on the roads.'

'And the roads lead to the workhouse!'

'Many a night I've spent in the workhouse already, Father, and many a bob or two I won off the old men in the Body of the House.'

'That's all right. You can go as you please now, but wait until you're old and the Master of the workhouse confines you to barracks — it will be a different story then. Take my advice and give up the rambling and settle down with some decent people that will look after you.'

Jimmy raised the canvas cover from his brushes, took off his coat, folded it neatly and stowed it in the cart. The priest watched him, his finger smoothing ·the top of the bicycle bell. Jimmy rolled up his sleeves, humming to himself, *Deirdre's Farewell to Scotland*.

'I'll be back in the evening,' the priest said, pressing both tyres with a finger and thumb. Jimmy continued to sing, and a smile flitted across the priest's face as he watched him. Perhaps, after all, he was mistaken that the remark about the Reverend Hope had hurt him. He wheeled the bicycle over the gravel, hesitated, and looked back at Jimmy with a quizzical expression: 'Tell me,' he said light-heartedly: 'Sure there's no truth in the story that the Reverend Hope got you to give up your Faith?'

He was sorry he had spoken. All the levity was crushed from Jimmy's face and he dropped a brush he held in his hand. 'It's a lie, Father! It's a twisted, crooked, damnation lie. If I knew the man spread it I'd throttle him. The Reverend Hope's a decent wee man. He's from Scotland. He learns me old tunes and the only prayer I heard pass his lips was: "Scotland's dead — May the Lord take care of her. Soon it will be nothing, only a name on a map".'

The priest put a hand on Jimmy's shoulder: 'I didn't mean to offend you. I knew it was only a rumour. Of course I knew!' and as he pedalled off and felt the cold morning breeze against his face and heard the larks sheering the air with song a confused feeling of joy and regret struggled within his mind. He pondered on what he had heard and realized that in exile the Reverend Hope foresaw the spiritual doom that engulfed his country — his people bartering the things of the spirit for the things of this world and losing with it their fine feeling of perceptiveness.

Back at the house Jimmy was still standing where the priest had left him. He was undecided what to do: whether to harness the donkey and go inland again or remain where he was until he had finished his jobs. Hadn't Ned Mason said the same thing to him in the pub in Downpatrick and now it had reached the ears of Father Toner: 'What harm did I do anyone that they'd fling cheap lies about me over the country!' He paused and glared malevolently at the kitchen window of the house: ''Tis the oul blade of a housekeeper has done it! She's wild because Father Toner is so great with me! As if a man like me would become a Protestant for any job! Jimmy Neil that never passes a chapel without saying a prayer for the soul of his father and mother. But I'll not let it annoy me. God damn them for their lies! I'll whistle it out of me! I'll damned well whistle it out of me!' and he lifted his brushes and began to sing. He would do the bedroom-chimneys first and arrange to come in the early morning and do the range — he could do it in comfort then, for Kate would be in bed and wouldn't be eyeing him like a hungry ferret.

He came into the house but already she had gone up the stairs before him, and locking her bedroom door and putting the key in her apron pocket she passed him on her way down again and was annoyed when he did not look at her. He went into the priest's bedroom but came out immediately and standing at the kitchen door he shouted as loudly as he could: 'Have you any old newspapers, Mam?'

'That's no way to shout. Ye'd think I was deaf,' and with her hands resting on the table she warned him that she would

61

stand for nothing only clean rooms. He didn't answer her. There was a great heat from the humming range, and a smell of bacon which lingered in the air made him hungry. For a minute she stared at him, his sooty boots laced with cord, his shirt open at the neck showing his hairy chest, his hat on the back of his head like a comic performer in a circus. The sight of him jigging about in her clean kitchen revolted her, and to get rid of him she hauled out a bundle of old newspapers and left them on the floor. 'There!' she said, pointing to them with her toe. 'And don't spend the whole morning at them chimneys for I have the rooms to dust yet.'

He rattled up the stairs, and singing away to himself he spread out the newspapers on the floor and laid his brushes on top of them. Then something in the months' old papers caught his eye and he lay over them, resting on his elbows like a child absorbed in a story book. Down below a door opened and he jumped to his feet, listening intently. The door closed again; he breathed freely and seeing a few cigarette butts in the fireplace he picked them up and sat down on the wicker arm-chair in the room enjoying a smoke before he would begin his work. The morning sun glided through the window and shone on a varnished prie-dieu and on the gilt edge of a prayer book that rested on it. He recalled the day that Dan Scullion had made the prie-dieu for the priest, made it without one screw nail and how he had waited till nightfall before carrying it up to him. 'There's nobody like Dan for doing a fine job,' he said to himself, the chair creaking as he crossed and recrossed his legs. He lit another butt. 'Maybe while I'm here I could get Dan to make a long box for the donkey-cart — a box with a lock on it where I could hide the brushes from the prying eyes of the peelers. If oul Kate knew I'd no licence she'd fairly inform on me.' With his head cocked to the side he heard her washing the dishes downstairs. He got to his feet and tiptoed to the window where three flies, having emerged from their winter hiding places, were struggling on the sunny pane. He teased them with the lighted-end of the cigarette and then with one swipe caught the three of them and tossed them through the open window and stood gazing over the fields and watched black-kneed lambs vigorously sucking their mother. A latch clicked and Kate flung out a dish of water and standing out from the house shaded her eyes as she peered up at the roof. Jimmy wheeled from the window, and screwing a few lengths on to his brush manœuvred it up the chimney, the soot falling into a sack that covered the mouth of the fireplace.

Kate turned the knob of the door quietly and came into the room. The curtains rose up with the draught and the papers rustled on the floor. Jimmy turned his back to her, and with a great flourish of importance screwed an unnecessary length on to his brush and levered it up the chimney. He knew she was eyeing him and he began to sing, stopping now and again to rub the small of his back with his fist. 'That's the lumbago he told me about when he used to be civil and polite,' she said to herself, and saw how he had worn a hole in his waistcoat with this constant rubbing. 'Let some of his Devlin friends go and patch it for him.'

Though he still kept his back to her he was conscious all the time of her staring eyes, and in his trembling excitement to do everything right he let the corner of the sack slip and a shower of soot spilled down on the hearth and rose up in a cloud around him.

'Get out of my sight!' he wheeled at her.

'The room! The room!' she cried. 'How'll I ever get it cleaned this wretched unholy day!'

'Me that has a name for clean work over all County Down! Get out and don't egg me to say what's flying round my mind!'

'You're a plague in any house! You've no respect for anyone. No respect for poor Father Toner's room. The poor man that gives you the shirt off his back, that has fed you and shod you, and all you do is to ruin everything you turn

63

your hand to. And then get drunk on his money into the bargain.'

His anger held him rigid, and a look of hard determination swept across his face.

'Get out, woman!' he blazed at her, a line of froth on his lips.

'You'll not order me in my own house. You don't know your place,' she answered feebly.

'Get out, you foul informer!' and he scooped up the soot in his hands; and afraid that he would fling it at her she backed out of the room.

By dinner-time he had cleaned three chimneys, mended a clock that was on the mantelpiece of the bedroom, and repainted the wall in the hall where it had been streaked by the bicycle. She called him for his dinner and laid it on a newspaper on the scullery shelf, a chair beside it. Without a word of complaint he carried it to an open shed in the yard, placed it on a box and sat beside it. She watched him from the window. The sun reflected on the finger nails of his sooty hands, and a few timorous hens, shaking their red combs, eyed him sideways. Kate sat down and squeezed her brow with her hand; her head throbbed and she drank a cup of tea to steady her nerves. What would Father Toner say if he found him taking his dinner out in the shed. It wasn't her fault — God knows she had tried to treat him decent. She picked a hair of wood from the scruffed table and dropped it into the tea-leaves in the bottom of her cup. She heaved a sigh and shuffled out to the scullery. It was colder here with the window open, and as she rinsed the cup at the sink she heard the ragged notes of Jimmy's mouth-organ. He wasn't right in the head, she told herself; and his other old crony, Dan Scullion, was as bad. It was a queer parcel for Father Toner to be mixed up with. He doesn't know them, poor man! If he did he'd hunt them from about the place. And why, in God's name, did he allow that tramp to sprawl about his bedroom; and why did he worry about him when he was safely out of the way in Down-patrick.

She saw him scrape the plate on to the yard and the hens snatching up the cold scraps of potatoes. But two chickens, hunched and gasping with the croop, stood forlornly against the sunny wall; their wings drooped and they made no effort to scramble with the rest. 'Why doesn't he cure them two sufferin' birds,' she said aloud to herself, 'him that pretends to Father Toner he can do everything.' Then she fled from the scullery, afraid that he might return with the plates.

In the evening Father Toner came back. Jimmy had cleaned the spouts, cut the grass and the edges of the lawn, and had fastened strips of leather to the branches of the rose trees that straggled against the boundary wall of the house.

'It's good to get a man to do an honest day's work,' Father Toner said to him, already arranging in his mind some jobs that might employ him for another few days. 'And what, Jimmy, will I pay you for the chimneys?'

'Now, Father, as man to man and none of this I'll-leave-it-to-yourself-business — a shilling for each of the chimneys and one-and-six for the range that I'll do early in the morning.' They walked together round the yard. The sun had gone down and a cold wind roved about the corners, clutching bits of straw and swirling dust under the spouts. The priest pointed to the gable where a patch of cement had broken off revealing the brickwork underneath, and he asked Jimmy to replaster it. Then he examined doors that needed a new hinge and the roof of the hen-shed where the felt was dry and cracked. Jimmy rubbed his hands together and wiped off a drop that dangled from his nose. Then noticing the two gasping chickens, their feathers blowing up in the wind, showing their pink flesh, he lifted them in his arms. He asked the priest to get him some turpentine. Then he searched the yard for a long feather, dipped it in the turpen-tine, and with the tip of it tickled the inside of the chickens' throats till they coughed up the worm that was choking them.

'Get Kate to give them something warm and they'll be all right in a day or two. And when I get time, Father, I'll run you up a few loads of sleechy wrack from the shore, and when they hoke and scrape through that, divil the pip or ache will harm your poultry.'

It was dusk when he left the priest and went round to Dan Scullion's where he was to spend the night.

CHAPTER VII

THE wind was blowing in fierce gusts and the night settling coldly upon the land when The Curate reached Dan's. The oil lamp was on a newspaper on the table and Tessie was bent over it with the glass globe in her hand. He watched her hang the lamp to a nail in the wall and screw up the wick.

'My granda expected you round before this,' she said to him, wiping her oily fingers with a piece of the newspaper. 'Time and again he went to the foot of the field and gaped across at the priest's house wondering when you'd be finished. He's out in the shed now hammering away at something and working the annoyance out of himself.'

Under the yellow light of the lamp The Curate pared a bit of tobacco, and his face which had been knotted in anger the whole day began to relax as he chafed Tessie about Paddy Boden and asked was it true that they were getting tied up at Easter.

'Not a glimmer of truth in it,' she laughed. 'They say more than their prayers in this part of the country . . . Pull your chair close to the fire or my granda'll think I was short with you. He'll be in in a minute or two for he has no light out there except a candle.'

The Curate filled his pipe, his eyes glinting roguishly as he gazed at Tessie stirring a pot that simmered on the hob. Her dark hair was shining, a red-knitted frock moulding her fine figure. 'Paddy will have a snug wee partner when he gets her,' he said to himself, fastening his eyes on her as she swung across the kitchen and put bowls with spoons in them on the table.

The latch clicked and as Dan came in, a draught dimmed the lamp and the smoking wick blackened the tip of the globe. His trousers and beard were dusted with shavings and in his hand he carried a wooden frame, a scythe blade screwed to it.

'There's what I was makin' while you were paughlin' around cutting grass with a child's toy,' and he handed the frame to The Curate. The Curate looked at it puzzledly: 'What kind of a contraption is it?'

'Aye,' says Dan, rubbing his frozen hands over the flames of the fire, 'I thought mebbe you'd tell me it was somethin' from the wilds of Africa. It's a cradle-scythe,' and he gripped the two handles on the frame and rhythmically swung it backwards and forwards across the floor. You could mow all day with that and never be tired. I made it for myself to cut thistles. It used to be in the old days I'd make them and take a man's measurements like a tailor makin' a suit of clothes. But nobody wants them now — the young fellas are all out for the shop-made article. A child could use that and never be tired,' and he swung his scythe again.

Tessie handed each of them some stew, and The Curate took his seat on the settle, the warm bowl resting on his lap.

'The young is changed and changed for the worse,' Dan continued. 'They don't want to listen to the likes of me nor you. There was a time when a man could tell you a good yarn but now they haven't time to bid you the time of day. They're always in a hurry — all out for gallivantin' and ridin' on their bikes to see the pictures. But I'm happy out

67

there in the shed — planing away at a few boards. It gives me an appetite and eases my mind.'

Outside the wind dunted against the house and died away again, and he recalled, when he was a young lad, crouched around the fire, how his father used to question him about the different natures of the winds. He licked the back of his spoon and looked at The Curate: 'Do you hear that wind, Jimmy? How'd you know it was a nor'-west wind supposin' you didn't know the lie of the land?'

Tessie took the empty bowl from him.

'It's a cold-rifed wind,' said Jimmy, taking a pin from the lapel of his coat and dislodging a piece of meat from between his teeth.

'Sure every north wind is cold — that's no answer,' and his rough hands rasped as he rubbed them together. 'Listen to it — do you remark anything peculiar?'

They all listened and heard it lurch and bump against the back of the house.

'They've all the same sound, Granda,' Tessie said.

'They have not! Listen again with the ears the good God gave you!'

'Don't heed him,' Tessie turned to Jimmy, who was sitting as patiently as a watchdog, his fidgety hands on his knees, his ear cocked to the windward side of the house. Dan had the pipe in his fist, a shining spittle on his beard. In his mind he was seeing the wind like a living thing, rubbing its shoulders against the corners of the house and snatching up every feather or twig that it found about the yard.

'I notice sweet damn all!' said Jimmy, with a hopeless shrug of his shoulders.

Dan took a patient draw at the pipe and pointed the shank of it at Jimmy. 'A nor'-west is a listening wind — that's what it is. A listening wind! You'll hear that wind blarging against the house, then it will dull away till you think it's died down. But it's only listening, man. It'll come again like a pounding of horses, and then you'll hear it dulling away . . . dulling away . . . listening to everything and gathering strength for another brattle. It's a queer wind — the nor'-west. It's very human in its ways.'

They sat quiet for awhile. A moth flurred around the lamp-globe and Dan spat into the fire. Then the wind came with a plump, snuffling like a dog under the door, and bumping, bumping, bumping on the thatched roof.

'You're right, Dan,' said The Curate, and he got to his feet, whispered something to him, and both of them buttoned their coats to go to O'Hare's pub.

'Don't stay too long,' Tessie said to them at the door.

'I'm sure you're botherin' about us,' Dan said. 'Me brave Paddy Boden is skulkin' around some corner till the coast is clear.'

They shivered leaving the warm house, and out in the night air they struck the road sharply, for the wind was growing in strength, the sky chipped with stars, and a broken moon shining frostily above the sea. Once or twice snails crackled under their feet and trailed silver snotters on the road.

'Do you know, Jimmy, a snail is the only animal that carries its house on its back. . . . I heard tell of a man once that lived on the edge of the sea. He had a big wall round his garden to keep the waves from spitting on it, and one night he gathered a half-bucket of snails in his cabbages and dumped them in the tide. And do you know what happened? The next morning his walls and slates was covered with snail tracks — every damned one came back to the garden again. Would you believe that?'

'I'm sure it's true, Dan. There's pigeons can find their way back from foreign countries.'

'Pigeons be damned. They've a fine pair of wings and a good pair of steady eyes. But you'd think a snail had no sense in its head once it left the house at its heels.'

They argued loudly, and a peewit which was guarding its young, mounted on the wind with weird calls. They drew near Luke's and saw the shadows of a lamp striding across the yard; and Dan began to launch forth about the day of the fire trying to convey the impression that he, himself, was there and had directed the men in staunching the flames; and he told about Ned Mason and how he did the right thing by his neighbour, rushing out to help while his own father had just closed his eyes in death: 'There's not many fellas like Ned left in this part of the country!'

They argued about Luke's new roof; Jimmy contending that it was better than the thatch, Dan maintaining that it was a cold, lazy, ugly contrivance and a shame and a disgrace for anyone related to him. 'And do you see the branches of the sycamore hanging over the roof?' Dan went on. 'Luke will need to cut them down or the drip will rust the tin. It'll be a lovely sight then with a cock-eyed tree!'

Luke was whittling hazel rods for his lobster pots, Barbara was reading a book by the fire, and Mary was scalding the can after milking. They coaxed Luke away from the heat, and when they were on the sea-road again The Curate pestered him about John: did he hear from him often, when did he expect him home, and were his letters well-lined with £ s. d. Luke, his head bent, answered evasively, saying that John was never in the same port for long: a week maybe in Liverpool, then a month or two in Montreal, and short spells in South America.

'Wherever he is,' says The Curate, 'he'll not be shirking his work,' and he described with great vigour how John, after playing a football match and doing more than his share, had rowed him all the way from Ardglass and had arrived in below the house in time for milking the cows. Luke remembered that day well, and how John, fresh and lively and singing about the house, had gone that night with Mary and Barbara to a dance in the schoolhouse. Luke sighed, and a great weariness like a hood seemed to close down on him.

They walked in silence now, for the wind buffeted them

with thick, soft blows, and time and again they had to stand and pillar themselves against it. Turning on to the sweep of bay that led to the village they heard the waves crash on the beach and fiss amongst the sea-rods that slithered about on the stones. They had to shout to be heard above the noise, and when they spoke, their lips were wet with salt. Squares of light from the little homes warmed the air, and in the gaps of the wind was the sound of a melodeon from a cottage and the noise of couples dancing. The Curate fumbled in his pocket for his mouth-organ, and without taking it from his pocket, rubbed his finger along its metal fastenings — maybe he'd give them a tune or two when he had a few drinks to warm him up.

CHAPTER VIII

THERE was great confusion in the pub: men talked and argued from all corners of it, but nothing could be seen distinctly through the wedge of smoky light from the over-head oil-lamp. Old Dan sat on a barrel under the light, but the lamp had been filled too full, and when a drop dripped from it on to his knee he edged away from it to the fire which a youth was fanning with a tin advertisement he had lifted off the wall. The Curate stood the first round of drinks, and at the first sip from his glass he gazed round the room and noticed the police sergeant leaning against the counter, having a drink with the auctioneer. He suddenly became aware of the soot on his hands, the smell of soot from his clothes, and knew also that it lay embedded in every wrinkle on his face. He pulled the hat down over his eyes and manœuvred Dan and Luke to the edges of the light. The sergeant had his back to them, but when the door opened and whorled the smoke about the pub and set the lamp swinging, he would turn round, look sceptically at the light and listen for a moment to the whinge of the wind as it swept across the roof. The Curate watched every move of the sergeant, and at the same time was listening to two men at his back who were arguing about the date of the Big Wind.

'It was a couple of years before the famine,' one was saying.

'I'm telling you it was after the famine,' the other maintained, and then he shouted over The Curate's head to the sergeant for his opinion.

The Curate lowered his head and saw a cockroach struggling in a beery spittle on the floor. The sergeant was talking, his back against the counter: 'Well, you know, you might be right and you might be wrong. There were many big storms in the country in the nineteenth century,' he evaded, not wishing to display any ignorance even about an unimportant date. 'Let me see — there was a Big Wind that ravaged County Antrim, then there was a Big Wind that devastated parts of County Down, and there was a Big Wind that did untold damage in the County of Tyrone, and there was another Big Wind . . .'

'Leaning against the counter,' added someone from a corner.

Everybody laughed except The Curate, who still had his head down watching the cockroach. The sergeant's neck reddened and he turned and asked the auctioneer when he thought it was.

'I think you're right, Sergeant,' he said. 'It was after the famine!'

'That's what I thought,' said the sergeant, getting ready to go.

Old Dan drained his glass of whisky: 'The Big Wind was before the famine!' and he shouted so loudly that The Curate almost raised his head. 'I mind it well for I was lying in my box-bed at the time,' and he called this after the sergeant who was going out the door with the auctioneer, and when the door had closed on their heels The Curate breathed freely. He looked compassionately at the cockroach: 'I'll give you your liberty too,' and he released it with the toe of his boot and saw it meandering round the barrels and disappear into a hole at the side of the grate close to the warm ashes. He rubbed his hands, pushed back his hat from his brow, ordered another round of drinks, and told Dan to go on with his story of the Big Wind.

'I mind it as well as if it happened last week,' Dan said, 'for when the storm broke loose my mother brought me into her bed and propped me against my da's back, and then I heard my ma say to my da: "Get up, Tom, for the love of God, and bolt the front door for it's lying wide open."

' "Go asleep, woman," my da yelled back at her. "I bolted and locked the door afore I got into bed."

'And then there came to the window a sound of hens flitterin' at it with their feet and wings, and when my ma looked over the blankets she saw a tree blown right up against the pane and scrapin' at it with its twigs. I opened my eyes then, and looked up at the roof, and there was no roof there, only the stars and wrack and stoor flying like rooks across the sky. And there was one rafter with a few straws hanging over it like a moustache.

' "Ma," I said. "Ma, look up. There's no roof above us at all."

' "Tom," she spat into my da's ear. "Tom, for the love of the good God, wake up, before we're blown into the lake."

' "Go asleep!" my da hurled back at her. "Let me rest. You're dreaming — you and that changeling of a child. Go asleep."

'My mother began to cry: "It's the fearfullest night . . . It's the end of the world," and then a great belch of water came over us, and my da wakened up: " 'Tis an unmerciful and unholy night! Why didn't you waken me sooner!" he moaned, and when he looked up and saw a great eel coiled round the rafters where the wind had blown it out of the river, he got up on the bed and hit it on the napper with the potstick.

' "Be the holy," says he, "if we've no roof we'll have something to eat. If you were setting lines for a year ye'd never catch a lad like that."

' "Give him another crack, Tom, for the divil's in them eels, they're so hard to kill!"

'My father gave the eel another crack and coiled it round the rail of the bed. Then a tree sailed over the house and my da said it was an ash tree and my ma said it was a beech. They argued about that till another went over. Then a hail of water flew so fast over the roof that not a drop came into the house. . . . And in the morning when we looked out, the causeway was covered with bushes and trees and dead trout.' As old Dan finished his story he cleared his throat, spat into the fire, and watched the spit forming a ball with the ashes and rolling out again.

'That's the bloodiest, damndest pack of lies ever I heard,' a man commented, and before Dan could reply, the door opened and Ned Mason came in, and Dan got up from the barrel and hailed him. And while they were talking Luke slipped unnoticed out of the pub.

With one sweep of his eye Ned saw James, his servant-man, who had given him his notice earlier in the day. He had been standing idly about the yard when Ned had asked him to search the rocks for driftwood. 'I've done more than a man's work and I'll do no more,' he had answered sullenly. 'And what's more I'm leavin' now.'

'All right, please yourself,' Ned had replied, and went into the house to get him his wages and to plead with his mother not to coax him to stay. This had riled James, and when he was going down the lonin with his wages in his fist, he insulted Ned about leaving his dead father to put out a fire. 'So help me God, I wouldn't have done it to please any girl!' James spat out.

74

'I'd have done it for any neighbour!' Ned had answered.

'You would not — you damned liar!' James had yelled back to give himself courage and to cower Ned. But Ned caught him and flung him amongst the thorns of the hedge; James lifted a stone then, and Ned's sisters came between them, and while they pulled Ned back to the house, James stood in the lonin cursing the whole breed of the Masons.

And now, as Ned stood at the counter with The Curate and Dan, he deliberately turned his back to the barrel where James was sitting. The Curate stood drinks again and raised his glass to Ned: 'Here's to the day you put out the fire!'

'The day that he disgraced his father's corpse!' James put in, his courage strengthened by a few drinks. Dan and The Curate glared over at the barrel.

'Don't heed him!' Ned said and smiled with bitter contempt.

'I wouldn't listen to that insult!' The Curate said, wiping his mouth on his sleeve.

'Keep you out of it!' James said, rising to his feet. 'A man that'd turn Protestant for a ha'penny job!'

The Curate drained his pint: 'It's a damned lie!' and he said it so quickly that a shower of spits flew from his mouth. 'Come outside and I'll show you who turned his coat!'

'Order now!' said Mr. O'Hare from behind the counter. 'Order, please!'

'You turned your coat!' and James came over and shouldered the wee Curate against the counter.

'Be off, you foul-smelling instrument of perdition!' said Dan as he pushed him away with his stick. James caught it and made to break it across his knee. There was a scuffle; Ned gripped the stick and wrenched it so viciously that James stumbled against a barrel. He raced in at Ned and The Curate tripped him. He fell at their feet. He scrambled up again, and Ned, seeing the fierce stare in his eyes, hit him a short jab, James falling against a barrel, his head

75

striking the ground. He lay there for a few minutes while someone shouted for the sergeant. Then Dan bent over him and called to Mr. O'Hare for a spoonful of whisky.

The policeman entered, took out his note-book, licked his thumb, turned a clean page, and rested the note-book on the counter under the light. He breathed heavily through his nose when he saw that few men remained in the shop. .

'Now, Mr. O'Hare,' he said, 'I'll take your statement first.'

Mr. O'Hare took his arms out from under his apron: 'Well, sergeant, I've nothing to say because I saw nothing. I was below the counter, sergeant, rinsing the glasses in the bucket when I heard a scuffle and a groan. "Order now," I said, "or I'll have to close the shop," and when I raised my head, sergeant, somebody said a man was hurted.'

The sergeant grunted, rested his pencil on the open book, and bent down to examine the injured man. He wiped the blood away with a handkerchief and saw a small deep cut. 'But in case there'd be complications I must get a statement,' he said to himself. And then, standing up, he rapped out to no one in particular: 'Who hit him? What happened? Is there nobody going to tell me anything? I hold you all responsible.'

James, who was propped against a barrel, opened an eye and rubbed his chin.

'Who molested you?' the sergeant demanded from him, and James turned up his eyes and closed them again. The sergeant shook him: 'What happened to you?'

'I think I toppled off the barrel,' he mumbled. The sergeant lifted the book from the counter and tapped it under Dan Scullion's face. 'You've an old head and a wise head, Dan,' he flattered him. 'You'll tell me exactly what you saw and heard.'

Dan's eye ranged from the sergeant to Mr. O'Hare, and from Mr. O'Hare to the injured man, and from the injured man round the vacant barrels and seats of the pub, and then finally rested on the skimpy fire in the grate. He was glad that The Curate and Ned had cleared, and he smiled cunningly and spat into the fire as if he meant to put it out.

'Well, sergeant, I'll speak as an honest man. This is the way it was, sergeant,' and he traced the point of his stick through a spittle on the floor, raised it and poked it at the almost bare grate. 'I was gawkin' at the fire, sergeant, eyein' a bit of coal and a beard of flame wagglin' about on it. Says I to myself — in my own mind, sergeant — "When that beard of flame is burnt off that bit of coal there'll be no fire left in the backside of the grate and I'll clear home to hell out of this." And just as I was gettin' up to go home in orderly fashion, sergeant, I heard a groan — the same groan, sergeant, that Mr. O'Hare heard, and I wondered was it the wind —'

'You better go home now,' says the sergeant, getting into a temper and pulling out his pencil from the closed notebook. When Dan reached the door he turned and bade them all good night, laughed to himself, and hurried along the windy road, stopping with no one until he reached his house. There he found The Curate and Tessie and Paddy Boden clustered around the fire, and, before sitting down, he pranced about the floor, flourishing his stick, telling them what he said to the peeler and how O'Hare had given him a full glass of whisky to bathe the wound. 'What happened to you? . . . I fell off the barrel,' and he laughed so loudly that The Curate, who was seated in a gloomy silence, was forced to smile, and later, because Tessie had pleaded with him, he struck up a few tunes on his mouth-organ. But he played listlessly, without his customary vigour, and time and again he missed the notes, and Tessie, realizing that he was tired and his mind withdrawn, made up the settle bed for him in the kitchen and banked up the fire.

That night sleep came in snatches to The Curate. He heard the wind rising and falling, the mice scrabbling under the dresser, and saw the shadows of the fire wading across the ceiling. Before dawn he arose, and by the light of the fire he dressed so quietly that the mice made no move to scuttle away from him. The wind had fallen, and when he lifted the edges of the blind he saw through the branches of a tree the cold light of the coming dawn. He heard Dan snoring and he stole out and hurried to the priest's house. The back door was on the latch and he noiselessly cleaned the range, and before the first seagulls had risen from the shore he tackled the donkey and moved off. As the wheels crunched over the gravel the priest heard him, and pulling on an overcoat, ran out to him.

'You're not going away again, Jimmy?' he said.

'I am, Father,' he tried to say lightheartedly.

'But what about the other jobs. I need you for awhile yet. . . . And Miss Drennan was telling me last night that she would like you for a part in a play she is organizing.'

For a few minutes Jimmy did not speak. His eyes were lowered, seeing the priest's slippers and his bare feet thrust into them. He sighed and shook his head: 'I'll be back again, Father, some day.' But something in the tone of the voice, in the melancholy droop of his head, touched the priest, and pressing a hand on his arm he said to him: 'Tell me, Jimmy, what's troubling you?'

'Nothing, Father . . . nothing,' and he kept his head lowered and twisted the rope-reins round his wrist.

'You're not taking to heart what I said to you yesterday?'

Jimmy gave a pained smile: 'I'm not, Father. Sure I know you wouldn't believe what they say about me.'

'Stay for a few days.'

'I can't, Father. Not now, but I'll be back.' Jimmy would not yield to him, but before he moved off he promised that he would return again some time.

The priest was suddenly aware of the cold morning air and he hurried back to his room; it wasn't worth his while now to get into bed again, for he wouldn't sleep, and in a couple of hours he would be going down to the chapel to

78

say Mass. To-day he would offer up the Holy Sacrifice for Jimmy Neil, and as he thought of him he wondered what it was that drove him from the parish, and try as he could to explain it, only one answer insistently presented itself to him — his own remark about the Reverend Hope. It was that and nothing else: and the more he pondered on it ·the more a stiff feeling of anger with himself spread through his mind. He shrugged his shoulders. 'Hasn't Jimmy told me there is no truth in the story,' he said to himself. 'And yet do I believe him? I want to, but to say that I do believe is only a specious juggle of self-deception.'

He paced the room, took a cigarette, flicked open the lighter and immediately blew it out again. Do we know what men are really thinking, he asked himself; the life of the mind almost makes up the entire life of each of us, and still how little we know of the barrenness and desperation that each of us masks daily by a smile, a laugh, or a few tangential words. What are Jimmy's thoughts now as he jogs towards Downpatrick — that I can only guess at, and in guessing, blame myself for driving him away: away to someone perhaps who will show him an increase of kindness.

From a drawer he took out a small note-book in which he had given expression to a few thoughts as they occurred to him during retreats he had spent in silence and in prayer. He turned the pages carefully and his eye halted at a paragraph entitled: *The Shortness of Life* — Continue each day to dwell on my vocation and with it to dwell on the shortness of life. Dedicate my life to the service of God and to the service of others. Abandon all self-seeking and acquisitiveness. Give alms especially when it inconveniences my comfort to do so. Each day do something good and plunge myself into a routine of positive action. I must not be a fireside priest — nibbling my way through life in the hope of living long. *Labor improbus* — labour in the sweat of the brow ... He turned a few more pages and his eye rested on what he had written under: *Suffering* — Why does God

79

submerge me so often in suffering and disappointment? That I might draw nearer to Him by casting all my grief upon Him. For it is only in suffering that I discover my own cringing impotence. When I am well physically and not mortifying myself in little things, how selfish and self-sufficient I grow — praying with a lack of fervour and even indolence. But let suffering assail me: how closely then I turn to God, how earnestly I pray because I think of death. With me to be well physically is to be sick spiritually: my spiritual well-being is nourished by suffering and disappointment — I should greet them then as gifts from God: always rejoice in pain.

He put the book away when the clock on the mantelpiece chimed seven. Jimmy had mended it, and though he wouldn't admit it to himself he was sorry he had done so. He was glad when the clock went out of order, for he hated, lying awake at night, to hear its remorseless striking of the hours. And it would be weakness now to put it deliberately from the room or cease to wind it. Poor Jimmy, little did he realize what jangling conflicts the mended clock would cause.

He crossed to the window. A few curls of soot lay on the sash and he became aware for the moment of its penetrating smell. He blew them off, his breath moistening the pane. Across the quiet land, flat and cold after the storm, he saw the tufts of grass still holding the direction of the wind, and saw striding up the Mason's hill the figure of a man with a dog. On the hip of the hill, in the hard light of the wind-combed air, the man and dog were clipped against the sky.

He turned from the window, poured water from the jug into the basin, pressed in a loose tack at the corner of the splash-mat, and began to shave in cold water. He thought of Ned Mason. What controlled Ned's mind, he asked himself — was it the one thought of his love for Mary Devlin or an anxiety to talk his mother out of her piercing hostility towards the Devlins? He stropped the razor and tested its sharpness on a grey hair he plucked from the brush. How little do we know of one another, he said to himself; it is only in the writings of the great saints of the Church that we glimpse the fusion of our faltering desperation or the travails of our tormented joy. We are all actors — and the only thing we are sure of is the immediacy of our own pain. What pain I may have inflicted on Jimmy Neil, what pain Ned has inflicted on his mother and she on him and on the Devlins, we can only guess at. And John Devlin? — what is it that gets into a young man's mind to make him leave his country and his home and not write to his people?

He bled his chin slightly with the razor and staunched the cut with a bit of fluff off the towel. He brushed into place his thin hair, put on his collar and his soutane, and kneeling on the prie-dieu he said with all the simplicity of a child: 'O Jesus, through the most pure heart of Mary, I offer Thee all my prayers, works, and sufferings of this day for all the intentions of Thy Divine Heart. . . .'

CHAPTER IX

It was Sunday. Sunlight lay flat across the fields, the level sky was scored with a line of cloud, and from the sea came the splash of tired waves. Ned, after taking his dinner, was rambling across his fields, looking at his cattle, noting how this one was thriving, or that one a bit lame, or another with a dry, unhealthy coat. But he had nothing to complain of: his sheep were all dipped and no sickness amongst the lambs. He glanced over the fence at the fine beard on his corn; and at his potato field he halted, his hand on the warm bullwire, and looked with a pleasurable feeling at the rising tops of his potatoes. He threw his leg over the fence, and his dog crushed under the wire after him and then suddenly bounded after a rabbit. Ned walked down between the drills, the sleepy scent of the leaves rising thickly under the sun, and an odd butterfly with outspread wings resting itself on the budding tops. He would have to spray them soon before they flowered. As he walked, a light dust rose at his heels, settled on the leaves, and there was no wind to blow it off again.

He came out on the sea-road, and when he opened the door of the wee farm a slab of sunlight fell across the floor, and a hen with a brood of yellow chickens ran out from a box that lay sideways against the wall. A wet saucer, dirted by the feet of the chickens, rested near the mouth of the box. Delia hadn't been down to feed them yet, so he went into the room that was used as a store to get them a handful of meal. The hen followed him in, pecked at a grain of corn that stuck out of one of the bags, broke it with her neb, and called her chickens. Ned tossed some mashed oats to them, filled the saucer with fresh water and sat down on the table, enjoying a smoke and the quiet coolness of the house. He watched a chicken balancing on the rim of the saucer, dipping its beak into the water, its throat tremoring as it raised its head to drink. Others joined it, tilted the saucer, and spilt the water across the floor. 'Man dear, but they're stupid,' he said to himself, and patiently filled the saucer again.

He turned to the window; flies buzzed on the sunny pane and a few dead ones lay under the cobwebbed snib. With difficulty he rattled the window till it opened with a screech and let in the sun-sifted air. Nettles grew as high as the sill and their leaves were splashed with the droppings of birds, and he knew the sparrows or starlings must be nesting in the thatch above. He would speak to his mother soon and get the eaves wired or a new roof put on like Luke Devlin's. He went out by the back, and brushing his way through the nettles and crunching over broken crockery, he stood on the sill and pulled out a few untidy nests and stuffed up the holes with sods. A couple of eggs fell amongst the nettles, but in one nest he felt the warm scaldies trembling under his hand, and he left them alone.

The noise of girls laughing on the road drew him from the nests, and when he peered round the gable he saw Mary and Barbara and a few others out for a Sunday walk. He called to them and Mary and Barbara stopped, and he heard Mary say: 'Run you on, Barbara, with the rest, and I'll follow after you.' He watched her coming towards him, her green coat, the well-smoothed collar at the V of her neck, her black hair shining in the sun. Her face was flushed with laughing when he carried her in his arms through the nettles and sat beside her on the window-sill. She lifted a piece of straw and began to coil it round her finger, but seeing a blue egg too light to hide itself in the grass, she picked it up and held it on the palm of her hand and reproached him for robbing the nests.

'They're the divil's own pest,' he laughed, putting his arm about her waist and feeling the throb of her heart like the tremorings of the young birds he had lately touched. 'They'd ruin the thatch on us. How would you like to waken up some fine morning with the rain dribbling down on top of us from the holes in the thatch.' She liked the way he always coupled her name with his, and taking his hand, she raised it to her lips, and for answer he pressed her head back and kissed her. She sighed with a mixed feeling of joy and fear, and looked nervously from side to side.

'Nobody could see us here,' he said, and uncoiled the straw from her finger and threw it on top of the nettles, and taking the egg, he flicked it into the hedge opposite without her seeing him.

They remained so still then that a sparrow with a worm in its mouth fluttered into the nest above their heads and out again. A young foal gazed unflinchingly at them over the hedge, its ears pricked, a startled expression in its wide eyes. Its mother stood nearby, its eyes half-shut, and no movement from her except a slight shivering of her flanks

83

when the flies tormented her. Sparrows hopped about, scolding harshly because they were deprived of their nests.

'After all, it might be better to put on a corrugated roof,' Ned sighed. 'And we could get your father to sling the ropes over it for us,' he teased. But she was barely listening to him, her mind perplexed with one thought, wondering if a time would ever come when she would have their washing spread out together on the top of the hedge and the twigs sticking up through them.

'What's on your mind?' he asked, pressing her towards him.

'Nothing,' she said meekly, 'I was just looking at the mare and wondering if there is anything more patienter. It hasn't budged a bit since we sat here.'

'That's her fourth foal. Do you remember the horse that took fright in the roller and went scatterin' madly with it at its heels over the roads and how your John risked his life by throwing himself round its neck — that was her first foal. Many an evening my father, God be good to him, used to talk about that and about John. We have still got that horse — a good worker but as nervous as a kitten.'

'I liked your father,' she said. And knowing what was in her mind he added quickly, 'And my mother's good at heart, too, Mary, when you get to know her.'

'It's hard to know a person that'll walk past your house with a hand always to her hat or a handkerchief to her nose and her face turned to the sea.'

'That's not like her,' he broke in.

'And only yesterday, when she was on her way to the chapel to confession, she passed my father on the road and didn't bid him the time of day. It fairly galled him — and he's not a man to take to spite easily.'

'Och,' Ned said, shaking his head, 'her poor mind's shattered and shod with worry since my father died. She's old now, and I wouldn't pay much heed to the crotchety ways of an old woman — they behave differently from what they're thinking,' and as he finished, his mother's words at the day of the fire tore through his mind with a raw persistency.

The door of the house opened and Mary jumped from the sill.

'It's only Delia,' he said, holding his hands to the side of his face to peer through the window.

Delia carried a can in her hand. 'I was wondering who opened the door,' she spoke. 'I came down to give the chickens a bite to eat.' The hen clucked round her legs, the chickens cheeping unceasingly. She lifted the lid off the can and steam burled out from it. Then she took a flat board from under the table and began to scrape the meal on to it with a stick. The chickens hopped about her hand and stumbled over one another. Mary, leaning her elbows on the sill, watched the chickens pecking the meal on the hen's bill and eating that which clung to her feet.

'My mother was asking did you go to the island to-day to have a look at the sheep,' Delia said to Ned.

'I was waiting for the tide to turn and then I'd walk over across the strand,' he said, and when Delia had closed the door and gone off he turned suddenly to Mary: 'Come on with me to the island and I'll take the boat.'

'But your mother would see us from the house.'

'And what if she does! She'll have to say "yes" to us some day. We've done no harm and we needn't be ashamed to face anybody,' and lifting her in his arms he kissed her and carried her through the nettles to the gable end.

As they skirted the house on the hill and made down the cliff-path to where the boat lay on the stones, his dog ran after them, his paws covered with clay, his panting tongue gritted with dust. The tide was going out, leaving pools of water and wet patches of sand drying under the sun. They began to drag the boat down to the water, but the keel sank in the sand and he had to put an oar under the bow to serve as a roller. They had the boat nearly launched when Barbara and a few girls came running along the strand, shouting to Ned to take them out. A rope from the stern wriggled over the sand and he saw them trying to stamp on it with their feet. He laughed as he stood up and pushed off vigorously with his oar. Barbara rushed to catch the end of the rope, but a wave swept over her shoes and they all screamed with delight. The sheepdog was barking, running to and fro in the shallow edges, the water dripping from his long hair.

'We'll take you some other time,' Ned called, as the boat coggled into deeper water, and when Mary looked back she saw Barbara standing very downcast, her friends around her. Then the dog ran amongst them shaking himself, and they shrieked and scattered away from him.

The bay was smooth and the little island lay at the far side of it close to the shore. Mary sat in the stern, her back to the house on the hill whose windows were innocently reflecting the sun. She was afraid even to take a furtive glance up, for she feared that the same woman who had already insulted her was lurking in some corner of it.

At that moment Mrs. Mason was sitting in her bedroom in view of the sea, the peaceful sunlight falling through the lace curtain on to the prayer-book which rested on her lap. As she raised her head to blow at two pages that were stuck together she looked out the window and saw the boat trailing its rough wedge across the bay. She took off her spectacles, blew her breath on them and polished them on the corner of her apron. She was sure there were two people in the boat. She pushed down the window to see more clearly. There was someone with a green coat in the stern. The window streeled into its place again and the snib fastened sharply. She knocked on the floor and called to Delia. She took off her spectacles and tapped them on the closed prayer-book. She opened the room door and called sharply. Delia came running up.

'Did you see Ned when you were over at the chickens?'

'I did. . . . He was down at the wee farm.'

'Was he his lone?'

Delia didn't answer.

'Was he his lone — I'm asking you?'

'No, I don't think so.'

'You don't think so! What way is that to talk! Who was with him?'

Delia smoothed out a crease on the quilt of the bed.

'Have you lost your tongue?'

'He was speaking to Mary Devlin.'

'I just thought there was someone out in the boat with him. Come here to the window — you've better sight than your poor mother.'

'I think there is somebody — it might be one of the dogs.'

'I never saw a dog with a green coat on it. It might be Mary Devlin if you ask me! A nice way to be carrying on of a Sunday and your poor father barely six months in his grave. You're as bad as he is for shielding him. I've told you, and I've told Sarah and Ann that Mary Devlin is not a suitable match for Ned. And now, after all my warning, you secretly encourage him. There's nothing in this house only deceit. God knows you'd think we had our share of trouble without bringing another burden of it into the house.' She tapped the book on her knee. 'Mark my words — no luck will come to this house!'

She took up her place in the embrasure of the window again. A few gulls swayed over the house, their shadows gliding into the room. Below, in a small vegetable garden, two blackbirds began to fight, and a cat which lay full stretch on the wall under the sun paid not the slightest heed to them.

Mrs. Mason tapped with her foot, and with the leg of her spectacles picked out a few shavings of a pencil that were embedded in the seams of the boards where she sat. She opened her prayer-book and her eyes alighted on a passage that seemed to her to echo the thoughts of her own mind: 'Let every soul be subject to the higher powers; he that resisteth the power, resisteth the ordinance of God, and they that resist purchase to themselves damnation . . .'

She put the book aside and looked across the bay at the green-humped island. The two of them were walking side by side, the sheep gathering in a group and moving away from them. And in her own mind she fancied she could hear the sharp protesting cries of the oyster-catchers as they dipped about their heads. She sighed heavily and plucked off a thread from her apron. Years ago, before she was married, a crowd of them had gone on a picnic to the island, and now the memory of that day rushed vividly to her mind — the man she loved lifted an egg from a nest at her feet where she had nearly trodden on it, made two holes in it with her hat-pin and blew a stream of yolk out of it on to the grass; he gave it to her as a keepsake and she kept it for a long time in a box filled with wadding. They played blind-man's buff, and when a girl was blindfolded they made a ring round her and shouted: 'You're near the cliff! You're near the cliff!' It was on that day, too, that her husband had proposed to her. As she recalled it all, tears glistened in her eyes, and when she raised her head Ned and Mary had crossed the hump of the island and the sheep were beginning to graze again. She got to her feet, a suffocating ache pressing in her throat. That side of the island was scooped with sheltered nooks — what took them there of all places! Her hands trembled. She closed the wardrobe door that was ajar and a faint smell of camphor flurried into the air. The room seemed unbearably close. She opened the window at the top, raised it at the bottom and propped a stick underneath it. Nothing stirred on the bay; the cat was still stretched on the wall and she could see the contented rise and fall of its sleeping body. She hurried from the window, the swish of her skirts wavering the ends of the curtain. She would go for a walk along the shore. She took her black coat from the wardrobe, and with the button-hook fastened the three top buttons in her boots which she had opened to give her ease. She went down the stairs. The kitchen door was open to the sun, and outside the dog was barking. Sarah was giving a saucer of milk to two kittens and Delia was swishing a newspaper at a hen that was venturing across the threshold. Sarah got up to go with her mother when a shadow fell across the floor and Father Toner came in, his hand ruffling the dog's neck. Delia got a plush-covered chair from the room, wiped it with her apron, and placed it near the fire for the priest. Sarah lifted the kittens' saucer from the floor.

'Now don't let me disturb you,' said Father Toner, waving his hand at the blue sky. 'The sun drew me out and this is the reward I got,' pointing to an L-tear on his coat.

'Come down to the room, Father, and give your coat to Sarah. She'll not be long mending it,' said Mrs. Mason, her composure slowly returning to her.

'I'll be all right here in the kitchen,' he said, as she took his hat and stick from him. Then he laughed as he saw Sarah take a needle and black thread from a wicker box: 'I suppose one could take a dispensation for work of this kind on a Sunday,' and he took off his coat, but noticing how abashed Sarah and Delia were to see him in his shirt-sleeves, he followed Mrs. Mason down to the cool room where a heavy album sat on the middle of the table and a mellow tick came from the grandfather clock in the corner.

She offered him a cigarette from a silver box which she reserved for visitors like himself.

'I'm off them for a little while,' he said.

'Is it doctor's orders?' she asked with mild anxiety.

'Not at all, not at all,' he laughed.

'It's not like you, Father, to refuse a cigarette,' and she tapped the box with her fingers and put it back on the mantelpiece.

He felt that his refusal had hurt her, and, seeking for something pleasant to say, he made a remark about the cool freshness of the room, and this agitated her still more.

'Wait, Father, and I'll get you something to put round your shoulders.'

'I'm quite comfortable, Mrs. Mason, thank you. It's lovely in here — and God's own sun sweetening the room,' and he motioned to her to sit down.

'Maybe, Father, you'd take a little . . .'

'All right now, Mrs. Mason, but nothing strong, please.'

She whisked out of the room. He felt that he had pleased her. He stretched out his hand to the album, moved a glass inkstand away from him, but noticing that it covered a big inkstain on the cloth, he hastily restored it. He flicked through the photos in the album: there was one of Aunt Rose and her three white dogs outside her house in Downpatrick, one of Mrs. Mason and her three daughters, one of Ned at the plough, and one of the pony and trap and Mr. Mason holding the reins. There was a panoramic photograph of an Irish Pilgrimage to Lourdes, and he picked out Mrs. Mason, and her husband with official ribbons in the lapel of his coat, and Ned, only a boy then, sitting cross-legged at his father's feet; and there he was himself in the front row, young and fat and fresh, and Father O'Brien, his hat on to cover his baldness, and a wing of nuns at each side of him. He was thinking about a number of people whose names had slipped his memory when Mrs. Mason tapped the door and put a tray with glasses on the table.

'Are you sure, Father, you wouldn't have something strong?'

'Sherry, now, Mrs. Mason.'

The cork gave a dry whistle as she screwed it from the bottle, and as she poured out the wine she saw the cuff of his shirt fastened with a button and remembered how her own husband — God be good to him — hated cuff-links and how she had caught him on a few occasions rolling the loose sleeves up to his elbows and pulling on his coat.

As she handed him the glass she noticed that the button on his right sleeve was sewn with black thread and was glad that she didn't let him saunter off to his housekeeper with the ripped coat — a nice mess she'd have made of it. It's strange now that he puts up with that fumbling old woman about his place — done and doddering, she is, years ago!

'How's Ned?' he asked, toying with the stem of his glass.

'Hm,' she started, 'out sporting himself — somewhere,' and instantly her mind clutched on the island, its sheltered nooks and the high bracken that was concealing them maybe as she spoke. She sipped at the glass: 'God knows where he is — he's seldom to be seen about the place on a Sunday.'

'Och, he gets it tough now with no servant-man to help him,' and as he took a drink from his glass he eyed a bit of cork that floated in it. He held the glass in his two hands and wondered if she had heard about the recent row in O'Hare's pub. He decided not to mention it.

' 'Deed, Father, he can find plenty of time for gallivantin'.'

'The young need it. I don't like to see them lounging about — moody and discontented. They need a bit of brightness, of relaxation to keep them from grumbling.'

'It's my belief, Father, they're too much given to sport . . . Not as in my young days.'

'The young, I think, are always the same, Mrs. Mason. It's we who have changed and we tend to deny to them what we ourselves desired when we were like them. If I had the funds I would build a decent hall for them where they could have whist drives, plays, and dances — it would help to keep the few youth that we have at home. It bruises my heart to see them heading for Belfast or across the water or marrying away. Those that return have lost their natural ways and some of them, I'm sorry to say, lose more than that,' he took another sip, his eye still on the bit of cork: 'No, Mrs. Mason, we want a bit of pleasure and colour in the parish — I feel when a man is full of gloom he's full up with the devil. A good Christian sheds some wholesome joy around him!' He drained his glass and held it loosely between his finger and thumb.

He was in a strange mood, she thought. She took the glass from him and saw the grain of cork clinging to the side. How did she not see that before she handed it to him! Her mind was upset — she could do nothing right.

The door was politely knocked. She opened it and took in the coat and examined the mend by the light of the window.

'Sarah has made a splendid job of this,' he said, his finger running over the outline of the patch. He stood up and put on the coat: 'If Kate hears about me bringing my mending to the neighbours she'll give me a rare scolding.'

They went into the kitchen and the dog rubbed itself against his leg.

'I don't see Ann about?' he said to Sarah and Delia who were standing smiling at him, both having changed into new frocks while he was in the room.

They told him she was in Downpatrick helping Aunt Rose, who was ill.

'If she happens to see or hear of Jimmy Neil maybe you'd let me know,' he said, bending down and tickling the dog's throat.

'Jimmy Neil!' they laughed with polite irony. 'Jimmy Neil — Ann is sure to see him!' and they laughed again, the priest smiling back at them as he stepped into the sunlit yard.

Mrs. Mason walked with him down the lonin. The potholes were filled with gravel and fresh netting wire covered the holes in the hedge that bordered the orchard. A bird was singing. There was a heavy scent of hawthorn blossom and some of the petals floated in a tub of water near the corner of a gate. She bade him good-bye at the foot of the lonin, and on her way back she felt weary. She plucked a twig of blossom and inhaled its sweetish scent. Somehow his call had not, as it always did, calmed her. She was always glad to see him, but to-day, she thought, he was in a peculiar mood. And that bit of cork! It may have been in the glass, she suggested to herself, and then immediately swept that from her mind for she remembered that it was she, herself, who had cleaned them last. And how did she manage to give him the one with the cork and not take it herself! And Ned — why wasn't he here to receive him: thinking of nothing only his own selfish interests. Why can't he be like his sisters — I've no trouble with them, no trouble at all. She shook her head and quoted a line aloud to herself: 'an obedient man will speak victories and in his house are riches forever.'

As she dragged herself across the yard a gull was pecking at a crust of bread; it ran away from her with half-spread wings and rose into the air in the space between the gable and the cart-shed. She saw the blue of the sea and a boat rippling across it. She hesitated, twisting the hawthorn twig in her hand. They have no pride, the Devlins — no pride at all! You'd think once was enough to speak to them! And as she reflected on the anxiety that that scene had caused her and on the spiteful gossip that had followed it, she shook her head to drive the ugliness of it from her mind. 'No,' she said firmly, 'I'll not lower myself to speak to her again.' She looked at the hawthorn twig and flung it on the yard: 'It's unlucky to bring that into the house,' and when she went in through the open door, the gull circled over the roof, alighted on the sunlit yard again, and walked cautiously towards the crust.

CHAPTER X

FROM that Sunday when she had seen Ned take Mary Devlin to the island she tried to get him alone so that she could speak her mind to him. For days she thought of what she would say to him. She would say it with all the earnestness of her love for him. And she would say it quietly. He was her only son, she would tell him, and she wished nothing for him only what was for his own good. She knew the tricks and wiles of the people in the parish better than he did. She'd point out the ruination he was bringing on himself. What could Mary Devlin give him, only worry. Look at the ragged, ill-kept place they had — a few potatoes, a patch of thin corn, and scarcely enough grass to feed their one cow and their handful of sheep. And their father — what was he but an idle man living only for his bit of a boat, a few fish that he'd salt for the winter, and an odd bag of dulse that might be sold, but more likely to be left on his hands to rot and stink. And then there was John — a galli-vanter that flew away from his home and God alone knows for what reason. And where was he now? — nobody knew, not even his own father or the priest. Surely that'd show what stock they were. And in what condition might he not tumble home some day — arrive, perhaps, with not a penny to bless himself, and expect to be kept in tobacco and food and drink: and who would keep him? His father could hardly keep himself let alone a big lazy lump of a son and two silly daughters that thought more of dancing and show-off than they do of an honest day's work. No, Ned, she'd plead, you must listen to reason — you must pay heed to the mother that bore you, to your mother that wrought hard to make this farm for you!

With these thoughts in her mind, day and night, she waited for the right moment to speak them to him. But a chance did not come her way for Sarah and Delia were always in the kitchen at the wrong time, and now that the sunny weather was here he was out working in the fields, would return for his dinner and not take time to smoke his pipe in the kitchen until he was out again. And then in the late evening when she heard the jangling of the horses returning to the yard and saw Ned and the farm-hand trudge about the sheds she understood that to open her mind to a tired man would only thwart her purpose.

Her sister, Rose, came from Downpatrick to convalesce—

and noticing how dry and moody Ned was with his Aunt she put all her thoughts of Mary Devlin from her until such a time when ease and peace had flowed through the house again. But one lovely Sunday morning when Ned was harnessing the trap to take them to Mass the idea occurred to her that she'd tell the girls to walk home from chapel and take their fill of the lovely day, and then when she had Ned to herself in the trap, the bells of the pony jingling and its hooves smacking rhythmically on the road, she would open her mind to him. She smiled as the girls squeezed their way on to the trap beside her, Aunt Rose, pale and frail, standing out in the yard and waving to them as they swayed down the lonin.

They arrived before Father Toner had come out from the sacristy. Mrs. Mason arranged herself comfortably near the altar, and the sunlight shining on the varnished seats and a bee buzzing on the window filled her with such a light feeling of happiness that it was with difficulty that her mind fastened on the meaning of the prayers in her prayer-book. During the Mass the heavy unwavering air in the chapel made her drowsy and time and time again she shook her head to prevent herself from falling asleep. And then when Father Toner had at length folded up the corporal she sighed with thankfulness that it was time to sit up while he read out the notices for the week or gave a short sermon.

Father Toner had his back to them, his eyes on two worn spots on the carpet at his feet. He could hear the congregation clearing their throats as they rose from their knees and sat up. Then came the clink-clink of coppers rattling on the two wooden plates as they were passed from seat to seat — up the men's side of the aisle, up the women's side of the aisle, until finally the two plates of coppers were placed at the side of the altar rail and the two collectors had tiptoed back to their places.

The priest lifted a note-book with slips of paper sticking out of it and turned to face the congregation. As usual the three front seats on the men's side were empty, and yet men were standing at the back of the church, some of them leaning against the confessional, and others bent on one knee, their heads lowered. But he would say nothing to them this morning — wasn't he tired asking them to fill the empty seats in front and not be lounging around the door and piling their caps on top of the Catholic Truth Society box. And in the gallery there was the back of the harmonium with its ragged canvas confronting him — how often had he told Miss Drennan to turn it the other way! He glanced at the note-book in his hand, put it back on the altar, and picked up another.

He gave a slight cough and was about to begin when his eye caught sight of a tilted candle on the brass candelabra, its tears falling with a ponk-ponk on to the grease pan below. Mrs. Mason and her three daughters in the front seat saw it and then lowered their heads; the altar boys gazed at it with stupid curiosity. Mr. O'Hare the nearest to it on the men's side pretended to read the memoriam cards in his missal but made no move to prop up or blow out the dripping candle. Father Toner stared directly at it and was going to motion to one of the altar boys when he saw Dan Scullion approach the candelabra blow out the candle and shuffle back to his place.

A smell of burnt grease waded about the altar smothering the smell of the hyacinths arranged in vases at the side of the tabernacle. The priest coughed again and said slowly, 'I shall read for you the epistle of to-day's Mass, the Fifth Sunday after Pentecost':

Dearly beloved: Be ye all of one mind, having compassion one of another, being lovers of the brotherhood, merciful, modest, humble: not rendering evil for evil, nor railing for railing, but contrariwise, blessing: for unto this are you called, that you may inherit a blessing. For he that will love life, and see good days, let him

96

refrain his tongue from evil, and his lips that they speak no guile. Let him decline from evil, and do good; let him seek after peace, and pursue it; because the eyes of the Lord are upon the just, and his ears unto their prayer, but the countenance of the Lord upon them that do evil things. And who is he that can hurt you, if you be zealous of good? But if also you suffer anything for justice' sake blessed are ye. And be not afraid of their fear, and be not troubled: but sanctify the Lord Christ in your hearts. . . .

He folded his hands under his vestments and raising his eyes saw a little boy with sticking-plaster on his head chewing the corner of his prayer-book. He lowered his eyes and let them rest on the vacant space of the aisle. My dear brethren, he began, I wish to say a few words to you this morning on this epistle of St. Paul. In it we have stated with sure and simple truth a way of life that each of us should seek after and establish — first of all in his own mind, then in his family, and then in the community, the parish, in which he dwells. But that way of life is not to be obtained easily or without constant watchfulness. To possess it we must struggle hard. It is not, I must say, a mere obeying of the commandments, for many of us could lead a life in which the commandments were rigidly obeyed and then find at the end of our days that our lives were as dry and sapless as a bit of withered wrack. And why? — because only one side of our lives had been alive and that a selfish one — pursuing our own sanctification by a method of standing still: declining from evil but failing to do good. It is impossible to lead a good Christian life by living for yourself alone. And those of you who have that inclination must fight against it. It applies to all of us — both you and me. We are all smudged with the same selfishness, seeking always that which is easy, being easy on ourselves, not doing our fair share of work in our homes, or in the fields, or for our employer. Going about our work as if we had diseased hearts which at any moment might stop. We have diseased hearts — but they are diseased and cankered with the growth of self-love. My dear brethren, as you go on your knees each evening examine your conscience and destroy that selfishness that is buckling and crippling the real spiritual growth of your souls — never cease to ask yourselves what good have I done to others. To do good we must help one another — each striving to aid and not to hinder, being merciful, modest, and humble and not rendering evil for evil. I know it is not always easy in our day-to-day meetings with our neighbours, in our buying and selling, not to meet with some rebuffs and annoyances. But it is our duty to smother spite and to smother that grudging spirit that surges within us from time to time: for the man who dwells on spite deforms his mind, the man who remembers the faults of people and not their kindnesses poisons his own soul. My dear brethren, life is too short to squander it in criticizing one another's faults or in hoarding spite and insults till they lie like a heavy load upon us. Peace on earth comes to men of good will — To men of good will: it means exactly that — for where there is no good will there is no peace. . . .

Father Toner paused, took a handkerchief from his sleeve and blew his nose; the lad with the sticking-plaster on his head was bending a memoriam card backwards and forwards. Miss Drennan seated at the harmonium was choking a yawn, and Mrs. Mason had lifted a black kid glove from her lap and was straightening out one of the fingers. Father Toner once again rested his eyes on the vacant space of the aisle. He would end soon — they were getting tired.

To obtain peace of soul we must let the centre of our life be God. It is of little use saying: 'Not my will but Thine be done, O Lord!' when in our heart of hearts we do not wish for any such thing, in case God's will would be contrary to the wishes of our own; in case He should have designed for us some suffering, some setback, which we feel we do not deserve. But who is he that can hurt you if you be zealous of good. Who is he, indeed, that can hurt you if your minds are constantly turned to God and are numbed and deafened to the things of this earth — not laying up treasures for ourselves on earth, not piling up money above our just needs but sharing it, while we have time, with the poor and needy, not with outward show but in simplicity and in silence. Money and the greed for it and the greed that grows with it are damning many of us, even some of those who think themselves exemplary Christians. Let us hunger after those things by which we truly live. If suffering and worry do come our way let us bear them in patience and in the light of God's design remembering that the grace of God is sufficient for us all, that power is made perfect in infirmity. Suffering tries us all; suffering wrings the prayers from us — it is only when we are in trouble or beset with doubts and fears that we do turn with fervour to God. 'Gladly therefore will I glory in my infirmities that the power of Christ may dwell in me.' Let us not try to shirk and escape from the little crosses that are sent to us — face them with prayer, and spiritual good will surely be ours. Suffering, too, brings greatness of character — or looking at it in a worldly manner I could say that personality goes with suffering, dullness with a life of ease. . . .

The little boy with the sticking plaster on his head dropped his prayer-book and a few people coughed.

And lastly, dear brethren, too many of us believe that if we could only keep the Sixth Commandment that our lives would be above reproach. Let me tell you there are far greater sins than the sixth — there are the sins against charity of which I have already spoken. The sixth is in many ways the most selfish and because of that the most insistent — but to be conscious of that, and that only, is to be half alive. And what kind of growth can we expect in a field if we cast the seed into one corner of it. No, we must nourish and broaden and strengthen the acres of our mind by working good to all men, and then we would discover that we inherit a blessing — that sweetness of God that soothes the mind of man. . . .

He blessed himself, turned to the altar and lifted a note-book and slips of paper. He read the notices: 'The sick and infirm of the Sea-Road will be attended on Monday morning, those of Killymona on Tuesday morning, and those in Ballylucan on Wednesday. There will be a football match to-day at 3 o'clock between Dunscourt and Drumferrin and in the evening at 8 o'clock there will be a dance in the School — admission one shilling for gents and sixpence for ladies.' He closed the note-book and asked for prayers for the deceased of the parish, for those of the parish living outside it, for our country and for the Christians of the world.

He turned to finish Mass and no one except Kate, his old housekeeper, went out of the chapel until he had gone from the altar. Then the men crushed out first and the girls in the gallery leaned over smiling to the boys who winked furtively up at them. Next came the women, taking their time, and Mrs. Mason came last, having told her daughters to walk home and make the best of the day. Her head ached as she pulled on her gloves, and as she moved down the aisle of the empty church the fetid air that was stirred by the congregation swathed about her in sickening folds. She glanced at a pair of lost rosary beads hanging from a nail in the porch, dipped her finger in the delph bowl of holy water and emerged into the white sunlight and the fresh air. She went to her husband's grave and after praying for his soul she decided that the ground would soon be firm enough now to erect a headstone.

Men were standing in groups outside the chapel and others were walking off wheeling their bicycles. She hurried past them with her head lowered and came to an old disused shed where Ned was harnessing the pony.

'I thought Father Toner would never finish,' she said when she was seated in the trap, 'and the heat to-day, phew!

There wasn't a budge out of the candles on the altar. Wouldn't you think now he'd have some regard for us cooped up in that wee chapel and no ventilation in it.'

'If it was raining,' Ned said, 'you'd be faulting him for keeping us sitting in our damp clothes.'

'You always have an excuse ready for Father Toner,' she laughed lightly. 'But when I think of poor Father O'Brien that was here before him and the lovely sermons he used to preach — you felt your heart lifted after them! But Father Toner's make me feel dry.'

'That's because he has no soul plastering talk that the women of this parish want.'

'He's a queer man — and the way he never lifts his eyes.'

'He's a good warm-hearted man.'

'Poor Father O'Brien was a saint!'

'You must have canonized him yourself, mother!'

Her finger smoothed one of the buttons on the upholstery of the seat — it was better to say nothing, she thought, for fear she might cross him. She drummed with her bare fingers on the varnished mudguard above the wheel — how hot it felt! And before she realized what she was doing words of reproach were coming from her lips accusing him of not pushing the trap into the shade.

'It was in the shady side when I went into the chapel but the sun travelled too quick,' he explained.

'That heat is enough to buckle the boards. I suppose he preached too long.'

'He preached well.'

'God forgive me, for I was only half listening to him. I was thinking of poor Aunt Rose alone in the house and she maybe to fall down in a faint with that heat.'

A stone jumped from under the wheel into the hedge. The pony started but Ned gripped the reins and kept her ambling past the people on the road. He saw Dan Scullion walking alone and he hailed him: 'Man alive, Dan, you gave the candle a quare blow to-day.'

'Aye, Ned. I don't like to see things wasting their lives,' and then he motioned with his stick at Paddy Boden and Tessie who were hurrying a short distance in front: 'What do you think, Ned, of that pair since they were langled together?'

Ned laughed: 'If they'll not be happy with you, Dan, they were never meant to be spancelled.' And as he was passing them he flourished his whip with an impressive gesture.

When at last the pony got ahead of the people on the road it broke into a trot, its mane flopping up and down, the bells on its neck jingling, and a gentle stir of air eddying about the trap. Mrs. Mason settled herself more comfortably and looked at the cobbles of cloud on the far away floor of the sky. Then she glanced at her son and at the leather reins hanging loosely between his fingers. Now and again she saw him lift the whip and wave it at the cloud of flies that tormented the pony or occasionally stretch out his hand and kill a few clegs that had alighted on the pony's back.

'I never saw such a plague of clegs as there are the year,' he said.

'You said that like your poor father! How he hated them too.' Ned smiled to hear her saying that, and once again he killed a few clegs on the pony's back and saw their specks of blood drying in the sun.

The pony turned on to the sea-road and as they drew near the Devlins' cottage Mrs. Mason, knowing they would not be home from Mass, decided to take a good look at it as she passed. She saw the sycamore tree, and lying against its trunk a rusty barrel hoop and a broken cup. The tar was melting on the roof and strings of it were hanging over the eaves. She lifted her gloves from the seat beside her and tapped them on the palm of her hand. They crossed the stone bridge over the stream and saw the Devlins' geese asleep on the bank. The pony slowed down up the hill, snorting and flicking the foam from its mouth. The wheels gritted over the screenings on the road and overhead gulls glided down to the warm sand on the beach.

'Ned,' she said, surprised at the tremor in her voice. 'I've something to say to you,' and she stretched out her hand and clasped his. The tears came to her eyes as she unburdened her mind to him about the Devlins. He said nothing. The pony walked on, her head drooping from the slack reins, her ears shaking at the showers of flies that had risen from the rotten wrack on the shore.

When they had passed the empty house on the wee farm he halted the pony.

'Tell me, Mother, is it Aunt Rose that has roused you to this?'

'No, Ned, no! Leave that poor thing out of it. She's not well! As God's my judge she has nothing to do with it.'

'I doubt it!'

'Ned!'

'I said I doubt it! And if she thinks she can come out here to stir up trouble she can pack her bag, sick and all as she is, and go off to her dogs in Downpatrick. She married money.'

'It's not true, Ned!'

'It is. Everybody knows it.'

'Are you going to believe the words of gossipy, spiteful people?'

'I don't listen to spite. I believe what I know to be true. If there was any real love in her she'd have married long ago — married when she was fit to have children.'

'Ned!'

'Yes!'

'She could have married long ago — and to men of her own choice.'

'Then why didn't she do it. I'll tell you: because there was nobody to come forward with a sackful of money to give her the airs and graces and fol-de-lols that she wants! That's the life, Mother, she'd wish for me. But I tell you here and now that a batch of dogs and no children is not much use to a farmer. It's that woman that's filling your head with these notions!'

The trap swung through the open gate up the lonin, crunching over the pebbles in the holes, the dogs running to meet them and keeping well into the hedge.

'Ned, son,' and she pressed his hand, 'you'll not have words with your Aunt Rose and you coming from Mass? She'll be only here for another few days.'

He looked over the nodding head of the pony and said nothing.

'Promise me, Ned! ... I tell you she had nothing to do with it ... What I told you has been in my mind for a long time ... I wanted to give you my advice ... before ... before it is too late.'

He pulled up the pony near the door and his Aunt Rose came out leaning on a stick. He noticed how his mother's hand trembled as she gathered up her prayer-book and rosary beads from the seat of the trap, and as he helped her to put her foot on the low-hung step of the trap she looked at him and whispered his name.

'I'll say nothing!' he whispered back.

'He kept you a good wee while this morning,' his aunt said to them. 'Did he preach long?' Neither of them answered, and when his mother and she had gone into the house Ned led the pony to the tub to give her a drink. He unyoked the trap and pushed it under the open shed and went to the hill at the back of the house where he scanned the white road that swept past the Devlin cottage. He saw his sisters chatting on the road with Mary and Barbara, and saw the flash of Mary's green coat and Barbara's red one as they waved to his sisters before turning into the cottage. Suddenly his face became stiff and troubled, and he walked down the cliff-path away from the house.

CHAPTER XI

MARY was awakened by the scrake of gulls and by a rush of sunshine that pressed against the window-blind that faced the sea. For a moment she stared at the glowing fabric of the blind, watching the shadows of the gulls curving across it and breaking the threads of sun that stretched through every slit and hole. Beside her Barbara was asleep, the clothes cowled around her head. She got up without wakening her, unhooked the blind from the window and blinked at the glittering sun that heaved and broke upon the backs of the waves. A shower had fallen during the night and a few drops still lingered on the sycamore tree outside, but the road was drying rapidly and she saw a robin hop across it and alight on a rough stone. In a hollow of the stone some rainwater had escaped the sun and when the robin began to drink from it Mary, unable to restrain the joy it caused her, rubbed her hands and called: 'Barbara, waken up! Come quick!' But Barbara didn't hear her. The robin finished his drink and began to bath himself, his tail erect, his head ducking into the water and rolling the drops on to his outstretched wings. Then suddenly he got up, stretched himself thin, and flew off with a chirp.

She started to brush and comb her hair, all the time looking out of the window and feeling the clean warmth from the morning sun. She sang as she lit the fire and lifted the can to milk the cow. The grass in the field was damp and the blades stuck to her heavy boots. She crouched against the warm-damp sides of the cow, wet her fingers in the grass, and began to milk, the swallows sweeping low around her and the larks high up plaiting the sky with song.

Returning, she drove the geese down to the stream and on her way looked at the rainwater where the robin had washed himself and smiled at a tiny feather floating on top of it. She made the breakfast and called her father and Barbara. He scolded her for letting him lie so long on such a grand morning, and after hurrying his breakfast went out to the fowl-house, plucked two feathers off a hen to clean his pipe, and lifted the sail from the gable-end of the house.

'It's a lovely day for cutting dulse. Barbara and you can dry what's in the bags and have it ready for the buyer if he calls. And don't forget to weed the potatoes.' He walked across the drying sand to where his boat lay in the thin-lipped water. He lifted the anchor that was half-buried in the sand, coiled up the wet rope, and let the dog swim after him for a while before hoisting her aboard.

The boat slid out easily with the ebb-run and he gave an extra pull to the oars when he saw two other boats heading for the rocky point. He was there first and sought a sheltered bay out of the run of the tide. It was flowing out like a river, leaving whorls and wrinkles where it raced over submerged rocks. He flung out his anchor and standing in the boat with his long-poled hook he raised up the heavy masses of gleaming dulse and piled them around him. When he had stripped a few rocks he filled his pipe and sat back in the stern until the tide would ebb away from the deeper rocks. The sun came out strong and smarted the drying hacks in his hands. A small collier, its funnel dribbling smoke, lazed outside the bar waiting for the tide to turn and carry it up the lough. The sight of it filled his mind with a silent resentment about John and he wondered what unnatural twist had got into his son to make him forget his own father. And it wasn't that anybody was bad to him — when he was at home he had more than his share of everything that came into it: he had half the fishing money and the dulse, and when a sheep or heifer was sold he had more than a good penny out of it. If he'd only send a message on a penny postcard a body wouldn't mind — but this silence day in and day out makes you wonder if he's alive or dead.

The dog, her trembling forepaws on the gunwale of the boat, barked loudly and Luke told her to keep quiet. She lowered her ears, gave a muffled growl in her throat and sniffed the wind. Then she hopped on to the seat beside him but the water dripped from her hairy legs and he pushed her away from him. She barked again and a sheep bleated piteously from the land. Luke scanned the shore and on a sloping sandy bank he saw the sheep struggling on its side. It bleated again and the men in the other boats, who were further out from the shore, shouted to Luke to put in. He lifted the anchor and rowed into a sandy gullet, jumped ashore and strode towards the sheep. It struggled more wildly to escape, for the dog was barking and running round it. Luke yelled at her and when he reached the sheep he saw its back leg caught in the wire noose of a rabbit snare. He prized up the long staple that held the snare and snipped off the wire. The sheep scrambled to get away from him but he pinned it to the ground with his elbow and with his free hand tried to loosen the noose. The wire had almost hacked its way through the bone and the leg was broken. He knew the sheep was Ned's and he carried it on his shoulder up the green sandy banks to the Masons' house. Other sheep with their legs langled with bits of rope hobbled painfully away from him. ''Tis a wonder they didn't langle this girl,' he said to himself, 'and she wouldn't have wandered down amongst the rabbit holes.'

Sarah was crossing the yard when he approached and he told her what had happened.

'Wait till I get Ned,' she said, 'him and the new man are thinning turnips in the field,' and she went into the house, took a whistle from a nail on the wall and gave a few blasts.

Ned, stooped between the turnip drills, raised his head: 'It's not dinner-time yet,' he spoke across the drills to the new hand. 'There must be something wrong,' and when he reached the yard he saw his mother and Luke arguing loudly.

'It's your snare and nobody else's,' his mother was saying. 'Nobody traps rabbits on our land only you — and your son before he left the country!'

'I trap rabbits all right but I haven't done much at them the year.'

'Much or more, little or big, you've done plenty of damage. A healthy sheep destroyed on us and our fences broken down!'

'What's wrong?' Ned asked in a wheezy breath. Sarah told him.

'Hm, is that all!' he said. 'Sure nobody could watch sheep — they're stupider than cows.'

'If the snare hadn't been there this wouldn't have happened!' his mother turned to him.

'Haven't they fallen over the cliff before now? You may as well say the cliff shouldn't be there,' Ned said with feigned light-heartedness.

'I'll soon put a stop to the snares. I'll have a trespassers' notice nailed to a board where all may see it.'

'It'll be a waste of time where I'm concerned,' said Luke. 'I'll not pay heed to it and it'll only be a dung-board for birds. You should be paying me for destroying the rabbits and not obstructing me.' The two Mason dogs started to fight with Luke's. Sarah rushed at them with a brush but that only encouraged her own and they leapt at Luke's and toppled her.

'Let them fight it out! They'll soon tire of one another and make friends,' Luke said with a bitter smile.

His dog whirled to her feet again and catching one of the Masons' by the throat she swung it to the ground. Mrs. Mason backed away in fright and called to Ned to stop them. Without hurrying he filled a bucket of water from the tub and flung it over them, and they scattered from one another with a surprised yelp.

'Come on out of this, Nellie, till we get our work done,' Luke called, his dog running after him and licking his hand.

He walked down the fields to his boat, a restless annoyance agitating him as he pondered her lean angry words. Hadn't himself and John saved many a decent man's crop by thinning out the rabbits! Were they to be kept away from the very place where they hatched and swarmed and bred ruination. Be God — she nor any of her name wouldn't stop him! He'd smash to smithereens any notice, big or small, board or concrete, that she'd erect. It's time somebody faced up to her. He was a fool not to tackle her about her insults on the day of the fire — he was too soft with the likes of that one. Let a bad-tempered body off once and they'd toss you aside like an old rag.

His dog with her nose to the ground crossed and recrossed a patch of ground, her breathing quick and loud. Then suddenly she shot in a line to a clump of whins; there she stood rigid, her tail outstretched, one forepaw lifted. She glanced sideways at Luke and he picked up a stone and tossed it into the whins. A rabbit flitted out and the dog scrambled after it down the hill, tumbling it as it tried to turn into a hole. There was a spurt of dust from the sand and the dog came up with the rabbit in her mouth and laid it at Luke's feet. He stuffed the rabbit into his pocket, examined the dog to see if she had any cuts after her fight at the Masons' and then patted her on the head.

The tide was full out now and his boat was high on the sand. He sat for awhile smoking his pipe, lifting handfuls of the warm sand at his feet and letting it sieve through his fingers. The dog lay at full stretch beside him, her paws soaked with sand, her coat drying in the sun. Across the water he could see the sheen from the tarred roof of his house and clothes drying on the hedge. 'Two good hard-working girls,' he said to himself. 'I hope Mary'll take my advice and not be carried away on Ned Mason.' The wing-rush of shelduck streaked over him and he saw their tracks in the sand at his feet: 'Dan and me will give them a good belt or two at the harvest,' and when he scanned the sea he saw a line of young ones escorted by their parents. He got up and called to one of the boats to give him a hand to launch his own.

'Did she wet your whistle when you brought her the sheep?' one of them asked.

'She did like hell! She's for sticking up a trespassers' board.'

They laughed and spat into the water. 'Oul Mason wasn't like that when he was alive. There was no side with him. You'll find she'll not do it — she'd only make herself a laughing-stock throughout the parish.'

'I hope she does,' one of them smiled. 'And I hope she uses a good bit of timber for I'm badly in need of a bit to patch the hen-house.'

Luke rowed away from them and cut more dulse round the little island where the Masons grazed sheep. He lifted his lobster pots, caught a few codling with the handline and made for home with the flood tide. He ran up the little sail, and when the boat heeled on her side the dog curled herself under the stern-seat and fell asleep. The other boats had gone up the lough sometime before him, and there was nothing now on the sea except a few gulls and young wild duck. At his back lumps of cloud cowered above the sea and he hoped it wouldn't rain and that the girls were keeping an eye on the dulse that he told them to dry. But when he landed below the house Mary and Barbara were there to meet him. 'It might rain,' he told them and they began to stuff the fresh dulse into sacks. Mary sang away to herself as she tied the bulging sacks with ropes and heaved them on top of the water. She watched them rise and fall with the incoming waves, the air sizzling out, the sacks getting heavier, and then slowly sink and sway to the bottom amongst the rocks.

'No rain will wash the juice from them now,' she laughed. 'And anyway it won't rain — it won't!' she said, carrying the oars up to the gable, her father lumbering behind with the fish. She stood at the gable, brushing back her hair, and saw on the horizon the rain falling like sand from the heels of a cloud.

'Now what's it going to do?' Luke smiled, his eye on the cloud.

'The wind will sweep it east. Not a grain will fall on us. And anyway, we've as much dulse dried as'll keep you in tobacco for a month.'

'Before we've finished our dinner you'll hear that squally shower belting on the roof,' and he crossed the threshold with a furtive glance at Mary.

The stone floor was swept clean, a white cloth on the table, a print of freshly churned butter with drops of water on it, and on the window ledge a tumbler hidden with nasturtiums. The girls took turn about at the cooking, each trying her best to please her father. To-day it was Mary's turn and in a pot at the side of the fire she had roasted a young rabbit.

Luke washed his hands in a basin at the back of the house and sat down at the table. The dog crushed beside him, her nose on his knee.

'You may enjoy this rabbit and the one I'm after hanging at the back door for I may have to travel far to get the next.' He ate a few mouthfuls of potatoes, stripped a rabbit bone easily, sucked it and gave it to the dog. Mary sat near him, the slow emphasis on each word severing the mood of joy which had lightened her since morning.

'We're in this house for the past sixty years,' he continued gravely, 'and there was never any bad blood among us and any of the neighbours. But this past while things have changed. Mind you I've nothing against any of the Masons. Ned's a decent fellow if he had his own way. His sisters are all kindly spoken girls with always a word for you. Old Paddy Joe, the Heavens be his bed, was always willin' to help if you were cornered with work. Many's a time he treated me on a fair day in Downpatrick. And he never forgot till his dying day the time our John caught the runaway horse after she'd taken fright in the roller.' He put down his knife and fork, and the dog nuzzled its wet nose on his knee. Mary and Barbara ate silently, afraid of what he had yet to say. 'But God forgive me — Mrs. Mason is a flinty, ill-natured woman. Since her sister, Rose, married a pile of money in Downpatrick and her brother became a Canon somewhere up the country she's become that stiff and proud this place isn't grand enough for her and the people in it not big enough for her.'

'She has no brother a Canon. It's a far out cousin that's become a parish priest — and there may be no truth in it for he wasn't at the old fellow's funeral,' added Barbara.

'There's some connection, anyway, for she talks about nothing else when she marches into the village for her groceries.'

Mary sat silent. Barbara lifted the plates, scraped what Mary had left on to a tin dish and gave it to the dog. She wet the tea and poured it into three cups and sat at the table again. Luke split a farl of bread, spread butter across it, a skite of water streaking his thumb. 'You're the girl for the churn,' he said to Barbara, licking the salty water off his thumb. He poured the tea on to his saucer and drank it. 'As I was saying the people in this country are not worth a pinch of salt to her. To-day, as God's my judge, she gave me orders not to catch a rabbit or set a snare on her land.'

'She did not!' said Barbara.

'Yes, she did! She's to stick up a notice,' and he laughed so loudly the dog jumped on to his lap. 'But let her do it and I'll pay as much heed to it as I would to a scratching-post for a cow.'

A burst of sun glided through the back window, dimming the flames of the fire, and shining on the nasturtiums opposite the table. At that moment Mary saw specks of dew in the throats of the nasturtiums and the tiny web of a spider across the flat leaves. But she glanced at it without interest and turned to her cup again.

'You're right, Mary, it's not going to rain after all,' he

said to her. She nodded and picked a few crumbs off the cloth and put them on her plate. He blessed himself, pulled on his cap, and went down to the shore.

The clouds had broken up and the lowering sun was warm on his back. He pulled a sack from the water, lifted out the cold weed, and sitting on a rock he took a knife and stripped the dulse from the long sea-rods. Later, Barbara helped him to spread it on the flat rocks where in the last of the sun it gradually lost its wet-brown colour and became crusted with salt.

As Mary washed the dishes she opened the back door to let the sun and air through the heavy house. In the morning when she was washing the dishes in very hot water a great gloss came on each plate and she had held it sideways to see the light stretch off it. She had polished them vigorously and when arranging them on the dresser she smiled with joy at the way they shone. But now nothing could wrest from her mind the vague foreboding stirred up by her father's words. Through the open door she saw the mouth of the drying churn tilted to the west, the growing shadow from the byre, and at the side of it the quiet sunlight falling on the nettles where the turkey lay with her young. Above them young swallows rested on a wire fence and their yellow beaks opened when their parents flew to feed them. The air was filled with their chattering and the turkey scolded and flapped her wings when a swallow swished low over the nettles. From the fields came the sound of a reaper cutting hay. Mary closed the door against all that was expressing a different mood from her own. Even then she still could hear the cry of the young swallows and see their parents streel past the window.

'What on earth had happened between my father and Mrs. Mason?' she asked herself. 'Why didn't he tell us it all — and not in bits and scraps. That was my father all over — you could never get him to tell you anything at one go. He gives it to you in inches and makes a long, long story about the slightest thing. Och, it mighn't be as bad as he has painted it.' And she took a brush and swept the floor that didn't need to be swept, made a mash for the hens, and collected the eggs from the fowl-house. Noticing a hen beginning to clock she lifted it off the nest, fixed a string to its leg and to the other end of the string tied a large stone and put her out on the grass.

In the evening herself and Barbara got ready to go to Dan's, Barbara carrying milk and butter for him and some dried dulse to cure his rheumatism. She chewed some dulse herself as they walked along the road with the silence of evening settling drowsily upon the land.

'What do you think of her impudence this time?' Barbara said to Mary.

'I don't know what to think,' she said tonelessly. 'I'll say nothing till I see Ned to-night and hear what he has to say. Maybe our Nellie was worrying the sheep — that would vex any woman and urge her to say things she'd later regret.'

'Sure you know our dog never went after the sheep in her life! And you'd believe what Ned'd say and not believe my father!'

'Why do you deliberately twist my words! I only said I'd like to hear Ned's story of the whole thing.'

'You know full well what his mother is! She has so much hardness in her she can't find words enough to let it out!'

'You've no right to judge her,' Mary said crossly. 'Everybody has more good in them than bad if we'd only take the trouble to look for it.'

'That's right — give me a nice little sermon,' Barbara said mockingly. 'What good word did she ever say to you or any of us! If she was sorry for what she said on the day of the fire why didn't she drop in some evening and say so to my father. Does she even cast one glance at the house when she's passing by on the road — you've remarked that many's a time yourself.'

Mary didn't answer her. She knew what Barbara had said was true but if she agreed with her she'd rake up other signs of Mrs. Mason's ill-nature and confront her with them. She walked on as if enjoying the quiet of the evening. A few ripples of red lay on the sky where the sun had long set, and after the heat of the day a damp mist was steaming off the land, filling up the hollows and shaking itself out till it had covered the fields around the shore.

Old Dan was leaning over the half-door when they approached, and behind him the lamp was lit.

'Not a word to them about Mrs. Mason,' Mary said, holding Barbara's arm.

'All right,' Barbara said reluctantly. 'But sure they all know the sort of her!'

'You'll not say anything till I see Ned?'

'I'll not,' she said, feeling Mary's arm tightening on hers.

'My hair's quite damp with that mist,' said Mary when they were within ear-shot of Dan.

'So is mine,' said Barbara, giving a joyless laugh as Dan swung the half-door open and stood rigidly to attention. 'Here are the princesses,' he shouted, his hand raised in salute, 'and they carry with them milk in a silver can, butter from the churn, and dulse from the salt sea.'

CHAPTER XII

WHEN Mary and Barbara sailed into the kitchen past Dan, Paddy Boden and Tessie were sitting on the table with their backs to the light.

'I'm glad you came early,' Tessie greeted, hopping down and taking the milk and butter from them. They left their coats on top of her bed, combed their hair, and sat at the fire in the kitchen waiting for a few more lads and girls to drop in and start a bit of a dance. Dan resined the bow of his fiddle, and leaving the door ajar so as to give a welcome to the neighbours he struck up a few jigs and reels. They all kept time to the music with their feet, and then Paddy with a wild whoop lifted Tessie on to the floor and forced Barbara and Mary to form a half-set. They danced for awhile till Dan suddenly stopped and hammered with his bow on the table: 'It'll not do at all —it's not natural to see two girls as partners and Barbara dragging her feet like a plough horse. It knocks me off my rhythm. Away out, Paddy, and rattle up a few of the lads, for by my soul when you and Tessie get going and the first infant squalls from the cradle there'll be few dances in this house.'

'You shouldn't say things like that, Granda,' said Tessie with pretended indignation after Paddy had gone out.

'And why wouldn't I say them. What do you think, child, you married him for — was it to sit up on the table and look at one another like a pair of wintry jackdaws.'

Paddy was back in a few minutes: 'They're coming now, Dan. I hear them whistling and carrying on along the road. Strike up again and they'll not hang round the door.'

Dan was fiddling for all he was worth when the boys and girls came and pushed each other through the door. The girls stumbled on to the floor, and laughing and giggling they squeezed themselves on to the settle and on to stools and chairs arranged along the walls, while the boys hung in a group around the door. A ten-year-old lad had come in unnoticed with the crowd and sat on an upturned bucket in a dark corner by the dresser. The ridge of the bucket hurt him and he pulled an empty sack from the corner and spread it over the ridge. His black hair was fringed on his forehead and parted in the middle like an inverted V. Nothing could be seen of him, save when the dancers broke apart and the light fell on his face, on his bare knees and on the brass eyelets of his boots. He sat there quiet, watching the shadows, now broad, now lanky, now thin, coming and going, bending and stretching in time to the music. The lads danced with their cigarettes behind their ears; their hobnailed boots rasped on the stone floor and the swirl of the girls' skirts put an edge on the flames of the fire and made the wick in the lamp leap up the globe. The young lad crouched farther into the corner when the men's boots belted around him, but when the girls swayed towards him he stuck out his head to feel the cool swirl from their dresses. The air was thick with heat. Beside him was a bucket of spring water with a board covering its mouth and he yearned to take a drink from it but he was afraid to move in case his big brother would spot him and send him home. He saw Paddy and Tessie holding each other's hand aloft and striding forward between two rows of men and girls. Everyone whooped and clapped and the young lad rattled his knuckles loudly on the side of the dresser. He had made sure to serve Father Toner's Mass on the morning they were married, and now the memory of Paddy slipping him a half-crown when he had come into the vestry to sign the register made the lad shout with fearless delight from his corner. Then he saw Barbara sitting on a stool opposite him and he withdrew again into the shadow for he thought she was glaring at him. Nobody had asked her to dance and she was sitting glumly and trying to fix a string of beads that had broken from her neck. She glanced at Dan, but old Dan paid no heed to her for he was fiddling like mad, not taking time to spit in the fire, seeing nothing only the sweep of his bow and the dust of the resin bobbing below the strings.

'Keep at it! Keep at it!' he shouted when he saw the tired dancers faltering. 'Another round — yer gettin' soft the lot of you!' A couple of girls gave up and staggered laughingly against the wall. The dance stopped. The men leaned against the dresser, struck matches on the soles of their boots and lit their cigarettes. Girls sat on one another's knee, took handkerchiefs from their sleeves and wiped their clammy hands. The little boy gazed at a black shiny button on the floor — it had four holes in it; a man's trousers button, he thought. He'd lift it when he'd get a chance. The men and girls rearranged themselves on the floor for another dance. Barbara was still sitting but her beads were now fixed round her neck. The boy's eyes rested on her for a moment and then irresistibly turned to the button lying untouched on the floor. A girl's shoe grazed it, and then a man's boot crashed down and the button shot towards the boy in the corner and lay about a yard from him. He was stretching out his hand to get it when dancing feet backed towards him and he withdrew into his corner again, his eye watching the shiny button. It was dragged away from him again, and as the boots lifted and stamped around it he shut his eyes but when he opened them again the button was still there, catching a rim of light from the lamp. He'd lift it now. He rose from the bucket and darted on to the floor just as four dancers were surging backwards. They stumbled over him and fell in a heap against the dresser, upsetting the bucket of spring water. The little boy grabbed the button and as he raced through the open door he fell against Ned Mason who was standing at the threshold.

The music had stopped and everyone was laughing at the water that was wriggling across the floor. The men who had fallen were dusting their sleeves and Mary Devlin, with a hair-pin in her mouth, was fastening up her hair which had come undone in the scramble. Ned saw her, and a sudden spurt of jealousy hardened the look on his face. Why did she let fellows toss her about like that! He leant against the jamb. Then Mary saw him and hurried across to him. 'I'm glad you've come,' she whispered, standing beside him and taking his hand. The back of it was wet with mist and she saw his clothes and hair covered with tiny drops. She felt the sleeve of his coat, her fingers pressing his arm, trying her best to cheer him.

'Is the mist thickening?' she asked when they had squeezed their way on to the settle.

'No, Mary, it's lifting,' and he caught sight of Barbara on

118

the other side of the room. He waved to her but she pretended not to see him and talked with forced animation to a young girl sitting on her knee. Mary noticed how Barbara had avoided him and she pressed his sleeve again and sought his eyes. The strained look on his face made her uncomfortable and she yearned to go out with him and run with him along the roads until that heavy swaying mood was swung away from him. On her way home she'd get him to tell what had happened to-day about the rabbits. It was that that was worrying him. She tapped her toe on the floor when somebody gave Dan a rest by playing a melodeon.

'Ned,' she whispered to him, looking down at her hands. 'Lift Barbara for the next dance.' He nodded his head and put his pipe in his pocket. She smiled as he crossed the kitchen to Barbara. But Barbara was shaking her head: 'I can't. I've a headache!' she was saying, and without coaxing her he came back to Mary who had already jumped to her feet. She brought him to the middle of the floor to make a set in an eight-hand reel, and as he felt her hand tightening on his he braced his shoulders intending to fling off all the doubts and fears that had beset his mind throughout the day. He shuffled his feet on the floor, and then when the dance started he paced through its intricate pattern with many a whoop and exaggerated flourish of the shoulders. The sweat broke on his forehead. Someone opened the back door wide and the light struck across the fields startling the rabbits feeding on the cold grass. The dewy air drenched with the smell of hay rushed into the room. At every opportunity he manœuvred Mary to the door where they twirled and turned and gazed at the sky now sharp with stars.

'The night's lovely now,' she said.

'The mist's gone,' he laughed, and when the reel ended they rushed for their place on the settle.

On the road home he walked between Barbara and Mary. He linked Mary but when he tried to take Barbara's arm she shrank from him. The land was stripped of mist, the moon high in the sky and every bush and stone stooped over its own shadow.

He caught Barbara round the waist: 'What ails you to-night! You're not the Barbara we all know!'

She wrenched herself free and a button broke from her coat: 'Leave me alone, Ned Mason! Do you think you can say and do whatever you like with us!'

'Barbara!' Mary said.

'I'll say what I like!' Barbara shouted back. 'We've stood too much from the likes of them already!'

'What have I done?' Ned said.

'For the love of God, stop!' Mary intervened.

'You've no pride in you,' Barbara hurled at Mary. 'I'm ashamed to say you're a sister of mine! That you allow people to trample on you, to insult you, and not raise one word of complaint.' She turned sharply to Ned. 'Tell your grand lady of a mother I'll settle with her one of these fine days. She'll not ride roughshod over me!'

'Listen, Barbara,' Ned said. But she fled and left them standing on the road.

Neither spoke. Around them were the still hedges, snails crawling over the stones, and a cow tearing loudly at the dew-cold grass.

Mary caught his arm: 'Ned, I'm sorry!' She burst into tears and covered her face with her hands. He kissed her hands that were wet with tears, took them from her face, and when he looked at her he gathered her to him so that she wouldn't see him cry. His voice shook and he kicked at a pebble on the road.

'Don't be sorry, Mary. What Barbara said is true. But I can't do anything. To-night I threatened to leave the house if she warns your father off the fields. Did he tell you?'

She nodded.

'I called with him on my way to Dan's. There was a light in the window and I knocked a couple of times but couldn't get in.' Then he told her about the accident to the sheep and added: 'My mother can't bear to see an animal suffer, Mary, and she'd say things in anger and then be sorry she said them.' Mary listened to him in silence and wondered why he always sought to excuse his mother.

They came to the moonlighted cottage, the tarred roof gleaming coldly and the shadow of the sycamore leaning against the walls. There was no sign of a light in the windows. Mary shivered in the sharp air from the sea and he held her close to him while below on the shore the breaking waves jabbled the moonlight amongst the wet stones. A candle-light in the bedroom window drew them apart and they saw Barbara kneel on the ledge and hook up the blind, and then against the fabric they watched the flame of the candle struggling against the light of the moon.

'I'd better go in now,' Mary said, but he wouldn't let her go, and seeing on his face a look of pained suspense she rested her head against his breast.

'Everything's against us,' he sighed, 'and when I saw Paddy and Tessie bright and free to-night and old Dan happy with the pair of them I thought of the empty house that should be given to us and the rats and the birds making their own of it. But she'll have to bend! She'll have to meet us, Mary. We can't go on living away from one another and the years flying from under our feet.' He shuddered, and holding her arms stiffly by her side he kissed her.

'May God guide us to do what's right,' she said and turned to the house.

'You'll not fret, Mary,' he called to her.

'I'll not,' she called back and stood at the door till the sound of his footsteps were smothered in the sounds from the shore.

She walked through the kitchen to her room. Barbara was in bed, the candle blown out, and a smell of burnt grease lingering about the room. She took the blind from the window and began to undress in the light of the moon. Barbara coughed.

'Are you asleep, Barbara?' she asked.

'No.'

'Then why in God's name did you speak like that to Ned?' she cried. 'I never knew there was such bitterness in you,' and she sat on a chair and covered her face with her hands.

'I was tired of his mother getting off with everything.'

'But why did you lash out at him?' she looked up, her lip trembling. 'He can't control his mother.'

'I don't know — I was sick of everything: sick of the dance and the fellows here trying to make a fool of every decent girl. But I'm going away from it all. What is there here for any girl — there's no life; the same grind, day after day — getting up in the morning and going to bed at night just like one of the fowl. The same sea and rain and dulse. Working here and getting nothing for it.'

'What do you expect for it, Barbara?'

'I want something out of life that this place begrudges me. Everything moves but myself. I'm like one of the rocks out there — battered by everything.'

'And what about me — haven't I to live in it?'

'You've something to live for — you've Ned Mason. But I have no one. Now do you understand?'

'I do,' said Mary gently. 'But surely there's someone. . . .'

'There isn't anyone that I care about. At one time I thought Ned Mason cared for me but I see now it was for your sake — nothing else. Would you have me remaining here and growing old before my time like his sisters — slopping about the yard in a pair of men's boots.'

Mary got up from the chair and crossed to the window. She could find no words to answer her — she had often thought that way herself before she had grown fond of Ned. She lifted a brush from the window-ledge and brushed her hair.

'Many a girl that left here was glad to come back — I may tell you.'

'I'll not be one of them,' said Barbara. 'Let me once get

out of it — away to Downpatrick or Belfast or Glasgow and I'll never want to set eyes on the place again.'

'God forgive you for despising the place you were reared in. Someday you'll rue all this!' She brushed her hair from around her ears and then plucking the combings from the brush she pulled down the window and let the loose hair fluff away from her fingers. She propped the window open with the brush and stood back from the cold air that spread into the room. Taking her rosary beads she knelt to say her prayers, but before opening her soul to God she rested quietly for a few minutes to ease the painful throbbing of her head. She blessed herself, and to control the tumult of her mind she gripped the beads tightly. But her mind wandered — all the incidents of the day dragged across it, and time and again she shook her head to dispel the scene on the road which jutted sharply before her. And now if Barbara goes away, she thought, who would there be to look after her father if Ned happened to . . . She raised her head and a gilt cross around her neck fell coldly against her breast. 'God forgive me for such ragged prayers,' she breathed and wearily got into bed.

'Barbara,' she said, 'listen to me for God's sake. Don't let that mad notion ruin your life. Sure the place here will be all yours someday.'

'It will never be mine,' Barbara said coldly. 'If anything happened to my father, the place and all in it would be left to John. It wouldn't be long then till you'd see him galloping home to claim his own — I may tell you.' She shrugged her shoulders. 'Anyway I'm leaving. My mind's made up. There's nothing here for anyone.'

'Well, leave then!' said Mary, her patience gone. 'Leave — when and where you like! There's no one will stand in your way! But mark my words, you'll be glad to come back!'

'We'll see!'

For a long time Mary lay still, listening to the tick of the clock from the kitchen as it plunged and swayed through the

silence of the night. She opened and closed her eyes in fits
and starts, and when she saw the space of moonlight narrow
on the wall she knew the moon was riding across the sky. She
heard the lagging waves ebb from the shore, saw the moonlight fade from the house, and towards dawn she slept.

CHAPTER XIII

'DON'T worry yourself about Barbara — she'll be back again
before the turn of the leaf,' Dan was saying to Luke as he sat
with him making lobster pots, the sweet smell of shavings
at their feet strangling the smell of the tarred nets. Luke's
waistcoat was open, and now and again he would spit out
on the stones or gaze absently at the gander lying asleep in
the shade of the sycamore tree, or look at Mary's washing
drying on top of the hedge.

'Poor Mary has the burden of the work now,' he said.
'But God knows I don't want to hinder any of them if they
want to break out for themselves. It's hard, Dan, to hold
children together where there's no mother . . . Father Toner
pleaded with her to stay but she wouldn't say aye, no, nor
yes to him and he went away from her affronted. The
pictures and the dancing is dragging them all to the town.'

'Is it that eating-house fornent the station that's given her
the job?'

'The very place.'

'The one with Queen Victoria on the wall scowling at
every bite you ate?'

'That's the one!'

'Well, do you know, Luke, you'll have her home after next
fair day. I knew a girl that wrought in it for a spell, and she
told me that on a fair day she had two baths of spuds boiling
on one stove and three buckets of spuds boiling on another
stove and when the day was over she had a stack of dirty

dishes to wash, and what with all the standing the varicose veins grew out on her legs as thick as brambles. Wait'll me bold Barbara meets the heavy days and you'll find her walking out and what's more — walking home.'

'You don't know her, Dan, if you think that. She's as headstrong as a jennet and she'd not run home for fear we'd laugh at her.' He lifted a hazel rod, bent it in a semi-circle and nailed the ends to a flat board. When he had three rods nailed and curved over the board he covered the framework with the net, all the time old Dan advising him how to get rid of the bulky stones that Luke had anchored to the board. 'Cover the whole board with a half-inch of cement,' Dan was saying. 'You'd find that would steady it on the floor of the sea and give the lobsters more depth to ramble about in it and content themselves.'

Mary, her hands white with flour, came to the door and flung a dish of water on to the cobbles, the sleepy gander opening its black eye and closing it again. She leaned against the jamb looking at her father and Dan sitting on empty sacks and their backs resting against the limewashed walls of the house.

'Your back's all white, father,' she said.

'It'll dust off, child ... You're baking? Make a farl or two of potato bread for Dan. He'll stay for a bite to eat.'

Dan cocked his head sideways and looked at Mary: 'I hope you're not thinking long about Barbara — she'll come back as sure as the tide turns.' Mary smiled and withdrew, leaving the door open to the stir of air that came from the sea.

'Such unnatural heat!' says Dan, and he took off his cap and fanned himself. Then he saw the rooster chase a hen round the trunk of the tree and he nudged Luke: 'That hen wasn't running her best!' and he gave such a loud laugh that the other hens under the hedge chuckled excitedly and shook their red jollers. 'Your hens are in great trim,' he said, but noticing that Luke was in no humour for talking he put on his cap again and began to pare the ends of some hazel rods. Then a motor drew up on the road beside the house and Luke got to his feet when he saw the driver descend and open the door of the taxi. A man in a grey tweed cap and a blue suit was coming out backways on to the road. Luke's penknife dropped from his hand when he saw his son, John, standing on the road, a yellow walking stick in his hand. Luke hurried over to him. 'I'm back again,' John said with a weak smile, and when he limped stiffly forward his father went to support him. 'Och, it's not as bad as that,' he laughed, 'it's the rough stones is the killer,' and he guided himself towards the cottage, holding himself erect. The gander awoke and stretched his neck at him but John warded it off playfully and watched it seize the rubber-covered ferrule in its beak.

'And Dan,' he said as the old man held out his rough hand to him. 'Not a bit changed. The same old playboy!'

Mary withdrew to the shadows of the kitchen and only went forward to greet him when his shoulders bulked in the doorway and his head stooped below the lintel.

'You didn't expect me back like this, Mary,' he smiled and sat on a chair at the window, the dog smelling round him and licking his hand. 'Ah, Nellie, after two years you'd think you'd forget the smell of me,' and she jumped up on him, whining with delight and trying to lick his face.

'A dog's smell is its best memory,' said Dan, standing on the floor beside Luke. Luke pulled the dog away from John and she bounded out through the door and raced at the hens and the gander.

'Take the weight off your feet the pair of you,' said John, and when they were seated he pulled up the leg of his trousers and showed them a swelling on the right leg just above the ankle and launched into an account of how he had broken his leg in a storm at sea and how when his boat had put into St. Malo a young doctor had set it badly and for three months afterwards he had lumbered about the cobbled streets of St. Malo waiting for the return of his boat. 'I was going to write to you then but I knew you'd worry, and I said to myself, "Why write to them now when I'm not well, when I didn't write to them when I was well?"'

His father stooped and cautiously smoothed his hand over the swelling on the leg: 'Does that pain you, John?'

'What are you talking about! Not at all!' and he stamped his boot on the floor to convince them that it wasn't as bad as it looked. 'It gets a bit stiff on me when I sit long, but, please God, when I massage it every night and get the salt water at it it'll bècome as hard and as strong as a bit of seasoned oak.'

Mary swung the pan on the fire and as she prepared a meal for them all she heard them talk about Paddy and Tessie's wedding, about Barbara's flight to Downpatrick, about The Curate, and about the death of old Mason and how Barbara had set fire to the thatch on the same day.

'Come out, John, to you see the new roof I put on,' Luke was saying proudly, and all the time as he walked round the house and stood out from it the better to see the fine points of his work he thought of Mrs. Mason and wondered if he should tell John about what she shrieked out to the whole countryside on the day of the fire. 'I'll not tell him,' he decided, 'what's the use of torturing the lad's mind and maybe fill it with spite that'd do more harm than good.'

Mary called them for the tea, and when they were seated at the table eating the bacon and eggs she had fried for them she went into her father's room and seeing John's bed and the mattress rolled up on it and tied with a bit of rope a heavy feeling of sorrow swept over her and she covered her eyes with her hands and wept: 'O God,' she cried, looking at a crucifix on the wall, 'what's to be the end of it all!'

She got up and carried out the mattress to the smooth wire fence at the back of the house, and when she unrolled it to the sun a mouldy smell rose up from it and she noticed a few spots where the moths had scuffed it. When would she ever get time to attack those with a needle and thread — and their own patch of corn to be saved yet, and the potatoes to be gathered, and bread to be baked every day. And now that John was home and he badly lamed she'd not get much help from him. Maybe if she went into Downpatrick and told Barbara about him she'd be able to coax her to come back and help. She saw a moth struggling out from the seams of the mattress and when she swiped at it to kill it it fell amongst a clump of charred nettles and escaped. She searched the mattress for more and beat it vigorously with a rod, and then returned to the house and gathered sheets and blankets from a drawer and spread them on the grass at the back of the house. She heard her grandfather leaving and when she came into the kitchen John had lifted up his jersey and was showing her father a leather belt with many brass-studded pockets. From one of them he drew out a roll of pound-notes: 'There's twenty-five in that, father. I'd had more than that for you only for the months I was stranded in St. Malo.' From his canvas kit he took out three leather handbags that he had bought in a café from a travelling Algerian. He handed them to Mary: 'There's one for you and Barbara and Tessie. You can take the first pick.'

He filled his pipe and stood at the door looking at the sycamore tree, the edges of its leaves bitten by the salt winds and a few spots like tar appearing on others. He remembered as a boy climbing up it in the autumn plucking the winged seeds and letting them flutter to the ground. He picked up a seed at his feet, stripped off the outside covering and looked at the damp seedling embedded in its silky fibre. He squeezed the juice from it and flicked it on to the stones, and taking his stick he crossed to the road walking as steadily and as unconcernedly as he could, for he knew his father would be gazing after him from the window. He took off his cap and filled his lungs with the soft, clean air. There wasn't a breath of wind now and the cattle in the fields were standing still and gazing with a strange alertness at the yellow smoky sky that pressed close above them. At the stream he rested and smoked his pipe, listening with a sweet unrest to the sound of a reaper, to a man sharpening his scythe, to the voices of girls tying and stooking the corn, and to the excited shouts of children as they scampered after the corncrakes that had been exposed to the bare air by the advancing reaper. He put the pipe in his pocket and spat into the stream; the water was clear and still, the rising trout leaving ripples that quivered the rushes at the edge. He got up and climbed the little hill and at the top he looked back at the house and saw his father peering after him from behind a bush. John pretended not to see him and he turned his head away quickly and twirled the stick in his hand with all the abandon of a leisured gentleman enjoying the air.

At one of the Mason's fields below the wee farm a chestnut horse with a white throat was standing with pricked ears watching other horses working in a field some distance from him. John recognized it as the one he had caught when it was galloping along the road with the stone roller clattering at its heels. 'Afraid to yoke him up again,' John said to himself and thought of old Mason and the praise he had given him that day.

He opened the gate and made across the field to the horse, stretching out his hand and calling softly. The horse turned its head to him but did not move. He approached it cautiously and at the first touch of his strong fingers on its neck, the horse relaxed and yielded to him. It sniffed his coat and pawed the ground with its forefeet. 'So they're still afraid of you,' he said pulling a few bits of whins from its mane. He stood out from it looking at its legs corded with veins and at its flanks shivering from the flies. He strode back across the field and the horse followed him, and closing the wooden gate he hung his stick on the top bar and stood for a long time scratching the horse's head, and when finally he moved away from it along the road it followed after him on the inside of the fence until the field came to an end, and then it hung its head over the barbed wire and gazed after him.

When he reached home again Mary had finished airing his bed, and his father, fearing that the heavy heat foreboded a storm, was down on the shore fastening an extra mooring rope to the boat. John sat at the fire and as Mary tidied herself after her day's work he talked to her about Barbara and called her a right glipe to be skimming off on her own.

'Now, John, you have no call to blame her,' she laughed, 'you that set her the fine example!'

'But somehow a man's different in his ways. It's the life of him to rush off for a spell before he gets too old and fixed in his ways. It gives him something to think about when he comes back and something to talk about. But somehow a girl was made for the one spot — when she starts the roaming she's like a dog that goes after sheep: never contented.' He pushed a cinder off the hearth with his stick. 'I thought you and Ned Mason would have fixed it up long ago.'

'Och, we're only friends,' she evaded, knowing that in another hour or so she'd be away with Ned over the brackened banks near the shore.

'Only friends!' he laughed. 'That's like talk out of a book. You needn't come off with that to a man that's covered the world.'

'It'd been a poor look-out for you and my father if Ned and me had fixed it up. The two of you in the house and no woman in it would make a sorry sight!'

That thought never crossed his mind so he remained silent, staring at the fire and making designs with his stick in the ashes. Then he heard a step on the stones outside and Paddy and Tessie came in, shy and awkward, laughing at nothing, Paddy sitting up on the table with his cap on his head. At their heels came old Dan carrying a bottle of whisky which he had stowed away amongst a pile of shavings since Tessie's wedding-day; he had hoped that The

Curate would have arrived some morning with his usual un-expectedness and then the two of them could have drunk the health of the fresh couple, but as the summer days drowsed by and the harvest weather set in Dan took an odd slug from the bottle with the excuse: 'Och, The Curate will never come back!' The bottle was now half-full as he brought it round to celebrate John's home-coming. He spoke to none of them when he came in but straightway went to the dresser and took down three tumblers, one for himself, one for Luke, and one for John — he wouldn't encourage Paddy to start this game.

They sipped the whisky slowly and flung the door wide open to catch the last of the light. Outside the sea splashed without hurry, and under the sycamore tree and the hedges the heat of the day still lingered. Before the lamp was lit Mary slipped away from them and later in the night when she came back from meeting Ned, her shoes wet with dew, the lamp in the kitchen was lowered and the kettle simmering on the fire. She heard her father and John talking in their room and she made them a cup of tea and brought it in to them. After that they lit their pipes and talked for a long time. John couldn't sleep; the room was heavy with heat and he blamed his father for raising the thatched roof and for putting on an iron one that was as hot as a griddle. He flung aside the blankets and lay under the sheet and fell asleep.

The rumble of distant thunder wakened him, and as it drew nearer he sat up and stared into the solid darkness of the room.

'What ails you, John?' said his father, awakened himself by the distant grumbling of the thunder.

'Whisht, father! Do you hear it?'

'I do — it's a long way to travel before it comes our length. Bless yourself and lie down. It's been hanging overhead for a long time and I'm afraid there's a brave sup of rain with it.'

His father struck a match to light his pipe and he saw in

the black pane of the window the reflection of the match and the glow on his father's face. When the match had burned itself out the room was crushed in a bulging darkness and once again there was the sound of thunder falling like a load of stones.

'I'm going out!' said John.

'What's that — out?'

'The horse! The horse!'

'What horse?'

'The Mason's — the horse that broke off with the roller at her heels! She was put in the field this evening. She'll smash herself in fear.'

'Light your pipe and we'll smoke till it passes,' and he tossed the matchbox over to him. 'Let the Masons look after their own beasts.'

John wasn't listening to him — he could feel the nervous throbbing of the horse yielding under the touch of his fingers.

'It'll be a wild night. Take your beads, John, and lie down.'

'I'm not afraid of the night. Thunder and lightning is nothing to the likes of me.' A flash of lightning like the outline of a river on a map wriggled down the pane, and in an instant John was out of bed groping for his clothes. Great barrels of sound rolled through the sky and the rain fell like hailstones on the ribbed roof.

'You'll get your death, son. What concern is it of yours?'

'I must go!'

The father sat upright, the pipe in his fist; he'd tell him now about Mrs. Mason and the things she shouted to the whole countryside on the day of the fire; he shouldn't keep the boy in ignorance any longer — it'd not do a bit of harm to tell him.

'John!'

'Don't worry yourself, father. I'm not afraid of a scratch of lightning. The sea knocked that out of me.' He was struggling into his clothes. Another flash flung its glittering branches against the window-pane.

'The Masons is not worth a puff of bother. Wait'll I tell you this.'

'That horse'll rip itself to shreds in the barbed wire.'

'It'll shelter under the hedge. John — the Masons is a worthless pack. I've something to tell you about them.'

'It'll not go stale till I come back.'

'They insulted us when you were away.'

'As long as they didn't steal from us we'll get over it.'

He lifted the stick from the rail of the bed and rattled his way through the dark kitchen. He opened the door and the dog followed him out into the rain. He sent her back. The lightning struck deep into the sea. For a moment there was a fearsome gap of stillness. He gripped his stick firmly and splashed through the puddles on the road. The masonry of sky broke in fragments above his head, and the rain fell, warm and heavy as his own sweat. Gulls called weirdly from the shore. As he drew near the field two flashes swept a greenish light over the fence and he saw two horses galloping madly.

'Woa, there! Woa!' he shouted, hearing the drish-drash of their hooves in the rain. There was a flurry of lightning and he saw a white horse charge through the barbed wire fence and smash on to the road below. The ping of the strained wire quivered through the air. John halted in fear but when he heard the cries from the fallen horse he hurried to open the gate, calling all the time to the horse he had come out to help. He heard it galloping and he raised his stick to guard himself. He whistled and called again. The horse stopped. He approached it and caught its mane. He rubbed its neck firmly, the sweat hot as blood under his hands. 'Woa-a-a, now!' he said as he felt it shivering with fear, the last of the thunder trailing on inland away from the sea. Ned appeared with a lamp and as he came through the field the rain fell like wire around the edges of the light.

Behind him Luke was calling out: 'John! John! Are you all right?'

'I'm here!' John shouted back.

Ned held the lamp head-high, seeing John pillared against the horse and gripping its mane.

'God in Heaven!' he said. 'You shouldn't have stirred on such a night! Mary told me you were back,' and he gripped his hand excitedly. 'I'll never forget you for this — never!'

'I was a bit late. I seen the white one crash through the fence on to the road.'

'The young mare!'

Luke came over to them and helped to stable the horse at the wee farm, advising Ned to leave a candlelight with it. They went down the road to the mare and in the light from the lamp saw stretches of barbed wire entangled in its flesh and blood oozing on to the road. She tossed her head and hanched the air with her teeth.

'Up! Up, girl!' Ned said in a husky voice, lifting her by the mane. She sprawkled vainly with her forefeet and then lay still, her head sideways on the road and her eyes bulged in fear.

'Her back's broken,' said Luke, and when they examined her they saw her hind legs twisted in a grotesque shape.

'Shoot her!' said John, 'and put the poor thing out of pain.'

'I haven't the heart to do it. I reared her myself.'

They stood in silence around the lamp on the road. The rain still fell and an odd rumble came from the passing thunder.

'Get the gun and I'll shoot it for you,' said John, and when Ned had hurried off he turned to Luke: 'She'll be a big loss to them and the harvest only half through.' His father said nothing; he stood with his hands in his pockets gazing at the silver hoof of the horse and the dark impression of the seven nails. Then he sighed heavily and John turned to him: 'You've something to say to me, father?'

'About — about what?' he said with a light tremble.

'About the Masons?'

'No, no, no!' he shouted. 'I've nothing against them! I was trying to get you to stay in the house and you not fit. God forgive me — I've nothing against them.'

Ned came back with the gun, his hands shaking; 'I've both barrels loaded,' he said, standing out from the rim of the light. John took the gun and cocked the triggers: he stooped and felt with his trembling fingers along the wet forehead of the mare: 'Move the lamp a bit to the left,' he said to Ned, his voice thick and husky. 'Will one barrel be enough?' he added.

'Give her the two,' said Ned and turned his head away.

'Is the front trigger for the right or the left barrel?' John said.

Luke stepped over to him and without a word took the gun from him. He put the gun to his shoulder. There was a crash, then another, the sound echoing from the sea. The smell of powder was sharp in the rain and the sound of the gun lingered in their ears like a throbbing pain.

'We'll head for home now,' said Luke.

'Good-night to you,' said Ned, 'and thank you!' He lifted the lamp, looked at the ragged wound in the mare's head, and plodded up the road. Sarah met him and carried the lamp. Away in the direction of the Mourne mountains they could hear the smothered and strangled rumble of thunder, while to their left there appeared a patch of green with a few watery stars.

'It's clearing up,' Sarah said to him.

'The harm's done now,' he said and relapsed into silence. The rain slackened and as they walked up the lonin a stray drop or two sizzled on the hot funnel of the lamp. There was a light in his mother's room, and in the kitchen Ann and Delia had a fresh fire blazing in the grate. They gave him a bowl of tea to drink and when he had taken it and changed his wet clothes his mother called him and he sat on the edge of her bed and told her what had happened.

' 'Tis strange,' she said, 'the good worker to be taken and that nervous tempery article to be left.'

'Only for John Devlin we'd have lost the both of them. He was there before me holding on to the horse's mane and giving it courage. There's not many about the parish that'd rise out of bed on a night like this.'

'Maybe so, maybe so,' she said, 'he has his own reasons for going out, I suppose, and him only returned home.'

He saw what was in her mind — it was sagged with grudges and she could think no good of John or of any of the Devlins; she'd believe of them only what she wished to believe. He got up from the bed.

'I'll turn down the lamp and let you sleep. The tail of the storm passed over a while ago. There'll not be another whisper out of it to-night.'

'I hope you'll not be thinking of giving John Devlin a start at the harvest,' she said, her mind following its own track. 'You've enough hands employed as it is. The more you have the less they do!'

'He couldn't work, poor fellow, even if I asked him. He's lame — crippled!'

'Crippled!' she repeated after him: 'Crippled!'

He nodded his head and went towards the lamp.

'Ned!' she said gravely: 'Ned, son, come here to me.' She took his hand and stroked it: 'Listen to me, Ned. The Devlins will ruin you — you'll not have a penny piece from the day you join them till the day you die.'

He withdrew his hand from hers and said quietly: 'I don't want money! I want to live in my own way.'

'You don't want money! You don't want money!' and she shook her head solemnly: 'The way the world is made you can have no happiness without it. You'll live to rue the day you scorned it.'

'All I ask from you is my just share. My father meant the wee farm for me — he had that in his mind when he bought it.'

'And why didn't he say it in the Will!'

'He thought you'd give it to me.'

'And so I will — and something more with it, please God.'

'Aye, when it's too late!' he said querulously. 'What's the use of leaving me a couple of hundred pounds in your own Will — and the best part of my life slipping away from me like sand through a sieve. Give me the wee farm now and I'm content. Give it to me without stick or thatch or plough and I'll make a fist of it!'

'I'd give it to you this minute, Ned, if you were marrying nice people.'

'Nice people!' he said bitterly. 'There's kind people and there's hard people. There's not many would rise out of bed in a wild night to help a neighbour with his animals!'

'They've their own deep reasons — I suppose.'

'No,' he raised his voice, 'No — you'll never change. Now let me tell you something — I'll take the farm if you don't give it to me!'

'You can't — the law's against you!'

'Is there not a law of God greater than the law of the land! Surely to the good God all the praying you do should tell you who's in the right. And the Rosary you make me come in for every night — it's all a mockery, I tell you. You only rope in God when it suits your own ends.'

'You're talking like Father Toner.'

'I'm talking from my own heart. I've worked hard — in haskey weather and in smooth — am I to go on slaving from morn to night and not get justice done to me? I love Mary. I'm going with her now for over two years. Do you want me to make a fool of the girl?'

'I've told you what's in my mind. I see nothing but ruin for you. What with a crippled man and a lazy father you'll have a nice handful! Let me be under the clay first before I see blight crawling over you.'

Sarah had heard the sharpened tones of their voices and she came up the stairs with tea on a tray for her mother.

Without a word Ned went to his room and stood at the bare window, looking at the stars glittering brightly and listening to the drips of water falling from the roof. 'I'll give her to the end of the harvest to change her mind,' he said, pressing his throbbing forehead against the cold pane.

CHAPTER XIV

THE strong afternoon sunshine drew Mrs. Mason to the orchard, and sitting on a wooden seat with her back to the stone wall, she laid her knitting on her lap and gazed absently at a few flies that darted in and out of the shade under the trees. She saw the apples hang heavily, some of them appearing and disappearing behind the leaves when the light wind stirred the branches. A blue bonnet was hopping smartly from twig to twig pecking at the underside of the leaves, and somewhere in the shadows a robin was singing clear and sweet. Mrs. Mason closed her eyes and felt the sun prickling the withered backs of her hands. She breathed easily. It was very quiet, and behind her she heard the sleepy sound of the sea, the rattle of the pump in the yard, and a calf lowing when it heard the clang of the bucket on the stones. She opened her eyes, and the green of the trees and the red dahlias swung together in a blur of colour. The flower-bed still held the tracks of the rake, and under the stakes of the dahlias the soil was dark where it had been watered the previous evening. That was Delia's job — and she did it well. Father Toner was always glad to get a bunch of dahlias or chrysanthemums for the altar, and now that October was approaching he'd need them to honour Our Lady. The year was flying but, thanks be to God, the harvest was saved — and she closed her eyes again thinking of the thatched ricks now comfortably gathered in the haggard.

A gate clicked and Ned, with a spade on his shoulder,

came into the orchard. He didn't see her and she lifted her knitting and watched him through the trees. He took off his coat, and before plunging the spade into the soil he knocked off a lump of clay from the blade. He deepened a few holes which he had already dug, and put down new posts to keep out the hens. With the head of his axe he hammered down the poles into the ground, shaking them with his hand to test their steadiness.

'Get out you devil's torture,' he shouted as a hen tried to pass him. 'You'll not break through this.' He unrolled the netting wire and stapled it to the posts, and when he had finished he strode off again leaving fresh splinters of wood on the grass. She'd gather them up for they'd come in useful when she'd be baking bread. She rolled up her knitting and stooped under the apple trees avoiding the wasps that were gorging themselves in the windfalls. She ran her fingers over the fresh wire: 'As tight as a fiddle string,' she said to herself, and began to pick up the scallops of wood and put them in her apron. Then she remembered with a crushed feeling of despair the evening she had asked him to chop up the plank at the back of the house. Since that day she had felt him slipping away from her. He never asked her now for advice about anything — about buying or selling or alterations to be made or his going out at night. There were times when he'd have told her where he was going; but he's terribly changed now — he's not the boy she knew and reared as a child. The Devlins were killing all the good nature that was in him, all the openness of mind that he used to show to his own mother; they were drawing him away from her — he was as much a stranger to her now as the servant-man. She'd be afraid to ask him to do anything for her — a message or a trip to Downpatrick; and yet there was a time when all she had to do was to raise her finger: 'Ned, I want you to drive me to Downpatrick. . . . Ned, I want you to bring your sisters to see the football match.' No, he had changed and changed for the worse.

The six o'clock angelus rang out and she paused to say the prayer, her racked mind flitting away from the meaning of the words. She'd go to confession — that'd bring her peace. She hurried into the house, washed her face, and set off alone. The sun stretched itself across the stubble-fields and now and again she smelt the ripening potatoes. If the weather held till they had the potatoes gathered they'd have nothing to complain of. She passed the wee farm and stopped for a minute to look at the hacked earth where the poor mare had crashed through the fence —'The poor, poor thing,' she said to herself, 'and that other useless animal to be left.' She crossed the bridge over the stream — the stream that separated their land from the Devlins — and seeing her side of the bank trimmed and deepened and the Devlins' side thick with mud and the rushes sticking up through it, she clicked her tongue: 'The old laziness — drain a field once and it will do a lifetime! A thoughtless pack!' And there they were cutting their bit of corn — the Mary one tying, the father and John reaping with cradle scythes. The last to sow and the last to cut! And they were singing too — that was John's voice she could hear, deep as a voice in a well. If it would rain they'd not sing much — but it was always the same with them as long as she could remember.

She passed the house. Salt fish was drying under netting wire on the hedge and the dog was watching them to keep the gulls away. 'Phew!' she said, and waved away with her hand a few flies that had gathered about her. She drew near old Dan's and could hear him hammering at something in the shed. What would he do for a living if he hadn't the old age pension — make a few rickety chairs, she supposed. Hm! — she was sure he hadn't one rusty penny to his name. What had he but the four walls of a house, a clay roof over it, and not as much land in his fist as would sod a lark. A nice home to ask Paddy Boden or anyone to share. But he'll make good use of Paddy — get him to hold the cracks in the walls together with a slateful of plaster.

She straightened herself when she saw Tessie in a red blouse run from the back of the house down to the potato patch which was nearly half-dug. Thriftless, shiftless people! Live for the day and forget the future! Cadge from your neighbours when your own potatoes are done — a rabbit or two instead of fresh meat, a bit of salty bacon, a dry stick of a fish in the winter, and a sing-song at night to make you forget about to-morrow. 'Well, let them have it,' she said aloud to herself. 'I'm not the one to begrudge them their bit of bread and their drivelling life. But my Ned was made and reared for better than that! And whether he likes it or not I'll better his life for him. To think of the poor simple boy to be pecked upon by that flock! God in Heaven, I wouldn't be doing my duty to allow it!'

She walked quickly to escape from the rawness in her mind. But wherever she looked there was always something to smart her — a rusty gate or an ill-kept fence — and once again the dread of her son's marriage would drag through her mind like a heavy chain. At last she reached the chapel, and before going in she rested on the fresh plinth of her husband's grave. On the grave to the right she saw a glass jam-jar with rusty-coloured water, and she turned her head from it and rested them on the solid limestone memorial in front of her. With a mixture of pride and sorrow she read aloud her husband's name, his age, and the date of his death — all cut as she had desired in small letters. No one could say she neglected his memory. But when she noticed the bare span below his name the realization that her own name would be the next made her bless herself and hurry into the chapel.

Some penitents, mostly women, were there before her, though Father Toner had not yet arrived. Mrs. Mason took off her gloves and knelt in a seat apart from them. In front of her the priest's old housekeeper was trudging up the aisle doing the Stations of the Cross and holding on to the seat every time she genuflected. Then she would struggle to her feet with difficulty and in a voice made loud by her deafness would say: 'We adore Thee, O Christ, and praise Thee . . .' As Mrs. Mason watched and listened her mind sped away from the examination of her own conscience and she wondered why Father Toner could put up with such an old, old woman. She bowed her head and covered her ears with her hands to shut out the distraction, but when she heard other penitents coming into the seat behind her she arose with stiff assurance and took up her place in the line. Presently Father Toner came from the sacristy, genuflected before the tabernacle, knelt for awhile in prayer, and walked down the aisle, his eyes avoiding the rows of penitents arranged round his box. The heavy curtain swayed as he passed behind it, the wooden slide rattled across and a woman's voice droned through the church.

The old housekeeper finished the Way of the Cross and took her seat beside Mrs. Mason. 'I'll have to let her go before me,' Mrs. Mason said to herself, and having decided on that she knelt to recollect her sins and knew that when she had confessed them all the priest would be sure to ask her if she had uncharitable thoughts. Surely she could say no; she never wished ill to the Devlins — all she wanted was that they'd leave Ned alone. That was all — surely there was nothing uncharitable about that!

She laid her fingers on the seat in front of her, and when she lifted them again four moist imprints were left behind. 'Perhaps,' she said to herself, 'now that I am here I should tell him who I am and ask his advice about Ned. It would do no harm — Father Toner was always treated with kindness in our house and surely he'd be glad if I asked him.'

The old housekeeper stumbled into the dark confessional and when she bellowed out the Confiteor, Mrs. Mason pressed her fingers to her ears, for she knew that she would bellow out her sins with the same unabashed loudness. She was out quickly, and Mrs. Mason entered, and in the warm fusty air she covered her eyes with her hands and tried to shut out all distraction. But the voice of the penitent on the other side of the priest would rise sharply and dwindle to a hissing whisper and then rise again. Mrs. Mason coughed — some of these women were long-winded. The voice died away once more and Mrs. Mason straightened herself and waited. At long last the slide rattled over and she was looking through the grille at Father Toner who, with head inclined, was listening to her Confiteor and at the same time lifting the edge of the curtain to see if there were many more to hear. He blew his nose and put the handkerchief in his sleeve, and when Mrs. Mason had told her sins and was waiting for the priest to give her his usual advice about leading a good life, he said: 'You're sorry now for all these sins and the sins of your past life'; and in a few minutes she was out in the light of the chapel again, having said nothing about Ned. A feeling of complete dissatisfaction overshadowed her as she knelt to say her penance. She knelt for a long time. She heard Father Toner leave the confessional, and when she stole a glance round the little chapel she found that the other penitents had gone off. She pulled on her gloves and went out, and instead of turning on the road for home she went in the opposite direction to the priest's house, and without having arranged in her own mind the exact words she'd say, she rang the bell of the hall door and waited. To keep her from thinking she looked at everything: the shine on the brass door-bell, the black-leaded door-scraper, and the fresh cleanliness of the red tiles.

'Old and all as she is, she's clean,' she said to herself as the door opened and the housekeeper stood before her.

'Could I see the priest?' she said quietly.

'Eh?' said the housekeeper.

'Is Father Toner in?' Mrs. Mason said a little louder.

'He is. . . . Do you want to see him?'

'I do!' said Mrs. Mason loudly.

'Eh?'

'Tell Father Toner I want him,' and she felt a flush to her cheeks as she again raised her voice.

'Is it important?'

'It is,' said Mrs. Mason and nodded her head at the same time.

The housekeeper brought her into the sitting-room downstairs and in a few minutes Father Toner came in.

'Is it you!' he said breezily. 'Here, take this seat, it is more comfortable than that stiff-backed fellow.'

'Father,' she said as she took off her gloves, 'it's about Ned.'

'Ned!' he said in surprise, and, noticing how agitated she was, he added: 'I hope he hasn't been robbing an orchard.'

'Father, he's changed. He's not like a son at all. He has taken up with Mary Devlin and she's not a suitable match for the like of Ned.'

The priest said nothing, allowing her to reel off from her mind all the faults and failings of the Devlins that she did not wish her son to share. And then, as she finished, she grew quieter and said: 'I came to you for advice, Father.'

'It's a subject on which we are not prone to tender advice except, say, in the case of a mixed marriage. We would do our best to dissuade a young boy or girl from such a step. Though some of these marriages are a success it is our experience that in nine cases out of ten they are a failure. Married people need to be of the one religion, and if their marriage is to be a happy one they need to be strong in that religion and have respect for it. Where there is no religion there is no real love and where there is no love there is no real peace.'

Mrs. Mason looked across the table at him and wondered what all this had got to do with Ned.

'Do you pray for direction in these matters?'

'Night and day, Father, I pray that he'll do the right thing.'

'And if Ned continues to do the same thing you feel he's not doing right?'

'No, Father; yes, Father. You see these Devlins . . .'

'The Devlins,' he broke in gently when he saw her lift her gloves, 'I know them all, and since the death of their mother they have struggled bravely and well. Luke had to be father and mother to them, fisherman and farmer, and it was a great pleasure to me to see how well he fitted them out on a Sunday and the way he kept them at the school.'

She fidgeted and padded with her fingers on the table. She'd not get much satisfaction from him. She was sorry she approached him. He wouldn't care who Ned married as long as he settled in the parish. That was his worry — the parish, the parish!

'I suppose Ned's about thirty now.'

'Thirty-four come next tenth of January.'

'Well now, Mrs. Mason, it is time he was married. It's a grand sight to see a young pair and their children young with them. They have more understanding of their children when they're near to them in years.'

She stood up and he tried to persuade her to wait for a cup of tea.

'Oh, no, Father, I promised Sarah that I'd come straight back. She'll be wondering what's delayed me.'

'Take things quietly, Mrs. Mason,' he said to her as she went towards the door, 'and when you go on your knees give God a chance to talk to you. Everything done for the glory of God will bring its just reward.' He opened the door for her and walked with her down the gravel path to the road. 'And don't thwart your son. Don't provoke him to anger. After all, what does a man want out of life but contentment — his own fireside and the girl he loves.'

'But the Devlins, Father,' and she shook her head. 'Look at — at how unsettled they are! They're not content.'

'No one knows that for certain,' he said. 'What we live in our actions is only a fraction of what we live in our

K   145

minds,' and he stopped and lifted a straw from the hedge where the carts had brushed too close to it. He knew she was thinking of Barbara. He had blamed himself when anyone had gone off to the town, for it was his aim to knit them close together with dances and plays and cards and football, and so keep them from the cities where they became submerged and lost their identity. He himself would be content if he could fulfil that. And now she had said something for which he could not find a direct answer.

'Thank you, Father,' she said, 'and I am sorry for giving you so much trouble.'

'No trouble at all, Mrs. Mason. Everything will be all right if you leave it in God's hands. You'll call to see me again?'

She nodded and swung off down the road, hurrying as best she could before the dew would fall on the grass and the sharp winds blow in from the sea after the heat of the day. The evening in which she had hoped to find peace left nothing in her mind only puddles of despair, and all the way towards the sea-road she rebuked herself for going near him when she should have written to her cousin, Father Christy, and told him all — he'd have understood. But it's hard to explain yourself in a letter and then Father Christy's handwriting is that bad, she nor none of the girls could make head or tail of it.

She reached the sea-road and hurried past the Devlin cottage. Near the stream she saw Ned and John Devlin talking and laughing with one another as if they hadn't a care in the world. She quickened her pace to show them the hurry she was in. She'd pass them with a 'good evening'. But as she neared them John Devlin got to his feet and touched his cap: 'A brave evening, Mrs. Mason,' he said. Ned still lay against the bank, a stalk of grass in his mouth. Why didn't he get to his feet — he that was taught manners?

'I was sorry to hear of your husband's death,' John said, his huge hands resting on his stick. 'Many's a good turn he done me.'

'It was a hard blow,' she said, 'a hard blow,' and as she shuffled on her feet and moved off she knew she should have mentioned his own affliction.

'I say, Ned, she stands it well,' said John, resting on the bank again. 'There she is striking the road as hale and hearty as a woman of forty.'

'She's seventy-four — you wouldn't think that.'

'Your father, God have mercy on him, was good to her. Och, sure he wouldn't let the wind blow cold on her.' They laughed and talked till the dew fell on the grass and a few snails made out on the road. Out at sea the gannets and gulls were diving into the oily swell and tearing the air with harsh cries. 'There's plenty of fish in,' said John, 'if my father was eager to go after them. I'll try them myself some of these days when himself and Mary is gathering the spuds. He's afeared I can't manage the boat with this,' and he tapped his leg with the stick.

Behind them Luke was in his stubble field admiring his rows of stooks. He had seen John talking to Mrs. Mason and he noticed with a feeling of pride the natural way he touched his cap to her. It was well after all he didn't tell him about her — what was the use of adding bitterness to bitterness, souring the lad's blood, and making him as awkward with her as a swan out of water. There was a crackling step behind him on the stubble and he turned to see old Dan with a sheaf of corn under his arm and a shot-gun over his shoulder. 'I'm in time,' he puffed, hurrying past Luke and bursting through the hedge on to the road. Ned and John watched him scramble to the shore, tie the sheaf round its waist with cord, and wade out with his boots on over the shallow, sandy water. About four hundred yards from the shore he left the floating sheaf and waded in again, slowly unrolling the ball of cord. He called John down to him and they lay behind a breast-high pile of stones, the old man with his gun trained on the sheaf. He handed the cord to John: 'Roll it up bit by bit when I tell you. And for the love of God don't talk or budge when the lads come down to feed.'

They waited quietly, old Dan kneeling and peering through the stones, and John sitting with his legs outstretched, the wet cord in his hands.

'Any duck yet?' John said.

'Shush! Not a feather and the sea as smooth as water in a well. Don't stir now. I suppose the dog's in the house?'

'She is,' and John lifted his stick and prodded a few pebbles that lay near the toe of his boot.

Dan took the stick from him and put it out of arm's length.

'Keep still now. I see a couple flying in from the south,' and he crouched closer behind the stones. There was no sound now except the drip of water from the ragged edges of his trousers. The air was clear and he could see the duck as black as stones in the level water. A huge moon as red as an orange bulged above the sea, and with it came the wild duck, flying in twos and threes.

'Not a word out of you, John. Not a breath — they've ears like a clocking thrush. They smell the sheaf. The buggers is moving up. They're feedin' now. Let them have their fill. Roll up a wee bit of the string, John, not much, like a good fellow — they're dead cute! O begod, there's a ball of them round it now.' John tried to rise and he pushed him down again. 'Don't look up!' he said, 'or you'll ruin the show.'

'My leg's stiffenin' on me,' John said, trying to wriggle himself into a more comfortable position.

'Roll up a bit more. The tide's on the turn — there's a good quick belly on it.'

'Are they in range yet? My leg's as stiff as a rock.'

'The water puts you off. Roll up a bit more. What looks a couple of perches on the water is out of range.'

'For God's sake, Dan, let them have it. I can't thole the pain in my leg.'

'Roll up like a good man. There's three more cruisin' up to it. Oh, great big fat burly fellows.'

'Let fly!'

'Did you come on a twist of red wool on the cord?'

'I passed it long ago.'

'Why the hell didn't you tell me that! They were in range then. Now I'll ruin them. I'll leave nothing only feathers.'

'Oh-h-h-h,' John groaned.

One of the ducks stopped feeding, and with head erect turned tail to the sheaf and moved off. Dan levelled the gun. There were two reports and the water ripped around the sheaf and Dan fell back on top of John, pinning him to the ground until those that had escaped had flown overhead.

Nellie came barking from the house with Luke at her heels. She followed old Dan as he splashed out to the sheaf and carried in the duck that were floating on the water. The water was spattered with feathers and one duck lay on its back on top of the sheaf. Below it Dan plunged his hand into the shallow water and, groping around on the bottom, he pulled up a duck that was clinging with its bill to a piece of weed. 'The old trick,' he said, 'but you can't dodge me and none of us can dodge death.'

'It's cruel way to trap them,' John teased when they were up on the road again.

'Cruel! Don't I give them a good feed afore they die. Is it crueller than the painted ducks the big bugs use!' and then he shook his head bitterly. 'If I could prevent them fellas from gettin' them it's not one sheaf I'd use but a whole bloody stook. When I was a lad at school I seen the landlords shootin' them for sport and leavin' them half-dead on top of the water.'

'Wait'll John's attacking these fellows with a knife and fork,' said Luke, swinging a pair of duck, 'and he'll not be talkin' about cruelty.'

'That groan you let out of you nearly crocked the evening,' said Dan. 'A big drake heard it and he was in swithers

149

whether to fly off or swim off. But he seen nobody and he just shook his backside at the sheaf and called off the feast. It was then I let fly with the two barrels,' and his eyes narrowed with keen delight as he re-lived it again. 'I'll give them another crack or two next week,' he added.

'You may bring Paddy Boden to roll up your string,' said John, 'for I wouldn't go through that agony again not for all the duck in Strangford Lough.'

'Good night to ye,' said Dan, and as he swung along the road with the dangling bundle of wild duck he began to sing:

> If with money life you could buy,
> The rich would live and the poor would die.

CHAPTER XV

In the mornings and evenings when the tide was favourable John would go down to a pool in the rocks and bathe the swelling on his leg in salt water, and when he would come up to the house again, his father or Mary was always ready to upbraid him. 'You might as well spit on your leg as do that,' his father would say. 'Have a bit of sense, man, and let the doctors at it. They'll break it and set it right, and by Christmas, please God, you'll be home in fine fettle and ready for a bit of a dance.'

'There's not much wrong with the leg,' John would say. 'There's nothing like nature's cure. Look at that!' and he would shuffle his feet on the floor to convince them. 'The salt water's hardening it already.' He would lift the leg of his trousers: 'There's no gloss on that skin. When I came home it was as tight and shiny as the skin on a child's balloon, and look at it now.'

'It's painful to see you pawing and groping about like a blind man,' Mary would say, 'and when I see you floundering about on the rocks I'm worried silly till you step safe

150

into the house again. Heed what my father says and go into the hospital in Downpatrick.'

He let them talk, reproach him, and contradict each other, but made no move to follow their advice. Father Toner, too, dropped in one evening and put his hand on his shoulder: 'Like a sensible man, John, do what I ask of you. It will be a simple operation and you will have the best of attention and friends calling in to see you every hour in the day. It won't be like languishing in a foreign country with no one for company but your own memory.'

'And what guarantee have I that they will completely cure me? They might leave me worse than I am. I have known that to happen.'

'They couldn't leave you any worse than you are,' said the priest. 'You're a young man with fine sap rising in his bones and they would knit together in no time at all. If you were an old man with dry and brittle bones I might side with you. Like a decent fellow go into the hospital before it's too late. You're only a burden to yourself and to Mary here. And look at what you are missing — the boat and the fishing you were always so fond of.'

John smiled and shook his head: 'Och, Father Toner, you'd coax the fish out of the sea. I'll think it over and I might take a look in at the hospital and I might not. And as for the boat I could handle one now as well as in the old days.' And the following morning, to show that he was in earnest about the boat, he lifted his stick from the back of the chair and without saying a word to Mary or his father, who were preparing to gather potatoes, he shambled over a neck of rock to the boat and when Mary looked out of the window she saw the boat driving across the bay with long even strokes. Luke came out on to the road and hailed him. John waved back and then swiftly wheeled the boat, shavings of froth cutting away from her bow. He guided her neatly alongside the rock where his father stood, and John looked up at him with a vigorous, happy expression on his face.

'I can manage her yet,' he smiled.

'I'd be careful and not go out my lone.'

'What are you saying! I could pull her to Ardglass and back without taking off my coat,' he boasted. He stood up to get out, but the boat coggling beneath him jolted him against the rock.

'Easy now,' said his father, 'you're not as supple as you think.'

'I'm all right,' said John, scrambling up the rock. 'Sure that often happened to yourself.' And as he walked up to the house with his father he asked him to keep the boat moored to the rock and put a few fistfuls of cement in the hollows of the rock to smooth away the roughness. 'I might try for a few whiting some of these fine days.'

'It's a bit late for them, John, and anyway don't go out your lone. Get one of the lads out of the school to go with you — they're on their potato holidays now.'

'They'd be hungry every half-hour and wanting me to put them ashore. What's in fishing for a few whiting — only sitting at your ease in an anchored boat and sinking your pair of hooks and lifting them again.'

'Couldn't you wait till we have the potatoes gathered and then we could kill them together.'

'You know yourself it'd be too late then,' John said. 'The fish'd have skipped our shores and you'd catch nothing only strings of silver snotters.'

The following morning he got Mary to waken him and when the tide was full out and the sun sending steam from the sand he showed her the places where to plunge the spade. She would topple the sand at his feet and he would bend over it seeing the dark worms moving sluggishly as they tried to escape from the glare of the sun. He filled a tin full of worms and as he washed the sand off them at the stream she gazed at him with a pained expression. He turned from the stream, stumbled on stones that were covered with green sleech, and she put out her hand to save him.

'John,' she said, her voice thin with anxiety, 'you can't go on living like this.'

'I'm telling you, Mary, I'll have no call for the stick by Christmas.'

'What'll you do if you want a girl to marry you?'

'I could get one if I was on a pair of crutches,' he laughed.

'I'm wasting my breath talking to you. You can go your own way from this on. I'll not give advice where it's scoffed at,' and she raced up to the house and hurried back again with a can of milk, a few farls of bread, and a couple of raw eggs to stifle his hunger while he'd be fishing. Luke saw him safely into the boat and when he was ready to push off, Nellie, the dog, hopped in and sat on the stern. 'Don't stay long out,' his father called and stood on the rock until the boat had rounded the point.

But before the sun had set and before Mary and her father had come from the potato field John was back again with a few whiting and some lithe sliding about on the bottom of the boat, and at their tea that evening he was as pleased with himself as a young schoolboy as he told how he had sat at his ease throwing in the line.

The following afternoon he again ventured out, taking with him a small net that he intended to shoot across one of the narrow gullets below the Masons' house. There was a good 'take' this time and he remained out till after sundown, but noticing a head-wind strengthening with the outgoing tide he lifted the anchor and rowed for home. He pulled strongly but when he marked his progress by a rock on the shore he saw he was making no headway. To avoid the strong race of the tide he pulled near the coast but even there it was strong, shiving past the rocks with a gurgling sound. The dog shivered in the wind that swirled the hair on its back, and when the spray in large drops struck across her she slunk under the stern seat and lay on a piece of canvas, gazing at John with wide, steady eyes. He winked at the dog and drove the boat stubbornly into the waves, the water streeling from the bows with a vicious hiss. A great branch of water broke over him and he shook his head like a swimmer and saw the fish-scales washed clean from his knife lying on the seat in front of him. All he had to do was to turn back and lie in shelter till the tide turned. But he'd not do it and have the whole countryside out searching for him with lamps. He'd break the waves before they'd break him.

With solid backs they lurched at him, first in herds, and then a huge one by itself hurtled forward with a ragged top and John, clenching his mouth with the determination of one sure and certain of his power, tore a gap through it with a shout of joy. In the lull that followed he peeled off his jersey. He felt cooler now. He looked at the sky and amongst its broken pavings saw the first stars blossoming. It'd soon be dark, and in a little while the neighbours would be coming along the shore, swinging a lamp, and yelling themselves hoarse. Already a few lights in the scattered cottages were warming the darkness. He rolled up his sleeves. He'd not have it said in the pub that they had to tow him home.

'Now, in God's name,' and he spat on his hands and gripped the oars. 'Up! ... Up! ... Up!' he encouraged himself at each stroke, the tide cleaving past him in a wedge of fizzing white. A windy light was moving on the headland — that'd be the first searcher. Let them call and shout, he'd not answer them. The boat nosed round the point and there he felt the full blast of the wind. A light was in his cottage and he followed the line which it shook upon the water. The dog crawled out from under the stern, the white bellies of the fish slipping from under her paws, and resting her forefeet on the gunwale she suddenly began to bark, and her barking was answered by men whistling and striking matches in the sheltered cups of their hands. The boat, now out from the edges of the tide, travelled easily.

'Is that you, John?' his father shouted, his voice thick with suppressed fear.

'I got a few good ones,' John shouted back, with assumed

indifference. 'I'll run her on to the sand for there'd be no water at the rock.'

His father directed him with a lamp and when the boat slooshed on to the sand old Dan, Paddy Boden, and the blacksmith gathered round him gazing at the fish and telling him how he had put the fear of God in them. They helped him on to the sand, his leg stiff and cramped, his body oozing a warm smell of sweat in the night air.

But the next day his leg was swollen above the ankle and he couldn't move it. He had to lie in bed while Mary attended him, bathing the swelling with cold water and wrapping a bandage tightly round it. And once again she began her rhyme: 'It's the hospital now, John. You see you're in the wrong.'

'The swelling will go down again. I give it a bad wrench when I was rowing hard.'

'It'd be best to get the doctor to have a look at it.'

'You'll get no doctor for me. If you do I'll lock the door and he can jig his heels on the doorstep.'

'But you can't go on like this!' she cried.

He turned his head to the window and looked at the sea.

'You'll not have me dancing attendance on you if you don't be sensible,' she urged.

'My leg's knit, I tell you. The doctor in France told me I'd have pain in it for a few months — that's all. Do you think I'm going to suffer the agonies of a hospital again!'

She shook her head in despair and left the room, and each day that followed she continued to bathe it while he lay up in his bed, and each day someone was sure to call and recommend a different cure — an eel skin, a linseed poultice, or goosefat; and when one old woman said she would cure it by pricking it with nine fresh thorns for nine days he told her to get to hell out of the house or he would send the priest on her tracks.

From his window he watched the leaves of the sycamore shrivel in the cold, and at night heard the wind stream through them like dry paper. Black spots came on them and one-by one they lost their hold and fluttered to the ground and were blown under the hedge. The waves pounded the shore and when the spray flung itself on the iron-roof he thought of the snugness of the thatch that used to spread low and warm above his head. Carts moved in the mornings to the shore to gather the seaweed for the fields, and when he saw the men pitchforking the slabby wrack he would move his ankle gently and convince himself that the pain which streaked through his leg would soon disappear and leave him strength to do the heavy work about the house.

Old Dan came in one day carrying with him a wooden frame, and stumping into the room he pulled the bedclothes off John and set the frame over the swelling on his leg, and when he had pulled up the clothes again he stood back with pride: 'A houl you that feels lighter? Them bedclothes is a bugger of a weight!'

'It's better already, Dan,' John smiled at him.

Dan looked out the window and seeing a heron standing in the water's edge he turned to John: 'If you've patience to lie and rest in your bed you'll be as lively as a trout before the year ends . . . Do you see that crane out there? He's the patientest of all birds. He'll stand there for hours with not a flinch out of him and he'll dab at everything that swims around his stiff legs. He knows how to keep still and in that way he fills his belly and lives. Take a feather out of his tail — learn how to keep still.'

'And if the leg doesn't heal with the long rest what'd you advise me to do?'

'I don't know.'

'The hospital?'

'What does the priest say?'

'The hospital.'

'Then I'd bide by his word. He's a knowledgeable man and he knows what's best for you. Anyway a big burly fellow like you shouldn't be afraid of a bit of a pain.'

'You don't know what you're saying — a man like you that never had pain nor ache in his life.'

'Thanks and praises be to God for that,' the old man said and took off his cap. 'I never had anything in my life and yet I had everything. I had my health and I still have it. I can enjoy a potato and a fresh herring and a jug of butter-milk and a bottle of stout. I like to have a bit of a chat on a Saturday night and I like to see the young enjoy themselves. That's all I ask for! And if you've a stime of sense left in your skull you'll give an ear to what I say to you. If your leg's in good health it'll cure itself with rest — if it doesn't then I'd heed the priest.'

'I'll not set foot in a hospital again!' John said. And Dan, seeing that he had angered him, sat on the edge of the bed and tried to take the sting out of his words by saying over and over again: 'John, son, you'll be all right by Christmas. I feel it in here,' and he'd thump his chest. But John wasn't listening to him; he was looking at a shower of rain falling outside, scoring streaks of light on the window-pane, and wetting the few remaining leaves on the sycamore. And as he watched he saw through the mesh of rain his father and the blacksmith and Ned Mason and Paddy Boden hauling the boat on to the road, lifting it, two at each side, and carrying it to the north end of the house to lie all winter against the house, giving shelter to the hens.

'God in Heaven!' John cried, closing his eyes and resting his face on the pillow. 'Will I always be like this — fit for nothing!'

Dan patted his head as he would do to a child: 'Man alive, John, by the New Year you'll be leppin' around the field of a Sunday beltin' the ball between the posts and tumblin' the Ardglass fellas over the line! Wait'll you see who's tellin' the truth!'

'I wish to God, Dan, I could believe you!' and he looked up at him with tears in his eyes.

'Fill up yer pipe and have a smoke. Don't be stokin' yer

157

mind with gloom. Where's Mary that she's not puttin' a bit of a song through the house. The house isn't like itself at all — a house that had always somebody singin' or play-actin'.'

'You got the liveliest when you got Tessie,' John said. 'And the flightiest took flight to Downpatrick.'

'Tessie's as kind to me as she'd be to her own father,' and he bent over the bed and whispered into his ear.

'I hope it'll be a little girl she'll have,' John answered.

'I'll not say "aye" to that,' Dan said, and hearing a sharp rattle of boots in the kitchen he put his pipe in his pocket and prepared to leave. Paddy Boden and Ned Mason came into the room, their clothes covered with the dust of rain, and when they began talking to John to cheer him up, Dan slipped out of the room.

Darkness fell quickly and early, and when the lamp was lit John took a pack of cards from the window-ledge and called his father from the kitchen to join in a hand. The cards were dealt on to the bedclothes and the stakes, usually a penny, were tossed into a delph bowl. They would ponder their hand of cards with tense silence and there would be no sound during a game except the glossy shuffle of a card or the wind crushing its way through the sashes of the window and crinkling the blind. Then as a game would draw to an end and each hold a last card they would slap them down on one another with sharp rapidity, and John's voice boom out: 'Beat that!' and he would laugh loudly as he scooped up the bowl and emptied its contents on to his lap.

'Och, there's no beating that fella since he went to sea,' Luke would say.

'He has the aces under the clothes,' Paddy would say.

'Damn all I can get the night only handfuls of rubbish,' Ned would say; and, when it came his deal, he shuffled the cards so clumsily that they spilt fanwise on to the floor.

'You're all thumbs the night, Ned,' Paddy Boden said to him.

Ned flung up his head: 'When a man's out of luck every-thing knocks against him — even the weather,' and he flicked a penny into the bowl and smoothed out the wrinkles on the quilt beside him.

Mary came into the room, but they were so absorbed in their cards they didn't see her, and she stood silently against the door, rising on her toes and looking over Ned's shoulder at his hand of cards. She smiled when she saw he held two face cards and an ace. As they waited patiently for John to lead she watched the ravelling cords of smoke from their pipes, blue-white for a moment before melting into the darkness under the roof. 'It's about time he put a ceiling of boards in this room,' she said to herself, and thought of the heap of burnt thatch that was now lying at the back of the house and the grass springing up through it. She jumped as the game ended and John gave out his barrel of a laugh: 'You threw that game away, Ned,' he said, picking out Ned's five cards and placing them face-upwards on the clothes. 'Man alive, what were you thinking about! Why didn't you play the Queen first, and you'd have robbed the shirts off our backs.'

Ned shook his head and pitched a penny into the bowl: 'That's my last cent. I'm going this time if I lose!'

He lost, and pushing the chair away from him he got to his feet. 'Come round for a hand the morrow night,' said Luke, 'and rob this son of mine. He can't win all the time.'

Ned passed through the kitchen and Mary pulled on her coat and went out with him. He put her to the leeward side of him for it was dark with a cold wind whorling in from the sea. They put their arms round one another as they walked along, but when they splashed into a puddle in the darkness Mary jumped away from him with a playful scream. He lifted her in his arms and tried to carry her, but on reaching the small bridge over the stream he set her down again and stood to gather his breath, listening to the purl of the stream and the rattle it made as it fought its way into the sea. For a long time he stood in silence and she gripped his arm trying to draw him to her and away from whatever thought was stretching through his mind.

'Forget about the cards, Ned. Sure it'll come your time again,' she said, smiling up at him in the darkness.

'I'm not thinking about the cards, Mary. I'm thinking of John and I'm wondering will you get him to move to the hospital.'

' 'Tis hard to know — he's terribly headstrong.'

'And if he doesn't — what'll become of him? He can't expect you to stay and mother him.'

The complaining strain in his voice frightened her and she tried to quell it with affected light-heartedness: 'Och, he'll go all right. He'll see there's nothing else for him.'

'And if he doesn't?'

'But he will, Ned. I'm sure he will. Father Toner was angry with him the other day.'

For a few minutes he stood without a word out of him, his head inclined as if he were listening to the shattering jabble of the stream going over the stones.

'Ned, what's wrong with you to-night?' she said, and though her teeth chattered with the cold he made no move to shelter her in his arms.

'Tell me, Mary, would you marry me at the New Year if I asked you?' and he drew her towards him.

She laughed and raised her head, her breath warm against his face: 'But, Ned, what about your mother?'

'I'm asking you! It doesn't matter what she says or does. We'll run off and get married and tell her after it's done!'

'But, Ned,' and as she spoke she felt his arms go slack from around her.

'You don't care a bit for me,' he said coldly. 'Not a damned bit!'

'I love you!'

'If you did you'd do what I ask.'

'But we haven't a house.'

'I've my two hands!' he said, and held them out in the darkness. 'Will you marry me?'

She put her arms round his neck: 'I will, Ned,' she said, almost in tears. 'As God's my judge I want nobody but you. But wait a wee while longer. There's John to . . .'

'I knew that was in your mind. So you care more for him — a fellow that's too much of a collie to get himself cured.'

'I don't, Ned. I don't! I love you! I love you with every bit of me.'

'Prove it then!' he said aloud. 'Prove it!'

She remained silent for a minute and took his hand that was stiffening away from her: 'I want nobody but you, Ned.'

'We'll get married at the New Year and let God settle the rest of it.'

'But,' and she toyed with a button on his coat, 'I can't leave them the way they are now . . .'

'I knew it! You care more for them than you care for me. I've fought and stood by you — in the house and out of it. I showed them nobody counted only you! And now this is the end of it!' He wrenched himself free from the arms that clung to him and hurried away from her. She ran after him. 'Ned,' she cried, 'Ned — listen to me. I'll do anything you ask,' and she rested her head on his shoulder.

'It's settled then,' he said, and kissed her face that was already wet with tears.

He left her at home talking now of nothing except the dance that there'd be in the school at Christmas and of the concert the teacher had organized. When at last he had said good-night to her she stood in the darkness for a while looking at the light in John's room, the grotesque shadows of his arms on the blind and his loud voice raised in laughter: 'Spades again . . . The lucky spade!'

'I'll go in on the bike and see Barbara,' she said to herself, and when she opened the door the wind zoomed through the house, clattering a tin-lid from the wall,

THE following day Mary wakened early and, pulling the blind aside, she peered into the chilly dawn of a December morning. With the aid of a lighted candle on the hob she raked out the dead ashes of the fire, listening with a cold feeling of despair to the dunt of the wind against the door and the slap of rain falling from the roof. She saw the rain lying in the crevices of the stone flags of the kitchen and heard it seeping through the empty sack that was stuffed around the threshold, and all the words Barbara had flung at the place drove remorselessly through her mind. She shook her head, as if a bad thought were in it, and tried to listen to the crackle of the sticks, but the cold drift of the wind about her legs and the snail-lines of rain on the sooty chimney made her shudder violently. Barbara was right — the winters here are long and dreary. And anyway, the house is too near the sea, with no shelter except a thin hedge and a small sycamore with a bough cut off it. She unhooked the cloth from the window and saw on the pane the melting pattern of rain, half sleet, half hail. Every wave on the sea was raw and white, and near the shore she saw them arch their backs and toss the sea-rods amongst the polished stones. A handful of sleet pitted against the window and she shivered and hissed through her teeth. Whether the rain would slacken or not she would cycle to Downpatrick and plead with Barbara to come home for a while — if only till Easter. With the wind on her back going in, she might be able to dodge the showers.

She hurried on with the breakfast and brought John a light for his pipe. She wiped up the rain from the floor, wrung out the sack, and put it back in its place at the threshold. When she was ready to go John called from the room: 'Get me a few ounces of tobacco. Barbara can give you the money for I'm sure she's earning a good penny. And tell her I'm vexed with her for not coming to see me.'

'Don't travel a coarse day like that,' her father said from the other bed. 'You could get your death. Wait till tomorrow.'

'Och, I'm bent on going. I want to get a few things for Christmas,' and with that she left them, went out the back door, chased a hen that was roosting on the handlebars of her bicycle and set off with the wind driving behind her. Except for her shoes she was quite dry when she reached the hill above Downpatrick, but there the rain burst upon her, and as she sped down the hill she saw Ned's aunt pressed close against the asylum wall for shelter, her three dogs on leads, sniffing at the grass. The hiss of the bike startled them and they entangled themselves in the leads, Mary laughing to herself as she heard Aunt Rose's thin voice: 'Rory, don't be bold!'

She whizzed through the deserted town, the reflection of the telegraph poles and houses sunk deep in the wet streets. She reached the restaurant opposite the railway where Barbara was employed and stood in the hall-way breathing loudly and shaking the rain off herself. 'Every place is miserable in the winter,' she thought as she saw the wet, flapping sheet of an advertisement hanging from the railway hoarding. A woman with an umbrella passed into an open doorway, lowered the umbrella, and shook the rain from it on to the street. When she closed the door with a bang its sound rattled forlornly, filling Mary with a vague dread that made her wish she were on the bicycle again on her way home.

She opened the door of the restaurant and passed up the aisle between the deserted tables. A middle-aged woman with sleeves rolled up came out and Mary told her who she was. She led her through a greasy kitchen where she had to stoop under the clothes on the line, through a scullery with a trickling tap, and out to the back of the house where a wooden staircase on the outside wall led to a closed door. 'G'on up there and rap hard. She's making her bed,' and the woman hurried off, leaving Mary standing in the rain. As she mounted the stairs and looked down at the mangle covered with a tattered canvas, a tub full of bulging clothes, and the rain falling on a heap of coal, she felt her acute feeling of despair rebelling within her. She rapped with her knuckles on the door, and when Barbara opened it she went past her without a word and, sitting on the bed, began to cry.

'What's wrong, Mary? Is anybody dead?' Barbara asked, her voice sharp with anxiety.

'It's this! It's everything!' and she swept her hand round the room, her eyes alighting on the window patched with a cardboard advertisement. 'Oh, God in Heaven, such a place!'

'What's wrong with it?' asked Barbara.

'It's . . . it's ugly. . . . To think you were in a place like this and we didn't know!'

'There's nothing wrong with it,' said Barbara, and her eyes ranged over the whole room as if she were looking at it for the first time.

'My father will go demented if he sees this. You'll have to come home out of it.'

'You're seeing it at its worst,' Barbara said firmly. 'And isn't it a change from the sea and the burl of it under the door in the winter — coming under the front door and you sweeping it out the back.'

'It's dreadful to think of you here all your lone,' Mary went on as if she hadn't heard her. 'You'll have to leave.'

'I'll not leave. I'm content here. I've everything. Look!' and she switched on the electric light, and Mary, raising her eyes, gazed dumbly at the fly-specked shade and the bulb with its illuminated wire struggling against the light of day.

'You wouldn't condemn me to a life of candles and oil-lamps after that! And, what's more, I can have a comfortable read in bed at night and can switch off the light from where I lie.' She lifted the pillow and pulled out a shiny-backed novelette. 'There's what I'm reading now. It's a lovely story and I'll send it in to you when I'm finished.'

'I don't understand you,' said Mary, ignoring the book. 'Living outside the house like . . . like in a hay-loft and being content,'

Barbara plumped down on the bed beside her and, clasping her hands round her knees, began to laugh: 'There's a fellow mad about me in the town, Mary. That's the God's truth. He's a baker — he delivers the bread here every morning,' and as she spoke he arose before her mind in his white coat, the name of the bakery woven in green thread on the collar, and the way he held up the bag to the light to give her the change, coming close to her at the same time and tickling the lobe of her ear. 'Oh, Mary,' she went on, squeezing her sister's hand, 'he's terribly fond of me,' and she told of the walks she had had with him to the top of the hills above the town and how he had said the other evening while they were gazing at the distant sea: ' "Barbara, the wind will never blow cold on you again. We'll settle down in the hollow" — them's his very words, Mary.'

'He's codding you, Barbara,' and she lifted the novelette and tapped her fingers on the cover. 'This old trash is stuffing your head with nonsense.'

'He's not codding me,' and she stooped below the bed and dragged forth a cardboard box, and rustling through a heap of tissue paper, she displayed a string of beads, a hair brush, a leather handbag, and a gilt flap-jack.

'There's some of the things he bought me,' Barbara said proudly, and watched her sister open the handbag and smell the newness of the leather.

The expense of the gifts convinced Mary that the baker was in earnest and she was ready to say something in praise of him when the sight of the room with its worn oilcloth showing the outline of the boards underneath pulled her mind back with a jerk. 'But he'll hanker after you,' she said tenderly, 'if you leave this rotten shed and come home. If a boy loves you he'll think nothing of cycling out to see you every Sunday.'

'Out of sight — out of mind!' said Barbara. 'There's too many girls in Downpatrick would snatch him from me.'

Aware that her journey had failed, and half in pity for

herself and a yearning for someone to whom she could spill out her inmost thoughts, she revealed to her sister with passionate honesty what Ned had asked of her. But suddenly Barbara sprung to her feet and gave her a searching look: 'So that's it,' she said bitterly. 'There's nothing wrong with the place and you want me to come home so that you can go off with Ned and leave me to shoulder the load.'

'No, Barbara, no! As God's my judge I didn't know you had a lover. And as for the place here . . . Ah, well, I suppose when one's in love nothing is wrong with anything,' and she held her head and flivelled the pages of the novelette.

Barbara, noticing how her lip trembled, regretted what she had said and sat down again beside her talking of John and asking why he doesn't go to the hospital.

'I don't know,' Mary sighed, smoothing out a dog's ear on one of the pages.

'Is he drinking?'

'He's not. He hasn't tasted it since he came home.'

'Then I'd marry Ned. That would open John's eyes and show him he can't have you to herd him all day long.'

A swing bell on a pulley above the door rang, its tongue trembling for awhile after the sound had gone.

'That's somebody looking for a bite to eat,' Barbara said with a contemptuous shrug of her shoulders. 'They'll not starve for a minute or two.' Mary looked at the splashes of distemper on the bell and at the wire on the pulley disappearing through a hole in the floor. The wire was jerked again and the bell clanged impatiently.

'I better go before she comes pounding up for me,' said Barbara, getting to her feet.

In the shop as they passed through, Mary glanced sideways at the customer and then drew up suddenly as she gazed into the dark eyes of The Curate. He had grown thin and shrunken since she saw him last, and instead of his usual black suit he wore a ragged tweed, a safety-pin fastening the neck-band of his shirt.

'Where were you this last long time?' Mary said, sitting opposite him and shaking his damp hand.

'I was in jail in Belfast for three months.'

'Jail?'

'A peeler caught me with the sweep brushes without a licence and they fined me and cautioned me. I was nabbed again and they jailed me. When I got out I wandered about the streets of Belfast and played in pubs and outside pubs with my mouth-organ. But it was no use. It wasn't loud enough to draw attention in the traffic — you need a big melodeon strapped and buckled to your shoulder. The people gave me money not for what I played but because I looked foolish. It broke my heart and I give up the music and left the city.'

'And what are you doing now?'

'I was gardening whiles in the autumn but I'm not fit for it. My stomach's out of order and there's a pain rests across my back like an iron bar.'

'Why don't you come back to Dunscourt. You'll always get a place to lay your head.'

'I know that, Mary. I know that. But tell me, do they still talk about me?' and he looked straight at her, his brown eyes hurt with sorrow.

'Everybody asks about you. Father Toner and my granda and my father and Ned . . . Ned Mason. Everybody,' she said eagerly.

He took a pin from the lapel of his coat and dabbed idly at the table. 'It's not that,' he went on, his head lowered. 'But . . . Do they still say I turned my coat?'

She smiled and put her hand on top of his: 'They were only jokin' you, Jimmy. Nobody believes that. Surely it wasn't that drove you away. Oh, I forgot to tell you, our John's home again. But he has a bad leg and has to trudge about on a stick.'

'Poor John,' he said, 'and him a strong lump of a man that'd do your heart good to look at. Och, Mary, a man's better settled in one spot. When you go roaming your mind's never settled and when your mind's not settled you have no peace.'

Barbara brought them tea and a huge plate of cold ham for Jimmy.

'It'll give my stomach hell,' he said, counting the slices of ham with the point of his knife. 'But it'd be a sin to let the good food go to waste. May God send the pair of you fine strapping husbands,' and he mortared the ham with mustard while Mary poured out the tea. Through a crack in one of the cups the tea oozed in a brown stream, and Mary took that cup herself and gave him the other one. She dropped a spoon and as she picked it up she saw his burst boots and a pool of damp soaking into the dry boards.

'Where'll you stay the night?' she asked him.

'In the workhouse. I'll be in the body of the house till the spring of the year. There's no work in the gardens, my sweep brushes is in the barracks, and I sold the donkey and cart. The poor man that owned them is dead and buried and he left them all to me by word of mouth.'

'You'll be out to see us,' she said when she had finished, and slipping him a half-crown, she whispered to Barbara to stand him his meal.

When she came out of the restaurant the rain and wind had died down, clouds had broken loose in the sky and were wading in the blue puddles of the road. She wheeled her bicycle round the shops, buying a few things for Christmas and a coloured tie for Ned.

Going out of Downpatrick she usually walked up the hill, and at the top of it turned to look at the straggle of roofs and the two churches and the fresh freedom of the fields stretching away to the hills of Mourne. But to-day, with her few parcels swinging from the handlebars, she cycled up the hill, going diagonally from side to side, and passing children armed with branches of berried holly. At the top she didn't look back. She heard someone scream from the asylum grounds and remembered the spring day she had come in the cart with her grandfather and Paddy Boden and how her granda had said: 'God's pity on anyone who has a friend locked up in there. God help them — waiting in hope for a glimmer of sense to come to the friend's tongue and for the eyes to lose that vacant upward glance.' She sighed heavily as she free-wheeled down the hills that joggled away to the flat sea. 'We have something to be thankful for,' she told herself. 'We have our health. We have our worries too, but surely to God if we bear them with resignation there must be some purpose in them which we do not see.' She searched her mind for some worry in her past life which, now that she examined it from a distance, turned out for her own good. She began to sing, smothering back a burden of thoughts that were leaping insistently to her mind, and when she reached the priest's house she got off to tell him that she had seen The Curate.

The front door was closed, and though she jabbed the bell with much impatience there was no answer, and on going to the back door she saw the hungry hens clustered around it. With her hands to the side of her face she peered through the window. Kate lay on the sofa with a handkerchief over her face. On the shining range a pot was boiling over, the lid rising and falling, and streams of meal flowing down the sides and sizzling on to the grate. There was a glass of water on the table, a bottle of tablets, and a red plush box with an ornamental design on the lid.

Mary hooshed away the hens and went into the kitchen. She lifted the lid off the pot and pushed it to the side, and going to Kate she called out to her. But there was no answer. Her breathing was loud and whistling, the handkerchief falling into the cavity of her mouth.

'Kate!' and she shook her by the shoulder and lifted the handkerchief from her face. 'The pot's boiled over on you, Kate.'

The old woman groaned, opened her eyes and closed them

again. Mary gave her another shake. Kate stirred and raised a hand to her head as if she were chasing off a fly.

'Your pot's boiled over on to the range.'

The old woman gazed around her with a stupefied, stricken look, and Mary held the glass of water to her lips.

'I took a weak turn,' she said, after the first sip. Her eyes sought the clock on the mantelpiece and then the pot on the range.

'My poor hens,' she said. 'They'll be starving.'

'Lie quiet for a minute or two and I'll feed them,' said Mary, and hastened to the scullery to get a basin. The old woman inclined her head on the cushion and with a bewildered look saw Mary empty the yellow meal into the basin and shake a handful of corn through it. And when the hens were fed she watched her scrape the meal off the range with a knife and polish it with emery-paper.

'I'm done, Mary Devlin. I'm far through,' said the old woman, sitting up and squeezing her head with her hands.

'Nonsense,' Mary almost shouted. 'Nonsense. Sure we all get weak turns now and again.'

The old woman shook her head: 'I've wrought hard all my days. I haven't a friend or soul of my own in the world. You wouldn't believe that and me to have lived so many long years. I want to die in harness and be buried here.' She wiped her eyes with the hem of her apron. 'But I'm afeared the workhouse will be the end of me yet.'

Mary patted her hand: 'Put that out of your head,' she said with assurance.

'Hand me that box from the table, like a good girl,' she said, taking another sip of the water.

She opened the red-plush box and drew forth a collection of photographs, postcards, and letters tied with cord. Never before had she confided in anyone, but now that death seemed to be close upon her she felt the desire to unlock her mind and leave some trace of her life behind. One by one she took the photographs and explained each in detail —

families that she had served and what had become of them all. 'Ah, that was a handsome, lovely boy,' she said, as Mary lingered over the photograph of a youth dressed in officer's uniform. 'He was killed in the Dardanelles and his people never set eyes on him again. He was a lovely boy and he sent me a card from Egypt and always asked for me in his letters to his father and mother. . . . Wait now till I show you the card,' and she searched for it amongst the postcards and read out the almost faded words: 'I hope your eyes will be all right by the time this reaches you. Don't forget to take Rex out for a walk in the evenings and shake his paw for me.' . . . Poor Rex, that was the name of his dog, didn't live long after him, he was poisoned going after sheep. Ah, Mary, I never forget Master Frank in my prayers since the day the news came that he was killed. Them Turks is a bad lot, but bad and all as they are they wouldn't have shot Master Frank if they'd known the lovely boy he was — a boy that wouldn't harm a living soul. To think of him, Mary Devlin, and the bullets flying around him, and him sending me that card and asking about my poor eyes that were smarting with the paint that had splashed into them. . . . That's his sister,' she went on, pushing another photograph into Mary's hand: 'Miss Betty was a sweet girl. She was always laughing and riding her pony, and she'd ride him over the front lawn just to hear her father scolding. When she got married far away in Southampton she sent me a bit of the bride's cake all the way from there. I have the box here wrapped in tissue paper. God take care of her wherever she is now. I never forget to say a prayer for her when I'm on my knees. She was such a sweet and lovely girl! . . . And that group,' she said, showing her a group of children in an orphanage flanked by two nuns with joined hands: 'I'm in that but you couldn't pick me out. That's me with the thick head of curls. You wouldn't believe that, but it is. I was a fine wee girl, and when I was leaving the nuns, Sister Laurentia cut off one of my curls as a keepsake,—she did indeed. I could have been married twice. The first time I was asked I was too young and I refused because he had bad teeth, and the next time I was too cautious and I held on too long, and he went and married a postmistress that was old enough to be his mother. . . . Och, Mary,' she sighed and blew her nose in the hem of her apron. 'I'm lonely now and can blame nobody but myself. And listen, Mary Devlin, I have served Father Toner for wellnigh twelve years and never a cross word did he say to me.' She took out a handkerchief and dabbed her eyes.

Mary stood up and packed the cards together for her and stowed them neatly in the box. The light was fading from the window and sharpening the edges of the outhouses when Mary buttoned her coat and prepared to go.

'I'll call again to see you,' Mary said, and then remembered why she had called. 'Will you tell Father Toner that I saw The Curate in Downpatrick.'

'The Curate! What curate?'

'Jimmy Neil.'

'Father Neil — what parish would he be in?'

Mary shouted louder: 'Jimmy Neil — you know, the sweep-man!'

'That tramp!' she said, closing her box and fastening the metal clasp. 'Is he still at large?'

'He is. He's in the workhouse!'

'The workhouse!' and her voice broke in a husk. 'Och, God take care of us, is that where he is, the poor man. God look down on him.' She rubbed the backs of her hands and stared at the glowing range and the ashes falling in the grate.

'I must go now,' said Mary, and Kate hoisted herself up from the sofa and shuffled to open the door for her. The hens had gone to roost except one which was huddled in the corner of the doorstep. Kate lifted it in her arms and looked at its swollen craw: 'That poor thing can't eat a pickle. Take it to your granda and see could he do anything for it.'

Turning the corner of the house, Mary met Father Toner, his hat at the back of his head, a ring of keys jingling in his hand.

'Is this where you are?' he said laughing, his eye on the hen under her arm. 'Caught red-handed. You don't know a good one if it's the like of that you'd steal for Christmas.'

She smiled as she explained about the hen, and then, glancing sideways at the window, she told him about Jimmy Neil and about finding old Kate stretched on the sofa.

'She's not fit for the work,' he said, 'and she'll let nobody cross the doorstep to help her.'

'She dreads the workhouse, Father.'

'What put that idea in her head,' he said, twirling his ring of keys.

'I'll come over some evening, Father, and give her a hand. I can manage her all right.'

'You have enough to do nursing that big brother of yours. Barbara wouldn't think of coming back again?'

'She's too well settled, I'm afraid.'

'When I'm rounding up the bold Jimmy Neil, I'll kill two birds with the one stone and ask her.'

As she wheeled the bicycle with one hand she smiled at the little chance he had of tearing Barbara away from Downpatrick, and when she reached her granda's there was no one in the kitchen except Paddy Boden, sitting up on the table near the window and reading the newspaper in the last dregs of the light. Dan was out in his shed and she could hear him singing above the whirr of the lathe. She knocked at the door and called through a slit at the same time, and when he shot back the bolt and saw who it was he flung out his arms wide to receive her.

'I'll attend to you in a minute. I'm just putting the finishing touches to the leg of a stool,' and as he pedalled the lathe with his foot and held the chisel to the revolving piece of wood, she watched the flying spurt of the shavings and his eyes glittering in the light from the oil-lamp. 'The teacher has me tortured and pestered. A dozen three-legged stools I had to make for her concert and this is the last leg of the last stool.' He drew a sleeve across his nose: 'Mary, my sweetheart, learn to make things with your hands and you'll never decay; your heart, my girl, will never grow old. You'll always have peace and you'll have no time to brood on what the world does to you.' The chips grew finer now, some of them clinging to his beard. 'I think that'll do now,' and he unloosed the piece of wood from the lathe and felt its smoothness in the cup of his hand. Sitting up on the bench, he plunged a piece of paper into the funnel of the lamp and lit his pipe, smoking at his ease and not saying a word as he listened to Mary talking about the ailments of the hen. He left the pipe down on the bench, the smoke dribbling out from the shank.

'Give her to me here,' he said with an air of importance, and held the hen up to the light, softly feeling the hard-swollen craw. 'Do you know the hen's full with grub and yet she's dying of starvation. Isn't that a queer predicament for anybody to be in — dying of starvation and you full. Hold her a minute, Mary,' and he went to the sharpening-stone and put an edge on his penknife.

She eyed him suspiciously: 'Are you going to kill it, Granda?'

'I'm going to save its life. I'm going to operate.'

She closed her eyes as she held the legs of the hen, and when it gave a few gulches with its throat she squirmed and turned her head away. With one stroke he had slit the craw and turned the steaming mess on to the bench, a hoking through it with the point of his knife till it struck something hard — a round pebble. 'It's all over now except for the stitching,' and he sent her for a needle and thread and sewed up the slit. He put the hen on the ground and it shook its head and crouched on the shavings. 'You may tell Kate her hen will be laying in the spring. I'll keep her under observation for a few days and give her as much attention as if she were my very own. You can tell her I'll do every-thing in my power for her.'

They crossed the yard where in the half-light they saw a goat leaning its neck over the half-door of a shed. 'Come here till you see this lady,' he said, 'and a pair of horns on her as sharp as Sarsfield's sword. I bought her a month ago. There's nothing like goat's milk for a growing child. I was reared on it, and you wouldn't think to look at me that I'll be eighty next March.'

'You would not,' she said, though she was thinking of Tessie and her coming child.

Tessie was in the kitchen when they came in. She was sitting at the fire knitting a baby's vest.

'That's lovely soft wool,' said Mary, feeling it with her finger and thumb. And she sat down for a minute to tell her about Barbara and the ramshackle of a place that she was living in, and the little bell that rang when you pulled a wire that came up through a hole in the boards. But as she spoke, her mind all the time was on the kitchen in front of her, its scrubbed table and shining fender, the soft rustle of Paddy's paper, the slow trudge of Dan across the floor to get a drink from the bucket of spring water at the corner of the dresser, and the shine of Tessie's needles as she twirled the stitches on to the garment.

'I must go now, Tessie,' she sighed, her eyes on the sharp flame in the lamp. 'They'll be wondering I wasn't home before dark,' and when she was out in the night air again, the close peace of that house seemed to follow her and descend like a chill about her heart.

CHAPTER XVII

DURING the following week Father Toner was preparing for Christmas, making arrangements for confessions and for entertainments. Miss Drennan, the schoolteacher, was organizing a concert, and in the evenings she had the girls learning songs and dances and the three biggest boys in the

school rehearsing Lady Gregory's *Workhouse Ward*. Father
Toner dropped in to see the final rehearsal of the concert,
and standing with his back to the door he looked across the
schoolroom at the cluster of little girls who, with ribbons in
their hair and wooden stools under their arms, were whispering and smiling, the more nervous ones hiding behind one
another's back and peeping shyly at the priest. The two
hanging oil-lamps still swayed after they had been lighted
and the priest tried to steady them with his walking-stick.
Miss Drennan emerged from behind the faded green curtain
on the stage and beckoned to the little girls with her forefinger. At once they all clumped towards her, eager to get
behind the seclusion of the curtain, but someone dropped a
stool and immediately there was an explosive laughter from
them all and a gentle clapping from Miss Drennan as she
hooshed them in a loud whisper: 'On your best behaviour,
please. Remember who's watching you.' Father Toner
smiled and sat up on top of a desk, glancing at the well-
swept floor, the nail-heads shining, the easel leaning with
human importance in the corner and the blackboard still
holding the whorls of the duster. Outside big boys were
raising themselves on the sills of the windows and trying to
peer in, and when they spied the priest they jumped to the
ground again, and he could hear the clatter of them as they
fled along the frosty road.

A bell tinkled. The green curtain parted in the middle,
moved with some hesitation to each end, and the priest,
taking off his hat, gazed expectantly at the bare stage and
the crumpled drop screen at the back of it. To the accom-
paniment of an invisible piano the little girls, smallest first,
marched in, singing in Gaelic, a stool in one hand and a tiny
bucket in the other. Forming in a line facing the audience,
they rocked to and fro in time to the music, their bows
nodding in their hair, their buckets giving a gentle whinge.
Two chords on the piano and the buckets stumped to the
floor, but three little girls eyeing the priest were late and

176

upset the rhythm. The music stopped suddenly and the big girls shook their heads accusingly at the offenders.

'We'll have that again,' said Miss Drennan. 'All of you lift your buckets quietly and march off.'

Father Toner clapped and Miss Drennan poked her head round the curtain.

'They did it better last night, Father. They're a bit nervous.'

'It was splendid, Miss Drennan. It was tip-top!'

She gave a pleased smile: 'I'll put them through it from start to finish,' she said and withdrew behind the curtain to admonish the culprits.

Once again the piano rippled out the opening bars and the children marched in again, a little more sprightly this time, their voices loud enough to quell the notes of the piano. Down went the buckets in unison, down went the stools, and down went the girls on top of them. They paused, listening to the piano giving out the interlude, and once again they took up the tune, singing in high sweet voices as they milked their cows. And when they were on their feet again, marching off and shaking their heads a little airily, the priest took a book from below the desk and slapped it down on the lid to swell his quota of applause, and Miss Drennan came out on the platform, bowed with an excess of pleasure and called the girls to take the curtain.

'You'll have to send them to Ardglass,' he said, 'on tour, on exhibition, and show them what Dunscourt can do.'

The curtain jigged across again, but stuck half-way till a big boy, red to the ears and wearing a beard, came forward and plucked them together.

The priest got off the desk and stood leaning against the wire guard in front of the blazing fire. Through the fabric of the curtain he could see them preparing for the next item: 'The Workhouse Ward'. Two boys with white shirts pulled on over their clothes were arranging desks to represent beds and flinging sheets across them. Above each bed Miss Drennan was affixing two cards displaying in large inky letters: NO SMOKING and SILENCE. At last a bell rang and the curtain parted jerkily in the middle and before it had reached the wings the two old men, with their heads raised on their pillows, were firing words of abuse at one another, their voices increasing in sharpness as the play proceeded. When, however, a boy dressed as an old woman came on to the stage and peered in silence at the two men in bed, the little girls who were now seated in the desk near the priest began to giggle until Miss Drennan came forward and told them that they'd have to keep quiet or she'd put them out of the room.

'They're enjoying it,' Father Toner whispered to her.

'You don't know them, Father, as well as I do,' she whispered back, 'they'd keep up that silly giggling till you wouldn't hear your ears.'

She looked at the stage herself and when she saw the old woman with her boots laced with cord and a piece of a red petticoat hanging down below the skirt she laughed so much that she had to turn her back to the little girls and gaze into the fire.

'Why didn't you give the part of the old woman to one of the bigger girls?' the priest asked.

'I have only three boys in the top standard and there'd have been jealousy if I had cut one of them out. . . . Have a good look at their beards, Father. Do you know where they got them?' and she laughed till the tears came into her eyes. 'They told me they snicked them off the goats.'

The priest laughed so loudly that the lads on the stage paused, as Miss Drennan had taught them, till the laughter dwindled away. Finally, when they had concluded their act, they jumped out of bed in their shirts and hobnailed boots and stood to take the applause.

'It's a splendid show, Miss Drennan, a splendid show. We'll have to give the performers a party when all this is over. They deserve it. You're doing great work with them,' and after shaking hands with Miss Drennan he went forward and shook hands with the three boys and playfully plucked one of their beards. 'You're great men,' he said, 'and you're a credit to your teacher.'

When he came out of the school the moon was high in the sky. He walked briskly in the frosty air, hummed a tune to himself, and now and again prodded the stick into the ice that glittered on the cart-ruts on the road. Passing a house he heard a sprightly tune from a fiddle and through the window caught a glimpse of the couples dancing and an old woman crouched over the fire with a mug of tea on her lap. He would have loved to sit by the fire and watch them, but he knew his presence would jar upon them and ruin the close companionship of their evening. It was good to know they were enjoying themselves, he thought, it shortened the winter for them and contented them in a little way. Some day, please God, he would soon have enough money collected to build a fine hall for them where they could all gather in the winter evenings and be united in one group and not split up as they were now, dancing and singing and playing cards in an odd house scattered throughout the parish.

Near his home he saw the moon shining coldly on the slates of the chapel, and each headstone in the graveyard cut its geometric shadow on the ground. There was no sign of a light about his house and, after the bright warmth of the school, it seemed to breathe a sense of remote desolation. He opened the door and the squeak of the hinges echoed as through an empty house. He coughed a few times and the sound of his cough emphasized the silence. Kate was in bed, his supper laid out on a tray in the kitchen, and a saucepan of milk for him simmering at the side of the range. He poured the milk into a glass and sat in the kitchen, drinking it slowly.

A red cinder fell out of the grate on to the tiles of the floor; it quickly turned black, and in the quiet he could hear it crackling as it cooled. He heaved a sigh as he remembered what an old missioner had said to him as a student: 'You mightn't believe what I am going to say to you: a priest's life in a country parish can be the loneliest of all lives.' He didn't believe it at the time nor, for himself, did he believe it yet, but on occasions like this, when there came to him a sharp feeling of melancholy, he always sought to dispel it by reading a spiritual book or re-reading his student notes and the inexperienced comments he had scribbled on the wide margins. Sometimes, too, he would look at the photograph of his ordination group on the wall, and on scrutinizing those pure young faces unscarred, as yet, by the hardness of the world, he would wonder what had become of those, whom he knew, that had no inclination to read, and how, in God's name, they would adapt themselves to the bouts of loneliness that would assail them in a country district where even the bark of a dog or the cry of some beast in the fields only lengthened the loneliness of a night. For himself, thank God, he had his books and a parish with plenty of work; it was as well that he had that, for he was a poor mixer and the few card-parties that he had ventured out to amongst the well-to-do people in his parish afforded him no satisfaction.

He finished the milk, dusted the biscuit crumbs from his knees, and threw them into the grate. He took out his pocket diary and glanced at some of the calls he had to make before Christmas. He halted at one entry: *Call workhouse to see Jimmy Neil*, and with his finger in the book he paused, trying to settle in his mind a day that would suit him best. 'I'll try to fit him in this week,' he decided, and extinguishing the lamp in the kitchen by blowing down the funnel, he climbed quietly up the moonlighted stairs to his room.

CHAPTER XVIII

CHRISTMAS and the New Year had gone by before Father Toner got an opportunity of visiting The Curate. Old Kate, his housekeeper, was worrying him. She did her best to keep the place in order, but it was evident from the dust that remained in the corners of the hallway and the colly that lay unswept under the beds that she was unable to cope with the work, and when he suggested to her that she should take a holiday she went off in a faint on her chair. He wrote to Barbara Devlin offering her the job, and when she refused, Mary did her best to come up to the priest's house on a Friday or a Saturday to give a hand, and so one Saturday morning after Mass, Father Toner hurried his breakfast and set off on his bicycle to Downpatrick. It was a hard, frosty morning, and as he cycled through the town shop-boys were flinging sand around their doorsteps or standing with buckets of steaming water wiping the frozen moisture from the window-panes. On the outskirts of the town he saw through the bare trees the grey workhouse with its ugly drainpipes scaffolding the outside walls. At the open gate an old man with a crutch touched his cap and stopped chewing tobacco when Father Toner asked him if he knew of a Jimmy Neil that might be staying in the workhouse.

'He is in troth, Father,' said the old man, eager to display his information. 'He's not long in residence and you'll find him in the body of the House. He's the very divil at cards, Father, and he won tuppence from me last night. There's nobody in the House can touch him, I tell you. And he has as many songs in his head as a blackbird in June. Isn't that your man? Will I get him for you, Father?' He glanced sideways at the priest, rubbed frost off a stone with the nose of his crutch, and blew his breath on his hands to warm them. 'There's no sight nor stime of honesty in the young fellas nowadays. I seen a young fella passing on the road an hour or two ago and I hailed him and give him the money to get me an ounce of tobacco in the town. I give the villain a penny piece for himself and I'm thinkin' he has decamped with the whole lot.' He blew his breath on his hands again: 'There's no honesty anywhere.'

'There isn't,' smiled the priest, handing him a shilling. 'Will you keep your eye on the bicycle till I come out?'

'I'll herd it faithfully till you've your business done. There's neither rain nor bird will splash on it till you come out again.' He touched his cap and dislodged the piece of tobacco from between his gums and began to chew as the priest strode away from him. 'Go straight through the door, lift the latch at the passage, and you'll find your man in the body of the house. Tuppence he won from me. I'll cover the saddle with the tail of my coat and keep it warm for you.' Father Toner was already at the door out of range of the volley of words that followed him.

Cinders crunched under his feet in the draughty hallway, and seeing no one in attendance he lifted the latch in the door in front of him, walked along a glass-roofed corridor and presently entered a long, narrow room where old men were hunched over bare tables, some playing draughts and others cards. He stood within the door and scrutinized the scattered groups for Jimmy Neil. A man standing erect was tossing rubber rings on to white-painted numbers on the floor, and as they fell flat an old man would call out the score, while another would take his place at the butt, awaiting his turn. Further along, arranged in a broad semicircle around the fire, other men were seated watching a man toasting a piece of bread that was held up to the bars of the grate by a pencil. None of them had seen the priest except a thin slip of a man who was forever seated near a window goggling his head and smiling as if he were engaged in conversation with someone outside. He kept his eye on Father Toner, and seeing him surveying the room he stumbled up to him and put his trembling hand on the priest's elbow. The priest started as if a dog had brushed against him.

'Would you be wanting to see me?' said the voice from near the floor. 'I haven't smoked since last Easter — you wouldn't believe that. There's my pipe as cold and clean as an old bone.'

'Would you get me Jimmy Neil?' said Father Toner, and he jingled a few coins in his pocket.

The old fellow bowed his back a little lower, his hand affected a more violent quivering, and putting the pipe in his mouth he blew a whistle of air through it.

'Get me Jimmy Neil and I'll fill your pipe for you,' said Father Toner.

'Follow me,' said the old man, and he led him down the full length of the room, and the other inmates stopped their games and gazed after them with keen suspicion.

'They'll torment me the whole day to find out what was your business but I'll not tell them,' he said when they were out of the room. 'I could have took you a nearder way than this but I wanted to show you off and keep them on swithers wondering what you wanted with me. Nobody comes to see me and I haven't smoked since Easter.' He led him through the barber's room where there were handfuls of grey hair on the floor and a towel over the back of a chair. 'I'll get him for you in a minute,' said the old man when Father Toner showed signs of impatience. 'Down these steps now. Follow me. Open that door and you'll find Mister Neil on his two bended knees scrubbing the floor. And now you'll give me something to fill my pipe.' Father Toner opened the door slightly and saw Jimmy with his back to him wringing out a cloth.

The old man plucked the priest by the coat.

'I nearly forgot about you,' said Father Toner, taking a shilling from his pocket. And then he watched Jimmy rubbing the small of his back with one hand and drying up his scrawl of suds with the other.

'You're not wringing it tight enough, Jimmy,' said Father Toner.

Jimmy turned round sharply, and then got to his feet, straightening his back with much evidence of pain. He cleaned his right hand on his trousers and held it out to the priest: 'I'm right and glad to see you, Father,' and noticing the priest glancing at his corduroy trousers and at his stiff unbuttoned waistcoat he added cheerily: 'That's the regulation outfit — dressed up like a gang of Belfast gravediggers.'

'I had a few messages to do in town and I thought I'd look you up while I was here.'

Jimmy unrolled his sleeves, lifted his coat that was folded in a bundle on the floor, and led the priest into a square garden that overlooked the road, and as he walked with him along the cinder paths he told him of the time he had spent in jail: 'And here I am in a place like this, labelled as an able-bodied man and me with a pain in my back like a cross-cut saw. But I get an ounce of tobacco in the week for the work I do but you'd need a watchdog to look after that ounce for you. They'd slit your throat for tobacco — they would in sowl! But they're a low lot. The other night I seen three men using the one pipe, taking a pull at it turn about. They'd disgust you. There's no culture among them. At Christmas I got the lend of a mouth-organ and when I played a few tunes they told me to give the blasted thing a rest and let them get to sleep. And here I am a fine musician scrubbing and scouring and cutting bread for the likes of them.'

'And why don't you leave it?' said Father Toner, restraining a smile.

'I came here to stick it out to the spring and I'll do it. It'll not be long now. Every morning I come out here and examine the sooty buds hoping to see a bit of life. They look dead but when there's a scrap of sunshine I can feel the sap inside them striving to break out. At the first speck of green I'll be off.'

'You'll settle down in Dunscourt.'

'Och, Father, they broke my heart when they said I turned Protestant. It was a wicked, crooked lie they told you. Man, if they'd seen me last Sunday they'd been ashamed of themselves. The clerk didn't turn up to serve the priest's Mass and I was the only one out of fifty-four men that could take his place.'

They had halted on the path and Father Toner was fingering the branch of an apple tree that spread towards him. He

184

bent it slightly, and on releasing it a few frozen drops fell on to the soil. He sighed, and turning his eyes away from Jimmy he let them rest on the thin smoke of the town that was lifting in the wind.

'Put that out of your head, Jimmy. They didn't believe a word of it, I am sure. Come back amongst them and take a job on one of the farms.'

'They'll not have any call to be talking about me now and mouthing their rotten lies. The Reverend Hope's away to an island in Scotland. There was no body in the life here, he told me, it was all broken into little bits. Wherever he is now, Father, may the world do well for him. When I worked for him he was decent to me and he didn't care whether I was black, yellow, or brown as long as I worked well and played a tune or two for him on my mouth-organ.'

'That's right, Jimmy, work hard and work well for those who employ you . . . I must leave you now. We'll see you again in the spring when you'll be out to cut that grass of mine.'

When he came out of the workhouse the old man with the crutch had, as he expected, disappeared. The bicycle rested against the tree trunk, the saddle wet from the thawing frost on the twigs. He avoided Downpatrick on his way home, cycling along byroads that were unknown to him. He went leisurely, and when a few flakes of snow dwindled from the sky and melted on the road and on the handlebars of his bicycle, he did not hurry his pace. He raised his head to the sky, a misty blue without even the trace of a cloud. And then a wizened sun burst forth and spread weakly across the fields, the few flakes vanished amongst the trees, and a swarm of gulls following a plough shrieked and screamed as though spring had come. An old man carrying a bundle of broken branches on his back trudged up a lonin to a whitewashed house, and looking at him the priest thought of the cunning old men he had just left. He felt no pity for them, he told himself, for though they were mostly strangers to one another there was no loneliness amongst them. They had everything, he felt, except the freedom of that old man with his bundle of branches. 'I suppose it is that that makes them yearn to get out of it and I suppose it is the loss of that that drives them into it.'

On reaching his house the parlour window was raised and Mary Devlin was shaking a duster into the air. The tiles of the hall were drying after being washed, the brass bell shining, and the foot-scraper polished with blacklead.

'It's well Kate lets somebody in to help her,' he said, sniffing the fresh cleanliness of everything, and when he got a chance of speaking to Mary by herself he asked if Kate had objected to anything she did to-day.

'I just started into the work and she didn't protest. She said that I was the only girl that did things to her satisfaction.'

'She has you well trained,' he smiled, leaving her at her work.

In the evenings when Mary had finished, Kate would have a cup of tea ready for her in the kitchen and while she would be taking it Kate would reel out to her how foolish it is for any girl to go through life alone, and with many a weary gesture of her hand and a daub of the apron to her eyes she would lament: 'When you're old nobody wants you. God help that poor man in there, but if I could get somebody to give me a corner to myself and a seat at the fire I'd leave him. I'm not much good to him now and I know he hasn't the heart to send me away. If I could get into a wee place in the parish I'd know he'd be calling in whiles to see me and to see that I was treated decent. I'm no charity, Mary Devlin, I'd have you know. I'll have the old age pension and I've a bit past me forby.'

'There's plenty in the city would be glad to have you.'

'It'd kill me, child, to settle in a strange place and me so long here ... I'd like to be buried here. It's homely to be buried around the walls of a church and people noising past you on their way to Mass and maybe one or two, like yourself, that'd kneel down at my graveside and say a prayer for my poor soul. But in the city there's no church in the grave-yards and there's always such a swarm of people to be buried you'd be lucky if they didn't topple some stranger down on top of you after a wheen of years. God preserve us from the likes of that.'

After she had finished the tea and they were sitting in the dim glow of the range Mary, with strained patience, would continue to listen to her, and when the subject would change from the talk of death to the brightness of Kate's young days Mary would get to her feet and point at the bare window where they could see the stars ablaze in the cold-looking sky. She would pretend to hurry but once out on the road she would take her time, expecting to meet Ned who usually came of a Saturday evening to see her home. Passing Dan's she listened at the door and heard nothing but the rattle of osier rods inside. She raised the latch and looked in. Old Dan was weaving a basket for fish, and it was the cold from the door and not the click of the latch that made him lift his head. 'There's nobody here, but my own sweet self,' he said. 'Did he not turn up?'

'Who?'

'That'll do you. You couldn't fool me at my time of day. Stay outside like a good girl. You might miss him on the road. And listen, girl,' he said, resting a rod across his lap. 'It's time you and Ned were tethered. There's a right time for everything. There's the right time to eat a herring and there's the wrong time. Eat them in season and they'll melt in your mouth — eat them out of season and they're hard and dry like a bit of old stick. It's like that with love!'

'Herrings and love! Phew!' and she banged the door with affected disgust and strolled off along the road. She kept close to the shelter of the hedge that broke the fingers of the wind, and at the sound of someone whistling or the sight of a bicycle wavering on the road she would press close to the hedge, hoping to surprise Ned. But he didn't come, and when she reached the sea-road there was still no sign of him. She sat for awhile on the upturned boat in the shelter of the gable, listening to the scrabble of grit around her feet or watching the stars scatter in handfuls in the branches of the sycamore. She rested her head against the gable and could feel the heat of the stones that faced the fire and could hear John's loud laugh or the rattle of the poker as it was tossed on the hob. She went inside and got the hurricane lamp. She walked slowly around the outhouses, looking in at the hens, at the geese, and at the cow, and whenever a step sounded on the road she would raise the lamp so that its light fell on her face and shoulders. It grew cold and she went into the house where her father was making a long line, John helping him to fasten the hooks. She took her knitting and sat near the window, expecting him to step into the kitchen, since he wouldn't find her on the road. But that night he didn't come, and on the following Saturday when he came to meet her he made no excuse that he hadn't seen her for nearly two weeks and she, in turn, sensing his sullen mood made no effort to refer to it. But at last his moody silence and the cold look that he gave her from time to time broke her patience.

'Ned, is there anything wrong at home?' she said anxiously.

'Nothing.'

'There's something. I feel there is.'

He laughed with slight bitterness: 'There's nothing, I tell you. Nothing!' and once again he looked at her coldly.

'Ned, for God's sake, don't look at me like that.'

'Like what?' and there was an edge on his voice that frightened her.

'You're looking at me as if I were a total stranger.'

'Stranger, is it! Sure you think more of strangers and of helping them than you do of me.'

'I'm not helping any stranger. I'm helping Father Toner.'

'I suppose if anything happened her you'd take on the job,' he said ironically.

'I couldn't. It takes me all my time to spare an odd Saturday,' and then she hurried on, aware that she had blundered. 'I wouldn't think of it. It wouldn't suit me and the great day that's before us.'

'It's a long way off, I'm thinkin'.'

'You haven't changed your mind, Ned?'

'Me! — to change my mind,' and he laughed scornfully. 'You don't know me or you wouldn't say that. I'm sick of everything, Mary, do you hear? I'm sick of waiting. I'm sick of seeing your brother, John, hobbling about on that stick again. And I'm sick of you thinkin' about everybody else except the fella you're going to marry.'

'Ned,' she said tenderly, trying to take his hand. 'There's nobody I want only you. I live for you. And I know, as well as I know the bends on this road, that everything will come to us before very long. Maybe at Easter.'

'Maybe — and John, God forbid, to grow into a helpless cripple.'

'John's changed. The other night he told my father he would go into the hospital if the swelling didn't disappear. We have stopped trying to force him and it's John, himself, has all the talk about the hospital and the sensible thing to do . . . Why can't you have faith, Ned?'

'I have plenty of faith. But you can't feed it on empty promises and expect it to keep steady.'

She tried to take his hand again. It was stiff by his side: 'You're like the pillar of a gate to-night. There's no softness in you. Could you not put your arm around me and cease worrying about to-morrow. Let things take their course.'

'If you let the stream take its course it'd soon flood the land on you.'

In the starry darkness he plucked a blade of grass by the roadside and put it in his mouth. She talked about Barbara, about Tessie, about Old Kate's early life, trying in that way to break down his mood of stiff resentment. He spoke little to her, and as she stood with him in the lee of the gable he

189

idly flaked the limewash from the walls or with his hands in his pockets gazed at the glimmering lights far out at sea.

'It's getting late,' she said, shivering. And as she turned to go into the house he held her arm.

'Mary,' he said, and he gathered her tightly in his arms, kissing her. 'Nobody can take you from me. Let anybody try it!'

'No,' she breathed, and there were tears of joy in her eyes.

CHAPTER XIX

FATHER TONER, having administered the Last Sacraments to his housekeeper and closing her eyes in death, was standing at the window rolling up his purple stole. A doctor, a nurse, and Mary Devlin were behind him in the room speaking in hushed voices. The priest was puzzled what to do next: whether to take the remains at once to the church or whether to follow the custom of the country and so endure for a whole day and night the fuss of the women who would visit the house to pay their last respects. He beckoned the doctor and asked him what would he advise.

'You've done more than your duty by her, Father,' said the doctor, his hands in his pockets. 'You should have her coffined and brought to the chapel at once.'

The priest gave a wry smile. ''Tisn't the custom here. A long-established burial custom is almost sacred with the people.'

'You've done as much for her as one would do for his own kith and kin.'

The priest fingered the snib on the window and looked at the sheep, heavy with their young, lying in the fields: 'It's hard to know what to do. There was great kindness in her. She served me well and faithfully, and when I was sick myself she gave me the best of attention.'

'And haven't you done that for her and far more?'

The priest shook his head: 'I did nothing except what I wished to do. Mary Devlin had all the trouble — day and night she was on the alert.'

'I wouldn't upset the house any more if I were you. No one could expect it.'

The priest took out his watch, pressed open the flap, and looked at the time: 'Seven o'clock — it's early yet. I'll think it over after Mass.'

At mid-day Mary Devlin spread the news that old Kate was coffined and laid out in the priest's parlour. And that afternoon the mourners, mostly women, began to gather, kneel at the coffin for a few minutes and then sit for a while on the chairs arranged along the wall. Before evening Mrs. Mason called and though it was Mary Devlin who opened the door to admit her she walked in past her as if the door had opened by itself. She knelt as the others had done and then suffered the boredom of conventional respect by sitting for a while amongst the other mourners. When she was seated in their midst and was fumbling in her bag for her handkerchief they continued the conversation that she had interrupted.

'Indeed, as I was saying,' said a stout woman with three chins, 'there's not many like him in the whole length and breadth of the country — not many like him.'

'He didn't affront her anyway,' answered a little woman, her eyelids quivering. 'The doctor in every day for a whole week. The expense of that. It'll be a power of money and I'm sure she hasn't left a penny piece to bury her.'

'Indeed, Mary Devlin was telling a certain party Kate was well respected by all the people she ever wrought for. She was saying she could count lords and ladies amongst her friends and had scores of letters from all parts and airts of the globe.'

'I wouldn't doubt a word of that. But they'll not gather round if there's trouble afoot.'

'Nobody likes bother if they can avoid it, nobody. And there's that fine wee man has her nicely laid out in a brown coffin with gilt handles. Indeed, my own family won't do as well for me, I'm thinkin'.'

Mrs. Mason sat erect, affecting to take no interest in the conversation. She glanced at the coffin, its polished wood reflecting the light of the candles. Then she blinked at the candles themselves, their flames nodding away from the door and burning down one side. It's a wonder no one would think of moving them out of the draught. H'm, they think of nothing only their bit of gossip. Dan Scullion would do it, she thought, remembering the day in the chapel he blew out the noisy, dripping candle. She blew her nose politely in her handkerchief, and resting her eyes on the only wreath of flowers on the table tried, from where she sat, to read the words scrawled in ink on the card affixed to it. She thought it read: 'From the Children of the School', but she'd correct that impression when she'd stand up to take her leave. It'd be easy for her to pretend she was having a last look at the corpse and if she'd take her stand near the foot of the coffin she could read it with the tail of her eye. It's a pity she didn't tell Ned, before he left for the fair this morning, to buy a wreath in Downpatrick. But how could she do that when she didn't hear the sad news herself until the twelve o'clock angelus was ringing and the blacksmith shouted it to Delia when he was passing by on his bicycle. 'Tis a great wonder the postman hadn't it this morning. He gives you many a thing less important than that. Maybe he had it and wouldn't give it to her because she went out to meet him when he was half-way across the yard and didn't invite him into the kitchen as usual for his sup of fresh milk. That's always the way — once you start a run of kindness it's dangerous to break it off. If Sarah hadn't had the clothes drying at the fire she'd have asked him in and he'd have given her the whole news and she would have had time then to tell Ned to buy a wreath in Downpatrick. It'd have pleased Father Toner to see that somebody in the parish was taking an interest in old Kate.

'There's many will find fault no matter how much you do and how well you do it,' said the stout woman, after a pause. 'There's many will say, you know, there's many will say he should have had a glass of wine and a biscuit for them who travelled a brave distance. Not that I would touch it myself. But for them who came at great inconvenience. You feel, somehow, that full respects are paid when there's a tiny glass of spirits. It's the usual thing for a person well respected.'

' 'Tis hard for the priest to think of everything, poor man,' sighed the little woman.

'Indeed, that's true,' continued the stout woman, the chair creaking under her weight. 'After all, what's a glass of wine here or there. Isn't it better, and I always maintain it's better, we should be thinking of the poor creature that's dead and saying a prayer for her and not thinking of these fiddle-faddles that make no matter one way or another. One never knows whose turn it'll be next. Indeed, one never knows,' and she sighed and put her finger to the side of her nose.

'He done well for her.'

'Indeed, he did. Nobody's finding fault. But there's always one or two busybodies to start talking and whispering.'

'He could have packed her off to the workhouse and let her die in disgrace and no one to follow her coffin to the grave,' shrugged another woman who had been silent until now.

The workhouse! The word broadened in Mrs. Mason's mind and she tried to narrow it away from her. She fixed her attention on the scars and dinges in the linoleum and teased her mind into tracing the causes of them. It might have been the castors of the table that disfigured it or maybe some farmer with shods on the heels of his boots and he scringing them into it as the priest talked to him. But the babble about the work-house continued and the stout woman recounted the number of people she had known who had died in it and were buried in nameless graves. Mrs. Mason fidgeted uncomfortably on her chair. She opened the clasp of her bag and put away her handkerchief. A sense of suffocation seemed to thicken the room, and she glanced at the blind-drawn windows and the blurred shadows of the sashes. What excuse could she make to leave so soon! Her bag dropped noisily on to the floor and a lull came in the conversation as she stooped to pick it up. She coughed and again took out her handkerchief. A step sounded on the gravel outside, and presently another mourner entered and Mrs. Mason rose to give her her seat.

'Now, Mrs. Mason, don't let me disturb you. I only dropped round for a minute,' the mourner whispered. 'I've a cake at the side of the fire and I wouldn't like it to burn . . . She's like herself, poor thing,' she added, turning to the corpse. 'As innocent-looking as a little child.'

'She is,' said Mrs. Mason, not thinking of what she was saying. 'She got a happy death anyway.'

'And why wouldn't she — and she lying in the priest's house and he there, day and night, to see that she had everything she wanted. I wish, Mrs. Mason, we'll all get away as happy. He's a good, good soul is Father Toner. We never had one like him and we'll never see his like again. And the work he does by himself. The man before him had a curate to help him.'

'His predecessor,' said Mrs. Mason.

'His predecessor, as I was saying, had a curate to help him, and I heard it said on good authority that Father Toner refused help. He wanted all the work for himself,' and she caught Mrs. Mason by the arm. 'Some of them when they get a young curate take to their arm-chair and work the poor boy off his feet.'

'Father Toner's not like that,' said Mrs. Mason gently disengaging her arm, 'a gentle quiet man that does his work and you'd think he wasn't doing anything.' The woman caught her by the sleeve again but before she had time to speak she heard the front door opening and she moved at once to the only vacant chair.

Mrs. Mason was glad to get out in the air again, away from the sibilant whispers of the old women that were lingering like an echo in her ears. She called at the graveyard, conscious all the time that she was repressing some thought she was afraid to face. A streak of bird-dropping stretched from the tip of the headstone and she scraped it off with a piece of slate and wiped her fingers in the grass. 'In another week it would be his first anniversary,' she said, kneeling on the plinth and blessing herself. The year had sped quickly, and now death had carried off another from the parish. 'God knows who'll be next,' she said with a melancholy sigh, noticing two men digging the fresh grave a stone's-throw from her own. She knelt on. 'Well,' she said to herself, facing the thought which was teasing her mind. 'That's over and done with more than forty years ago and why should I let it annoy me now. How did I know that the old woman-servant I had was as sick as she was. And even she did die in the workhouse she died with the priest at her bedside. It wouldn't have answered me to be attending her in my own house, running up and down the stairs, and my first child three months on the way. I did what was best for her!'

She dragged her way from the graveyard. The road was dry and a faint tinge of green on the hedges. Passing Dan's cottage she saw two women with their sleeves rolled up washing sheets at the gable and laughing away to themselves. She didn't know whether or not she had bowed to them as she passed.

Yes, she thought, Father Toner hadn't cast her out — that was true. And it was strange that after all the years he had been here, after all the sermons he had preached that there would be few things remembered about him amongst the people except that. And for herself, she asked, would there be anything good said about her when she had gone. Was there anything they'd hold in their memory. They'd be sure not to forget her action on the day the Devlin's thatch caught fire. But would they be ready to afford her the excuse of her husband lying stretched in his fresh shroud! No, that wasn't the sort of country people — they'd hold something

195

ugly in their minds about a family and never let it die. She knew them well.

A lark was rising, its drops of song freshening the air. For a moment she stopped to listen to it, and then walked on. 'What is wrong with me at all?' she said aloud to herself. 'Why do I feel so empty, so dissatisfied? All my life I've tried to lead a good life — haven't I? I've tried to avoid sin, I've said my prayers, and never neglected the sacraments, and now why do I feel as dry as old hay? God, what's wrong with me? Have I done anything good for anyone? If once in my life I had befriended a sick woman and given her a decent burial it would have been something to look back upon and treasure.'

She took out her handkerchief and daubed her eyes. Near the sea-road she saw old Dan and a barefooted boy belting along at a great pace.

'That's a grand day, thanks be to God,' puffed Dan, hurrying past her.

'It is,' she said, standing to the side. But Dan wasn't thinking of her, for when Tessie's baby was coming he had gone off to the shore, and now when a lad had brought word that a son was born he was racing home to produce a cradle he had made in secret.

'There's something happening to-day,' Mrs. Mason said, turning round to look at the retreating figures.

At the bend on the sea-road a smell of tar came to her through the hedges, and on the shelving bank of the shore Luke was working at his boat, a bucket of tar poised on flat stones, a fire whirring beneath it. John was standing near him, swinging his stick like a pendulum and singing at the same time.

Mrs. Mason stopped and glanced at the gloss of tar on the boat and the splashes of it on the stones.

'Getting her ready?' she said, surprised at the huskiness of her own voice. 'God send you luck with her this year . . . Is your leg any better, John?' she added, without giving Luke time to reply.

'It is, Mrs. Mason. I think it's on the mend.'

'It'll never be on the proper mend till you stretch yourself on the hospital table,' said Luke, holding a jug of tar on the palm of his hand and dipping his brush into it.

'One never knows,' said Mrs. Mason, 'one never knows. But take good care of yourself like a good man,' and walked away from them.

'It's lovely here in the early Spring,' she said to herself, facing the sea and its falling waves. ' 'Tis strange you never tire of the sound of the sea — it's quiet, like someone breathing deeply.'

At the stream she rested for a minute on the stone bridge and looked at the geese asleep on the bank and their reflections in the water troubled by the breeze. She breathed in the air with a sigh of thankfulness. Up the hill she strode and past the wee farm where grass was springing on the thatch. She must get Ned to run his eye over it and not let it go to rack and ruin.

The gate of her lonin was swung back against the hedge, a large stone propped at its corner to keep it open. She was ready to edge the stone away with her toe when she remembered that Ned was at the fair in Downpatrick. 'I needn't close it,' she said, 'it's nice to have the gate wide open for you and you bringing in the horse and cart.'

She went slowly up the lonin, a straw in her hand. She looked over the orchard-hedge at the trees hunched over their own shadows. There wasn't a stir in it. The ground was damp in places, the spears of the daffodils thrusting above the grass. A hen's feather clung to the netting wire. Ned made a fine job of that, she thought, though some people will tell you it's better to give the hens the run of the orchard. But it was her belief they did more harm than good, destroying the flower bed and putting holes in the hedges so that the cattle could break in and rub the bark off the trees.

For a minute or two she stood in the yard admiring how well it looked in the quiet light of the evening — its spacious cleanliness, the fresh whitewash on the walls and the clean hem of tar on them. She crossed the threshold, and as she came in Sarah kept her back to her. Ann and Delia were knitting.

'That's a glorious evening,' she said, taking off her hat and coat. 'Make me a nice cup of tea, one of you.'

'Ned isn't back yet,' said Sarah.

'Well, he's later than this many's a time and you not worrying. I suppose your Aunt Rose has delayed him with her chit-chat.'

A cry broke from Delia and then from Ann.

'What's wrong with the lot of you?' she asked, holding her hat in her hand and jabbing it with the hat-pin.

'He'll not be back, Mother,' cried Delia. 'He told me this morning he was going away to sea.'

'To sea! What would he know about the sea! What nonsense are you talking!'

'I didn't believe him. But he said if he wasn't home early I'd know what had happened.'

'I don't want to hear any more of this nonsense. I'm ashamed of you — big girls like you that should have more sense. You don't know when a person's making fun of you ... Never heard such trash. Poke up the fire and hurry on the kettle.'

She sat at the table and folded her hands on her lap: 'He never mentioned the like of this to you, Sarah?'

'No, Mother. I'd have laughed at him.'

'And was it only this morning he mentioned it to you, Delia?'

'Yes, Mother.'

'And did you say anything to him?'

'I laughed and he said, all serious-like, it's no laughing-matter.'

'And why didn't you tell me?'

'I thought he was joking until I saw other carts returning over an hour or two ago.'

Mrs. Mason tapped her toe on the stone floor and glanced at the twilight shrinking from the window. She opened the door to let in more light. Sarah spread a cloth on the table and laid five cups on it.

'Will I light the lamp, Mother?' she asked.

'Plenty of time,' she answered, though two or three stars were visible through the open door.

The tea was ready and four of them sat down to the table.

'And what would put the notion of the sea in his head?' she said. 'Isn't there enough sea, and to spare, at his own back door?'

Delia cried again.

'Delia, what's wrong with you at all? Are you hiding something from your mother?'

'No — nothing.'

'Well, then, control yourself or you'll be a laughing-stock for all the days of your life.'

They ate in heavy silence. A red glow came from the fire. Sarah closed the door.

'Will I put a glimmer on the lamp now?' she said.

'Isn't there light enough from the fire that'll do us?'

Sarah cleared four cups from the table and left Ned's with a knife and fork beside it. She opened the door and brushed the crumbs off the plates on to the yard. Stars were glimmering above the roofs of the outhouses. She paused. The dogs began to bark and run to the head of the lonin while across the still countryside came the jolting of a cart.

'I hear a cart now, Mother. That'll be him.'

'Light the lamp, Delia, and you and Ann give your face a wash. Not a word to Ned about this nonsense, do you hear?'

The light from the lamp shone into the yard. They smiled as the cart knocked its way up the lonin. Sarah wet fresh tea and put the frying pan on the fire.

The mother went out to the yard. Two carts came up the lonin, one towing the other. A neighbour hopped off the first one.

'Ned asked me to leave the cart and horse home,' he said.

She shuddered. 'Is that all the message?' she said, trying to steady herself.

'That's all he give me,' and he backed the cart into the shed and unyoked the horse.

'Thanks,' she said.

'Good-night to ye,' he shouted as he climbed on to his own cart.

She came into the kitchen. The three sisters were crying.

'Stop it!' she said. 'Do you think I don't know my own son. He'll come back. Some wild notion he has taken.'

She sat at the table again and put a hand to her brow. Sarah gave her a cup of cold water and she drank it slowly.

'The Devlins!' she said, after a pause. 'Not but I warned him time and time again.'

She heaved a sigh and recalled the day she had seen John Devlin talking to Ned on the bank of the roadside. It was he that was the cause of it — driving wild stories into the innocent boy's head. Oh, God in Heaven, didn't she advise him to have nothing to do with them?

'All of you go to bed . . . And say nothing about it to the neighbours . . . Lower the lamp a little, Sarah, it's too bright . . . and hand me my beads like a good girl.'

Ann and Delia went upstairs. From under her mother's hands Sarah lifted the tablecloth, the knife and fork and cup and saucer. She brought her her prayer beads and patted her mother's shoulder: 'Don't be fretting, Mother,' she said, 'he'll come back. We must have faith in God's goodness.'

'O God,' she moaned, 'what did I do that You're so hard on me!'

She lifted her beads but her mind sped from the prayers she was saying, her heart hardened to John Devlin, and bowing her head on her crooked arm on the table she wept bitterly.